Have I Told You

F. L. Jacob

Dedication

*I dedicate this book to my husband. Honey, you have been
with me through it all. My craziness, my happiness, my tears.
Without you I wouldn't be able to do any of this.
You are my rock. I love you.*

*Girls, you know who you are, without you
I wouldn't have started writing again!*

*Mom & Dad, thank you for being so supportive of my writing.
You have no idea how much it means to me.*

Prologue

"Mr. Black, thank you so much for coming to our Winter Gala. I'm sure you'll be happy with the performance this year. We have an amazing senior class. The senior dancers this year are especially good," Joe, the head of the Arts Department at State, says as he greeted me tonight.

"The pleasure is mine, Joe. You know how much I care about the arts."

I turned to walk over to the bar, leaving Joe behind. The mingling at these galas got on my nerves, and I needed a drink. The bartender slid my drink to me, and I sat back on the stool to scan the crowd for potential sweethearts. Work never ended.

I saw a couple girls giggling across the room. I nodded at them as I took a drink. One was a dark eyed, exotic beauty, and the other was a pale, stick thin blond. They were both students. If there was anything I learned from coming to these galas for years was the students were easy to spot.

There were two types here, and those two girls each fell into a category. Over confident, sexy as hell, and will do anything to advance themselves was one category. The other was the non-confident. No confidence was a total turn off for me. It meant you did not believe in yourself. You had no fight. I was not going to remake someone. They have to have the drive to begin with.

I got the biggest kick out of seeing these girls squirm when I winked at them. I wondered what they were wearing under those dresses. Taking the last sip of my drink, I set the glass on the bar. Never braking eye contact with them, I made my way through the crowd.

"Evening, ladies. How is everyone tonight?" I asked, stepping between them, delivering my panty dropping smile, and touching the smalls of their backs. The small touch gives me the ability to see how a woman will react to me. Just that little contact tells me if they are open, confident, and if they take care of themselves. I need that control.

The two girls looked at each other, giggled, and smiled goofily back at me. I lightly thumbed their backs. My exotic dark eyed beauty was perfectly muscular. Her friend felt like a skeleton, which made me withdraw my hand quickly. I did not like boney. I wanted a healthy girl with a figure to kill for.

"I'm Lana, this is Kristy," my dark eyed beauty said. She tentatively continued, "You're Caston Black, aren't you?"

I smirked, "Yes, I am Caston Black. Are you ladies in the show tonight?"

"Kristy is." Lana said, pushing her friend toward me. The girl stumbled, and I caught her before she hit the ground.

She whimpered when I asked, "Are you okay? I don't want Professor Lee to lose a dancer because of me."

"Oh, I'm okay, Mr. Black," Kristy said shyly, not making eye contact. No confidence, just as I suspected.

The lights blinked, and I looked up at the ceiling. Fifteen minutes to curtain call. Smiling, I looked back at the girls. "Ladies, looks like I must get to my seat. Kristy, break a leg. Lana, maybe I will catch you at the after party tonight?" I reached for their hands and brought them up to my lips, kissing them gently.

I saw their legs buckle, as I turned to walk away, and I laughed to myself. Seeing my brother and his wife across the room, I gave a quick wave. Jon was five years older than me and had dirty blond hair like Mother. When I reached them, Jon slapped me on the back. "Cass, you're going to have to stop making girls swoon. I swear that one was ready to suck your dick in the middle of this crowd."

"Really, Jon? We're in public," Sara said. "Caston, sweetheart, how are you tonight? Thank you for the invite. It's so nice to get away from the kids. A night to ourselves – what will we do?"

"I can think of a few things." I teased, pulling her in for a hug and a quick peck on the cheek.

She playfully slapped my chest. Sara was a beauty inside and out. Too good for my brother. She was tall, had dark wavy hair, and a beautiful genuine smile. She is an amazing mother to my niece and nephew. My heart still aches for her when I think about our past.

"Is that all you two think about?" she teased.

"Yup," Jon and I said in unison.

I offered Sara my arm. "As if you can talk, my dear. I bet you can't wait till this is over with, either."

"You know me too well, Cass." She kissed my cheek, then we turned to walk into the theater with Jon following behind us.

Each seat had a beautifully printed program tied with a large satin bow. Sitting down, we made small talk about the club and Black Hollywood until the lights went out.

The first half was opera singers. I tried hard to stay awake. Work had been crazy, and I had been up for over thirty-six hours. Getting a jab in the ribs, just as my eyes started to close, woke me. Shaking myself awake, I opened up the program to read about the next section. I turned to the back. The dance portion of tonight's performance.

That's when I saw her. Her big hazel eyes, her long, wavy brown hair falling over her shoulders, cascading down her back, her pale, creamy skin. Her picture spoke to me. I felt as though her eyes were pulling me to her, and her lips looked delectable. She was my next Hollywood Sweetheart. I could not wait to see her dance. Touching the picture, a shiver went down my spine.

The music suddenly changed. I looked up. She didn't have the typical ballet dancer body. The long muscular legs traveled up to a beautiful ass. The hourglass figure was pure perfection, curves in all the right places. Healthy, not like the stick figure I had seen earlier. Most importantly she had perfect perky breasts. The cleavage poking above her costume made my mouth salivate. Brunette hair, pulled into a tight bun on her head, showed off her long neck. She was absolutely perfect. My cock twitched, I had to meet her.

Once her face looked out into the crowd, I felt her eyes boring into my soul. I could picture her magazine spread already... Her naked, except for her pointe shoes, shot from the back, highlighting her muscles perfectly with light and shadows. I would also love to do a private picture with her, too. Bound on pointe with her ass in the air. My cock was straining in my tux pants, needing to be released.

I quickly took out my phone and typed in Sabrina Bennett, next BHS.

The images in my head were making it unbearably hard to sit still. I quickly looked around to see if I could find Lana, thinking it was probably impossible in the large crowd. Sure enough, I found her staring at me four rows back, biting her lip in contemplation of what she wanted me to do to her, no doubt. She was nothing compared to Sabrina, but she would do for tonight.

I excused myself to Sara and Jon. As I stood up I caught Lana's eye, and nodded toward the door, indicating for her to follow me. Reaching the lobby, Lana was on my heels. I walked toward the men's restroom, and held the door open for her. Locking the door behind me, I turned around to see her already on her knees in front of me, ready and willing to suck me off. As she reached for my zipper, all I could picture was the Sabrina girl's face. Letting my head fall back onto the door, I closed my eyes and tried to keep going, but Lana was not Sabrina. I could not do this; I tucked myself back into my pants and quickly exited the building. I had to meet my sweetheart, soon.

Chapter One

Sabrina

Six months later ...

Caston and I met my senior year of college. It was spring of 2012. I was dating Mark Baker. He was the quarterback of State. I always went for the type of guy that was big, strong, and blond. However, my big and strong guys always turned into big, strong jerks. Mark was no exception. He was overbearing and mentally abusive.

The night I met Caston, Mark and I were at a frat party. I hated them. I was never into the party scene, but Mark loved them, and where he went, I was expected to follow.

This party felt different. We were seniors this year, and everyone seemed to be psyched that graduation was near. Our football team was ranked number one, and Mark and his buddies got bids to go pro, so they felt they were untouchable.

Mark was drunker than I had ever seen him that night. "Hey, Bre, get me another beer."

"Not right now," I said tentatively, removing his arm from my waist, trying to get away. He tightened his grip on my wrist. "Ow. You're hurting me, Mark."

Leaning in to my face, he whispered, "You better get me a beer, now, before you regret it. Remember you were nothing before me, you're no use to any man now, after what happened, and if I decide to leave you, no one will want to be with you. Ever."

I sighed and nodded my head, he was right.

I made my way through the crowd. My head was down, trying to get back to Mark as soon as possible. I hated making eye contact with people, because I felt worthless and ugly. Why Mark was with me I didn't understand, but he made sure to remind me, every chance he got, that I was the lucky one to have him.

As I turned the corner I ran right into the back of a man. "Oh, I'm sorry, excuse me," I said.

"No reason to be sorry," he yelled over the music, "it is so crowded in here you are hardly the first person to run into me tonight."

Looking up, I came face to face with the most beautiful man I'd ever seen. He had the clearest silver blue eyes, dark black hair that was the perfect length to run your fingers through, and an angular jaw. He was tall, and had great hands that were now resting on my arms. He was dressed in dark blue jeans and a white oxford with the sleeves rolled up to his elbows. His forearms were muscular, adorned with a leather cuff on his right wrist. I wanted to run my hands along his chest and through his hair. Looking into his eyes made my legs feel weak. The electrical current that ran through my body when he touched me made a shiver pass through me, sending a pool of lust into my thong. I smiled shyly, and tried to sneak past him.

"Hey, wait up," he said, keeping a light hold on my elbow. He leaned down to my ear. "Can I at least know the name of the only person here who is as sober as I am?"

His breath felt cool on my hot neck, and it made me shiver. I have never reacted like that to anyone. My mouth went dry, as I thought about how I wanted to turn my head and kiss his delectable lips. Suddenly, I didn't remember my own name.

"I'll go first," he said, holding out his hand and giving me a smile that made me want to pass out. "I'm Caston. It is a pleasure to meet you."

"Sabrina," I responded without taking his hand. "I really must go. Nice to meet you, Caston."

I quickly turned to leave, before he said anything else. His smile made my insides quiver, and I knew I had to get out of there before Mark found me talking to another man, or I did something I might regret.

"Here." I shoved the beer into Mark's chest when I returned, and plopped down next to him on the dirty leather couch, my arms crossed over my chest. I tried to sit as far away from him as I could, but he slid in next to me, draping his arm around my shoulders. I felt sick to my stomach as soon as he touched me; Beth was right when she said it was too soon to go out. Closing my eyes, I tried to breathe slowly to calm myself down, but all I saw were silver blue eyes staring into my soul, and those hands making their way up my legs. I tightened my thighs in response to my dampening panties.

"Thinking about me?" Mark slurred, and I was harshly brought back to reality.

"Ugh, no." I tried to get up, needing air, but he pulled me back onto his lap, grinding into me.

8

"Feel me, babe?" His friends just laughed and egged him on. I struggled to get out of his grasp, as I felt the bile rising in my throat, but he pushed me down, pressing my back into the couch. I felt scared. Flashbacks of our fight two months ago racked my mind, and I panicked.

"Mark, get off me. No! Get off me," I yelled. The grunts and howls around us made me aware that he wasn't going to stop. His hands were all over me, and I felt gross. Closing my eyes, I prayed he wouldn't do this in front of everyone.

Mark's hand just started to travel up my leg when, suddenly, he flew off of me. My eyes opened to see what was going on. Everyone was backing up, anticipating a fight that would most definitely break out.

"I think the lady said no." It was Caston. Did he know who Mark was? What was he thinking? Mark was bigger than he was.

"Excuse me, she's with me. I know what she wants," Mark yelled.

I sat up, unsure of what I was seeing.

"You are drunk. You should step away to clear your head, and leave the lady alone," Caston said calmly.

Mark, trying to be the tough guy, repeatedly shoved Caston in the chest. "Do you know who I am? I can do what the fuck I want. She's with me, so leave us the fuck alone."

I couldn't believe this. Who was this Caston guy? I'd never seen him before today. "The lady said no." Caston calmly repeated.

Mark obviously had enough, and punched Caston in the face. The crowd gasped, Mark turned away from Caston, acting so proud of himself for punching him. Caston never flinched. He stood like a stone statue. Mark was staggering back toward me when all of a sudden Caston grabbed Mark and pinned his arms behind his back.

He forcefully linked his arm through Mark's and made him walk over to me. "Tell the lady you're sorry."

"Bullshit, I'm not doing that. Plus she ain't no lady, fucking whore. Let go of me." Mark spat, struggling to get out of Caston's hold.

I cringed at his words, tears welled up in my eyes.

"Tell the lady you are sorry, or we are going for a walk."

I just stared up at the two men with my mouth open like an idiot.

"Fuck off." Mark spit out.

With that, Caston tugged Mark out the door to the back yard of the frat house. Everyone watched them go, then snapped back to me to see what I was going to do.

I sat there for what felt like hours, trying to process what just happened. Then scrambling to my feet, I stumbled outside to see Caston talking calmly to an irate Mark in the corner of the yard. Then much to my surprise, Caston started walking back toward the house, and Mark just stood there, not moving.

"Sabrina, you'll never be anything without me. You little bitch, whore! Fuck off! We're done!"

Frozen in my tracks, my life stopped. What just happened? I sank to the ground and tears started falling uncontrollably. I felt relief wash over me that I was free of Mark, but I was scared. Where was I going to go? What was I going to do? I lived with Mark. I had nothing. I reached into my jeans pocket to grab my phone. I turned it on and went to dial, but realized I had no one to call. Beth was out of town at an art exhibit this weekend, and Mark just dumped me. I have no family, no siblings, and nowhere else to turn. I hung my head, defeated, thinking I was going to have to crawl back to Mark and beg for forgiveness.

Just then a hand came into my line of sight. I looked up, already knowing who it was offering it to me. Caston looked down at me. The light that filtered down around him made him look like an angel. My angel.

Caston pulled me up off the damp ground. I stumbled a little, but he caught me and pulled me close. I could feel his hard body beneath his clothes. We were face to face, and all I wanted to do was taste his lips.

"Are you okay? There was no reason for him to be rude."

I looked down, trying to avoiding his eyes. "Oh, I'm used to it. He really doesn't mean the things he says."

Not letting me go, he took my chin between his thumb and finger and made me look up at him. "Never look away from me. You are a beautiful woman, who deserves to be treated with respect."

My eyes started to water again. No man has ever told me I was beautiful before.

"What's wrong? Please, don't cry." He stroked my hair until I calmed down. "What's wrong?" he repeated. I shook my head.

Realizing I was still in his embrace, I stepped back out of his strong arms. "I'm sorry, I usually don't cry so much," I said, as I wiped my eyes with the backs of my hands.

The crowd around us felt thick, and was making me feel claustrophobic. "I have to get out of here. Everyone is staring at me, waiting to call Mark to report what I'm doing."

Looking around he noticed what I was talking about. "Can I drive you somewhere? I do not want you to be alone tonight." Panic washed over me once again. Where was I going to go? As if reading my mind, he took my hand and led me through the crowd, away from the party.

The sounds of the party grew fainter as we made our way down the street hand in hand. Caston retrieved a key fob from his pants' pocket and hit the unlock button. The lights on a blacked out Jeep Altitude flashed. He opened the door for me, helping me into the massive vehicle. I looked over the expensive interior; the technology alone on the console put my little flip phone in my pocket to shame. Caston climbed in next to me, started the SUV with a push of a button, and pulled out into the street heading away from the party. He played with some other buttons on the steering wheel, bringing the stereo to life. Looking over at me he asked, "What would you like to listen to?"

I shrugged my shoulders. "It doesn't matter to me, I like everything. Surprise me."

I saw him smirk in the dim light of the street lamps. "Fair enough." He pressed a button and Sweet Dreams by the Eurythmics played through the speakers.

I let out a laugh. "Didn't peg you for a 80s fan."

"You would be very surprised to see my iPod. I am very diverse," he chuckled in return.

Pulling off into the darkness, we rode in silence for a while. We were heading away from campus and out of the city. I turned toward him. "Thank you, by the way. I've never had anyone stand up for me before."

Watching the scenery fly past the window I became a little uneasy, "Where are we going? I don't want to sound ungrateful, but I don't know you."

He laughed. His laugh was intoxicating. "Sabrina, I am taking you to my house. I would hope you do not make it a habit to leave with people you do not know, but I could tell you had nowhere to go. I did not know anyone at that party, and since I did not want to leave you with a possible serial killer, I figured I would take you home tonight."

"Oh," I said, facing forward again, biting the inside of my cheek, "You can call me Bre, and Mark's not really that bad. He only gets like that when he's drunk." *Or when he's mad*, I said to myself, which was all the time. I didn't want to sound pathetic.

"Do not make excuses for him, Sabrina. Any man who makes a woman feel like they are worthless is a piece of shit. And I will call you Sabrina. That's your given name, and I think it is as beautiful as you."

I smiled, thankful for the darkness right now, because his words made me blush. He has called me beautiful twice now. I tried not to look over at him, because I knew he was staring at me with those eyes that made my insides flush.

We continued on in silence, listening to the music play. He did have a very diverse collection. It was fun to see what would come up next. *'Five O'clock Somewhere'* started playing and I laughed. "I could really use a strong one right now." I said.

"I'll help you out with that as soon as we get back to my place," Caston stated. My mind started imaging his strong one helping me out. I chuckled to myself, hoping he only thought I wanted a drink.

Chapter Two

Sabrina

We finally arrived at a huge gated mansion. "You call this a house? I'd say it is more like a palace or mansion," I stated.

He pulled up to the black iron gate and the sensor on the dash of the Jeep flashed, making the gate open. We drove along a winding brick drive, lined with landscaping lights leading the way. I wished it was light, so I could see just how beautiful the grounds were.

We pulled up in front of the house. It was beautiful, a huge three story beige brick house with multiple wings. The up lighting around the front made the exterior look magical. The front door had a large canopy over it, and the landscaping around the front of the house was perfectly manicured. I felt like I was entering a fairy tale. There was no way this guy was for real.

Caston parked under the canopy, got out of the car, and walked around to open my door. My mouth was agape and my mind couldn't process the magnificent house, or the angel, in front of me.

Caston laughed. "You will catch flies in your mouth if you do not shut it."

I quickly shut my mouth and bounced out of the Jeep, while tugging my skirt down, so he could shut the door. Caston grabbed my hand and raised it up to his lips to kiss the back of my hand, as a tall dark military looking man dressed in all black appeared in the doorway.

He looked like he was about to speak, but Caston started talking first. "Terrance, please put the Jeep away. Also, do not start with me about leaving without you tonight. I had to get out of here. Please, tell Jules we will have a guest for breakfast, so she will make an adequate amount of food. Oh, and I will pass on the daily security update tonight. Thank you and good night."

"Very well, sir. Oh, and sir, please at least tell me where you're going next time," Terrance said with a sigh.

Caston nodded his approval at the man's statement. I cleared my throat behind him to remind him I was standing there. "Oh, Terrance, this is Sabrina. Sabrina, this is Terrance. He is my personal security guard."

Terrance put out his hand for me to shake. "It is a pleasure to meet you, ma'am. If there is anything you need please let me know."

"Thank you, and you can call me Bre," I stated.

Caston took my hand and led me through the massive oak door. We walked through the two story foyer to a great room with floor to ceiling windows. The furniture looked comfortable and not uptight, like I thought it would. There were blankets hanging on the back of the couches, and the center of the wall had a massive fireplace that gave the room a beautiful warm glow.

"Make yourself comfortable," he said, as he gestured toward the overstuffed couch, "I'll be right back. I have to go check my messages." I nodded in understanding, and turned to walk into the massive room.

I stepped down into the living area. The carpet seemed to sink under my feet, and I realized my feet were killing me in the black high heels I had on. Suddenly, I felt underdressed in my fishnets, extremely short skirt, and tight tank top that definitely showed off my features. Here in this house, I felt cheap. Oh God, I hope he didn't think I was like that. Terrance must think the same about me with the way I'm dressed. I became very embarrassed and wanted to turn and run out of the house without looking back.

"What is going on in that head of yours, Sabrina?" Caston questioned with a smirk interrupting my thoughts. He had silently returned and was leaning on the pillar connecting the great room to the massive kitchen, holding two crystal tumblers of amber liquid. I wonder how long he was standing there watching me. He had changed, and was now dressed in grey sweat pants that hung low and a tight white tank top that showed off every curve of his hard chest. Instinctively I licked my lips at the site of him, my panties became damp. Running away from him became a distant memory and I decided I needed to find out everything about this man.

Caston strode toward me, and handed me the glass of liquid. I took it from him, and took a sip. The liquid burned my throat, but it was exactly what I needed to feel comfortable enough to stay. He sat on the couch, and patted the seat next to him. I removed my heels, curling my feet under me as I sat down. I leaned forward to set my glass down, and pull my skirt down as far as I could get it.

"You did not answer me," Caston stated.

My eyes dropped and said "I suddenly feel like a whore in this outfit, and I was hoping you didn't think that's what I am."

Caston sighed, and pushed my chin up to meet his eyes. They sparkled in the firelight. "Sabrina, you were at a party. A college frat party, no less. I would hope under normal circumstances you would not wear outfits like this and you would have less makeup on. It never crossed my mind that you were anything less than a beautiful woman. Please, do not let me hear you call yourself a whore again. Never drop your eyes for anyone, look them in the eye and show the confidence that I know is deep inside you. It displeases me to see you belittle yourself."

I didn't realize I was biting my lip while he was talking, until he used his thumb to remove it from my teeth. The sensation sent a shiver down my spine. He dropped his hand from my lip, and then ran it through his hair. His muscles flexed in all sorts of ways that I cannot even describe. He brought his glass to his lips, taking a drink. I watched the liquid flow through his lips and his Adam's apple move as he swallowed. My mouth was suddenly dry and my mind went blank. All I could picture was my lips on his neck and my hands roaming his hard body, pushing that tank up so I could feel his bare chest pressed against mine.

I shook my head to bring myself back to reality, trying to keep a clear mind. I needed to find out everything I could about Caston, before I let myself go down a path that I felt I wouldn't want to leave.

I felt stronger and more confident than ever before. I knew Caston was the reason. Turning to grab one of the blankets off the couch, I said, "Tell me about yourself, Caston. Do you have a last name, and how come I've never seen you before tonight?"

"My name is Caston Black." Looking surprised, he asked, "Sabrina, did you honestly not know my last name?"

I shrugged my shoulders. His name sounded familiar, but I couldn't place it.

He looked away, shaking his head in disbelief. "I am no one. Just a man with a big house,"

"No way. I'm not stupid. You saved me from Mark, you have a mansion, you have a housekeeper, and you have a body guard. People who have body guards are somebody." I reached out to brush his hair off his brow and questioned him again, moving closer to his side, "So, tell me Caston Black, who are you?"

Caston let his head fall back and let out the most beautiful laugh. It made my lower half come to life, and I squeezed my legs to keep the feeling alive. He turned to look at me and there was a fire in his eyes, "My dear Sabrina, I do not know your last name, much less anything else. You at least know mine."

"Bennett. Sabrina Bennett. Now you know everything about me," I laughed.

"Hardly, but I will let it go for the moment," Caston smirked. "I own a lot of companies. However, one you might recognize is Rose Builders. We are the leading construction company for commercial and residential building in the tri-state area."

"I think I've heard of it."

He continued, "I was meeting with the president of the university to discuss the new building I am donating and building. When I was leaving, I overheard someone talking about the party of the year. Since I skipped college, I wanted to see what they were all about, so I came home wrapped up my work and headed back. Thank God I did, because I would never have met you otherwise," he said, while lightly stroking my shoulder.

"It sounds weird, but I do get death threats, and even though I could handle things myself, my second in command at Black Enterprise insisted I do something about it, so I hired Terrance. In all honesty it has been nice having him around, because I get a lot done, while he is driving, and he is now the head of security for all my companies, so I know everything is consistent."

He stood up to refresh his drink. "Let me see—what else did you ask? Oh yes the housekeeper, Jules. She is the only reason I am still alive. If it was not for her, I would never eat and this place would probably be a pig sty. I work over one-hundred hours a week, so finding any time to myself is slim."

He walked back to me, but I couldn't focus on his words, because I was hypnotized by the big bulge in his sweat pants. My eyes glossed over. "Earth to Sabrina," I heard, and my eyes snapped back up to his, but I was heated with a full body blush. "Did I answer all your questions?" he laughed.

"Why did you skip college? How old are you, anyways?" I asked.

He sighed. "I started college, but never finished. I felt I was not learning real life skills, so I quit. My parents were furious, but I had to do what was best for me. I guess I did the right thing. I do not like to tell that story, though, because I do advocate finishing college. Let me see, how old am I?" He sat down next to me again. His closeness was sending shock waves through my body. I adjusted the way I was sitting because my panties were about to combust. "Well, my dear, I am the ripe old age of twenty-six."

"Oh, in that case," I moved to stand up, "I can't hang out with an old geezer like you." I squealed, as he grabbed my arm and pulled me back down on to the couch. I fell over his lap and our eyes locked. One arm was cradling my shoulders and his other arm was draped across my thighs, where my skirt had ridden up. I took a deep breath and licked my lips, willing him to kiss me. His eyes were full of fire. I could feel his cock grow on my back.

Caston suddenly sat me back on the couch and stood, walking away from me. I was left breathing heavy and wanting. What just happened? Am I not good enough? I should have known better. Of course, I'm not good enough. I hung my head and gathered the blanket, pulling it up to my chin, suddenly feeling more self-conscious than ever before.

"I am sorry, it is getting late. Let me show you to your room," Caston rambled, obviously as flustered as I was. I nodded, keeping my eyes cast downward in response to his statement, and stood up to follow, keeping the blanket draped over my shoulders, covering my body.

I followed him through the hallway and up the stairs. We passed many closed doors. I wondered what one person needed with so many rooms, and what was behind the doors? We arrived at the end of the hall to a large double door. Caston opened the doors and let me walk in first.

Once again, I was in awe at the beauty filling the room. It had magnificent dark cherry wood walls and coffered ceilings. There was a wall of French doors that were draped by rich, heavy fabric. The massive four post bed was sitting diagonally in the middle of the room and it was piled high with duvets and pillows that looked like satin. This bed had to be hundreds of years old. I would love to run my fingers along every hand carved groove into the beautiful headboard. The air conditioning made the hardwood floors cold under my feet, but there was a large oversized oriental rug under the bed that looked soft and inviting. There was a mirror, bigger than any I have ever seen, on the wall. It reflected the bed and the massive fireplace on the opposite wall. The lights were dim and the fire flickering in the fireplace made the room seem magical. There was no way this was the room I'd be staying in. This has to be the master suite.

I looked over at him in confusion. He had just turned me down on the couch and now he was inviting me to his bedroom? "Isn't this your room?" I asked, walking over to the bed to run my hands along the footboard.

"I am not sure if Jules has the other bedrooms properly stocked, so I felt this was the best place to have you stay tonight," Caston stated.

Caston walked into the closet and brought me out a black t-shirt. Handing me the shirt he said, "I will be in the room next door, if you need anything."

He turned to walk out, before I could even say anything. I stood at the foot of the bed, with the blanket still wrapped around my shoulders, holding his shirt. The tears that were welling up finally reached their capacity and began to fall down my cheeks.

My heart sank. I really wished there was another reason for bringing me in here. I felt all the rejection that Mark had made me believe for so long. He was right. No one else would want me.

Laying the blanket on the bed, I removed my skirt and let it fall to the ground. My tank top was next, leaving my breasts exposed to the cool air. I pulled his shirt over my head; his smell was on it, almost as if he had just taken it off. My nipples hardened and longed to be touched. I walk to the side of the bed and crawled on to the softest sheets I have ever felt. I snuggled down into the bed, still crying, and reached over to the empty side. How I wished Caston was there with me, looking at me with those eyes, feeling his hard body pushed up against me, cuddling, and kissing his soft lips. The tears began to fall harder. Eventually, I drifted off into a light sleep.

I was awakened by the bed next to me dipping slightly. I hoped this was not a dream when I felt him wrap his arms around me and pull me close. He didn't say a word. His face was right next to mine, and I was able to snuggle into his neck. My body was awakened by his scent, and I was able to finally open my eyes to look up at him. He was looking down at me with such feeling. "I couldn't sleep while you were alone in here crying," he said. "No one should have to be alone when they are sad. You are stronger than you give yourself credit for, Sabrina. Please, don't cry." He stroked my back with his strong hands.

"Why did you leave me?" I sobbed.

"I never should have left you, but I am not accustomed to having such strong feelings for a woman who is with another man." He kissed my forehead, letting his lips linger there for a few extra seconds.

"I'm not with him anymore. You heard him at the party. We're over."

"Oh, Sabrina, he is far from over you, and you from him. Physically, yes, you might be, but mentally you are not. Do not get me wrong, I want you. I want you more than you'll ever know, but I need your body and soul all to myself. I cannot share any part of you with anyone." I tried to respond, but he quieted me. "Sleep now. Tomorrow I'll take you anywhere you want to go, and we will figure this out together, okay?"

"Okay," I whispered. I snuggled closer to him and listened to his heart. His strong embrace and the slow rhythm soothed me back to sleep.

Chapter Three

Sabrina

The sunlight coming through the windows eased me out of my slumber. I stretched out, suddenly remembering I wasn't home. Sitting up, startled, I saw Caston walking out of the attached bath into the room. I've never seen perfection in the form of the male body before this morning. He had rock hard sculpted arms, abs to die for, and the deepest V that I've ever seen. I would love to run my tongue along it taking me to his most private parts. He held his towel in one hand, but it was barely covering his perfection. The water drops beaded up on his skin, I longed to be one of them. I was suddenly very thirsty and wondered if he would let me lick him to get refreshed. Gathering the blanket up to my nose, I blushed at the thought.

"Good morning, Sabrina. I hope you slept well. I know I have not slept that good in years. I think it might have to do with the fact that you were in my arms," he smirked.

I was smiling behind the blanket, hoping it was covering up my full body blush. I nodded my response, still not able to pull my eyes away from his hard body.

"You can get in the shower now if you would like, or you can wait until after breakfast. Jules should have it ready by now. Then I can take you to school."

"I'll shower quickly," I said, getting out of the warm covers and pulling the shirt down, so I didn't show my thong.

I tried not to stare at his backside when I walked to the shower, because even that was perfect. The sculpted muscles rippled as he walked to collect clothing out of his closet and drawers. Then without any warning he dropped his towel. Oh. My. God. He had the finest ass I'd ever seen. It was perfectly round and the right combination of hard and soft with the most amazing dimples above his cheeks. My breath caught in my throat. I was afraid I was going to faint. I could imagine myself grabbing that fine ass and squeezing it as he pounded into me.

My thoughts elsewhere, I tripped over a stack of books on the ground. Caston turned around, worried when he heard the commotion, strategically placing his clothes, so he was covered. Concerned, he asked if I was okay, but had the most devilish grin on his face when he said it. How embarrassing. I gathered myself and sprinted toward the bathroom, so he couldn't see how flustered he made me.

Reaching the bathroom, I shut the door behind me. I put my hand on my forehead and let my head fall back. Oh my God, what was I doing? I'd never acted like this before. I did a deep rub of my temples, and let a sigh escape me, as I walked over to the exquisite two person shower.

The walls were covered in a dark grey stone. There were multiple shower heads and a large rain head coming from the ceiling. There were built in shelves that held expensive body washes and shampoos. Benches on either side of the shower held more bottles and fancy sea sponges. The floor was still wet from Caston's shower. I bit my lip, as

I thought about him standing there with soap running down his body. I stepped out of my black lace thong, pulled his shirt over my head, and stepped into the shower. I figured out how to turn it on, and was greeted by a subtle cascade of warm water washing away my thoughts.

Letting the water flow over my body, my hand wandered south, massaging my sex. The other hand cupped my breast, rolling my nipple between my fingers. The feeling made me tremble. Remembering the fire in his eyes and thinking about his lips, so close to kissing me, had me hovering on the edge. I wished my hand was his. Unfortunately, as I was about to find my release there was a knock on the door and it opened slightly. Startled, I covered myself, embarrassed by what I was just doing.

Caston stuck his head in, keeping his eyes covered. "Just wanted to make sure you were okay and had everything you need." I groaned. If he only knew how much more I needed.

"Doing fine. I'll be out in a few seconds."

I chuckled at him standing in the doorway, looking so adorable with his eyes covered. I wondered if he was peeking through his fingers. I dropped my arms exposing my body to see if I could get a reaction from him. His lower body gave him away. I saw a very apparent bulge forming in his black pants. Smiling to myself and turned around to show my backside.

"I...I'll be downstairs at the breakfast bar," Caston stuttered slightly.

"Okay, sounds good," I said. He closed the door behind him, and I quickly finished. I didn't want to make him wait too much longer. Judging by his clothing, I was sure he had to go to work.

I stepped out of the shower, wrapped my hair in one towel and my body in another. Walking into the main room, I noticed that my clothes were laid out nicely on the bed. There was another t-shirt of his laid out, too. I ran my hands along the shirt and my heart fluttered. I got dressed, putting the t-shirt on in place of the tank that I had on last night. My feet were still a little sore, so I opted to carry my shoes downstairs. Bending over to fluff my hair with the towel, I noticed my phone on the floor by the chair. I cringed. That one piece of equipment would take me back to the reality. It reminded me that I couldn't hide in rescuer's castle for the rest of my life.

I reached down to pick up the phone. My hand trembled slightly. This is ridiculous. *Sabrina, just turn it on and face the consequences,* my mind told me. I sat on the edge of the bed and stared at the phone for minutes. Finally, I hit the little button on the side of the phone. I couldn't believe my eyes, thirty-five missed calls, fifteen voicemails, and twenty-five texts. My stomach twisted in knots as I contemplated if I should open the messages or not. Just then my phone rang. The caller ID showed Beth's picture. Letting out a sigh of relief, I picked up the call.

"Hello, Beth," I said flatly.

"Sabrina, where the hell are you? Mark is going insane looking for you. He was over here, drunk off his ass, asking for you at the ass crack of dawn. I know he didn't believe me when I told him you weren't here. How could you not even answer my calls? I've been worried sick. I thought you were dead on the side of the road," Beth rambled, not letting me get a word in.

"Can I please talk, now? Geez. I wish you would've been at the party last night. Mark was being the biggest dick. He tried to force me to do things with him in front of everyone last night, Beth. I was so scared." I started to choke up, remembering last night's events.

"Oh, honey, I'm so sorry I wasn't there. I knew I should have blown off that out of town poetry reading." Beth said.

"No, don't be sorry. Thankfully, there was this new guy there named Caston. I literally ran into him, while getting Mark another beer, and he suddenly became my knight in shining armor."

"I heard about some guy manhandling Mark. Broc said he's so pissed, and threatening to turn him into the police."

I laughed at that comment. "Mark won't turn him in, because that would tarnish his reputation. Anyways, when Mark left me high and dry, and I had nowhere to go, Caston offered to take me to a safe place."

"So where are you?" I froze.

"Please, don't tell Mark you talked to me. I need to decide what I'm going to do. I'm finally done with him."

"Don't mess with me, Bre. I've been telling you for months to kick that guy to the curb, especially after last time, and you ignored me. Do you really think I'd tell Mark I talked to you? I hate that bastard. Where are you?"

I took a deep breath. "Caston's house."

"Sabrina Marie Bennett, you did NOT go home with a guy you've never met before? Did you…you know?"

"Oh my God, no, Beth! Geez what do you take me for?" I said, but my subconscious was shaking its head, because I would have done him in a heartbeat, if he would have let me.

"Good. I thought I was rubbing off on you. Who is this Caston, anyways? The name sounds familiar, but I can't place it. It's such an unusual name, you would think I would remember.

"Look, I can't really talk now. I need to get downstairs for breakfast, and then I need to figure out what I'm doing."

"Fine, fine, but who is he Bre?" Beth questioned.

"Caston Black," I responded. I heard the phone drop on the other end. "Hello, Beth? Hello."

"You did not say Caston Black," Beth screamed when she picked the phone up again. "*THE* Caston Black? Like Caston Black of Black Hollywood?" My mouth hung open. No way is my Caston that Caston Black. Surely, there must be more than one Caston Black in the area, but even I have to admit that is highly unlikely.

Trying to not answer her questions, I quickly cut her off. "Beth, gotta go. I'll call you back as soon as I can. I promise."

Chapter Four

Sabrina

No way was Caston Mr. Black Hollywood. Mark and his friends always had a copy of that magazine lying around. I wouldn't lie, I looked at Black Hollywood all the time. The girls in there were beautiful, sexy, and tastefully photographed. I would describe it as a newer more tasteful version than some of the older magazines of its genre. Everyone had heard the story of the man behind the magazine, but the stories they told didn't reflect this Caston at all.

If it was him, though, it would explain the security and the big house…remembering the magazine called it the *'mansion of the east coast'*. Where were all the girls? Was that the real reason he was at the party, scouting? Was he looking for his new College Hollywood Sweetheart? No, he cannot be that Caston. I sat on the edge of the bed, with my head hanging low. I wanted him to be my knight in shining armor, not Mr. Black Hollywood. I would have to do more investigating.

I put my phone in the pocket of my skirt and stood up to examine myself in the mirror. This would have to do. I wished I didn't look like Julia Roberts when she was shopping on Rodeo Drive. I tried to pull my skirt down so it was a little longer, but it did no good. I let out a sigh, squared my shoulders, and gave myself a pep talk. *This is as good as you're going to look, Sabrina.*

This is the new you. I need to stand up for myself. I need to value myself. My parents didn't raise me to be worthless. I want to make their sacrifice mean something. I want to be someone they would be proud to call their daughter. I need to be strong again. I could feel my mental change reflected in the way I carried myself. My spine was straighter, my head was higher, and my thoughts were clearer. I congratulated myself, and turned to go down the stairs to join Caston for breakfast feeling like a confident, new women. The smile engulfing my face hasn't been there in quite a while.

Hearing commotion coming from the kitchen area, I figured he was in there, so I quickened my pace. He had been waiting for me too long. I didn't want him to wait anymore.

"I'm here, sorry," I said, as I rushed into the room. I stopped dead in my tracks when three people turned to look at me. "Caston?" I questioned. Just then Terrance walked into the room. Thankfully, someone I recognized.

"Good morning, Ms. Bennett. Mr. Black stepped away to make a phone call. He'll return soon. Please, follow me to the dining room, where Jules has breakfast set." I nodded my understanding. I glanced back over at the other people, who still hadn't taken their eyes off me, then back at Terrance. I ran to catch up with him.

"Hey, Terrance, who were those people?"

"Mr. Black's associates. There was an emergency, so they came over early this morning."

"Oh, I hope nothing bad."

"No, ma'am. Please, have a seat. Mr. Black should be in shortly," he said, while he pulled out a chair for me.

"Thank you, Terrance," I said, as I sat down, looking over the magnificent spread on the table.

"You're very welcome, Ms. Bennett. Can I get you anything while you wait?"

"No, thank you." Terrance turned to walk out. "Oh, Terrance?"

"Yes, Ms. Bennett?"

"Please, call me Sabrina or Bre," I said smiling, hoping he would.

"Very well, Sabrina." Terrance had a smile on his face, as he turned to walk out.

I sat at the table alone for only a few minutes before I heard Caston coming toward the dining room. I sat up taller in my seat, and my heart fluttered.

"Vanessa, not now. I have company."

"But, sir, we've been waiting all morning and these numbers need to be approved."

"Vanessa," Caston spoke firmly, "I told you I have a guest. I am not even sure why you are here. I am allowed to take a morning off. It is my company, and Ashton should be able to take care of things. He is my second in command."

"Yes, but..."

"No, Vanessa. Please, show your tagalongs out, as well as yourself. Go back to the office and go over things with Ashton, or you will not have a job tomorrow." Caston interrupted her. God, he sounded so sexy when he talked authoritatively.

"Very well, sir. I'm sorry we intruded. I didn't realize you'd have a guest, and I thought these figures needed to be addressed by you."

Caston was in the doorway now, finishing his conversation. He looked amazing. He was dressed in black dress pants, a white collared shirt with the top three buttons undone, and a black suit coat. Remembering the body that was underneath those clothes, caused my thighs to tighten. He was very animated while he was talking to Vanessa. I looked down at my clothing and cringed. I really did look like a whore. As if reading my thoughts, he turned around in the doorway and gave me a smile that would have made me fall to my knees, if I'd been standing.

I gave a small wave. He turned back around and shut the door in Vanessa's face mid-sentence. Then he turned and walked over to the table, where the morning paper was laid out for him.

"I hope the rest of your shower was satisfying." Caston said with a knowing smile. I blushed. He had to have seen me pleasuring myself. Oh God, how embarrassing.

I reached for a bagel, and avoided answering him. "I'm sorry if I caused you any trouble today. I mean, with taking off work. I really can't thank you enough for your hospitality."

"Sabrina," Caston said as my phone rang. I jumped and tried to reach for my phone, but fumbled it, making it land right in front of him.

"Please, don't answer it," I entreated him.

Caston reached for the phone and turned it over. I could tell by his scowl it was Mark. "Hello. No, you may not talk to her. I will not tolerate that kind of language." Caston flicked his thumb and shut the phone. Looking over at me with annoyance in his eyes. "Please, tell me you have someplace safe to go today, because I do not want you going home, until I can go with you. If not, you will stay here. Mark is a loose cannon, and I'm afraid he will do something to physically hurt you."

"Um, no not really," I responded, breaking eye contact. "Beth has class all morning, but I don't. I'll be fine. Really. Mark won't do anything."

"Sabrina, I am not joking. You will not go home, until I can go with you."

"But…" I said, looking up to catch the seriousness of his look.

"No, you will stay here. End of discussion."

I nodded my understanding. He was right. I didn't want to admit to him that I was terrified to go to Mark's, but I had to get what little belongings I owned.

"Caston?"

"Yes?" His eyes are softer now, relaxed.

"You're right. I'll stay here." I smiled. I could see him relax in front of me. He really did care.

We made small talk as we ate. I was interested in him. There was a connection that I couldn't explain between us, but was determined to explore. I still didn't know if he was Mr. Black Hollywood, but I didn't even care about that. His smile and genuine personality drew me to him like a moth to the flame. He made me feel comfortable and strong. His laugh did things to me that I loved. My heart fluttered and felt like it was coming out of my chest.

Breakfast flew by. Caston stood up to leave and I felt sad, as if a piece of me was leaving. Standing in front of him, I straightened his suit coat; feeling very brazen I took his lapels in my hands, pulling him close to me. He put his hands on my hips, under my shirt. His thumbs edge their way to touch my skin. It jumped at his touch.

"Be good today. I will leave an iPad for you to use." He leaned forward and kissed my forehead. I sighed, and looked up at him timidly though my eyelashes.

"Yes, Caston," I responded angelically. My mind was begging him to kiss me. Please, God, kiss me.

"I could get used to this," Caston replied, staring into my hazel eyes, while brushing my sides with his thumbs.

He was barely a hair's breadth away from my mouth now. He enveloped my mouth, and his tongue parted my lips, hungrily seeking mine. I allowed him entrance, and my knees buckled. He caught me, pressing me to his body. One hand stayed on my back, while the other skimmed up my back and tangled in my hair. Intertwining his hand in my hair, he pulled my head back, starting to kiss the sides of my mouth down to my neck. My mind went absolutely blank, and I felt my insides clenching. Just as suddenly as he started kissing me, he pulled away. Breathless, I leaned up against the table. Holy shit! Did that just happen?

"I'm sorry, Sabrina, that shouldn't have happened until you are done with Mark. It won't happen again," Caston said, and quickly left the room.

What? NO! I had wanted it since I met him. This afternoon couldn't come soon enough. I needed to be done, once and for all, with Mark. Please, God, don't let there be any problems.

When I closed my eyes, I could still feel him on my lips and neck, his eyes staring into my soul. I touched my neck to keep the feeling alive.

There was an unexpected noise in the doorway, causing my eyes to snap open. I was greeted by a little plump woman with gray hair, rosy cheeks, wearing a black maid's uniform with a white apron. Her smile was so warm and inviting.

"Hello, deary. You must be Sabrina. Are you done with breakfast yet, hun? Oh, where are my manners? I'm Jules. Anything you want to eat, or need cleaned, it would be my pleasure to help you with," Jules said, wiping her hands on her apron, before extending her hand to me.

I giggled. She was such a happy person, and her smile was infectious. She reminded me of Mrs. Potts from *Beauty and the Beast*.

"Very nice to meet you, Jules," I said, shaking her hand. I almost felt like I should curtsy, too. "I'm done with breakfast, thank you. I'm not too hungry this morning. I'm sorry all this food is going to waste."

"Oh, deary, don't be sorry. We have plenty of hungry men working around the yard today. They'll be more than happy with some leftovers."

She quickly cleared the table. "Mr. Black left you an iPad on the breakfast bar in the kitchen. Please, make yourself comfortable. He said he would be home about two, which really means four." She winked at me, and turned to walk out of the room.

I made my way to the kitchen and saw an iPad sitting right where Jules told me. There was a note written on top of it.

Sabrina,

Please make yourself at home. I will be back soon. I had my tech guy set this up for you. He preloaded your school email onto it for you so you can check your classes. I will be in touch.

Love, Caston

Love? I sighed as I ran my fingers over the note, and a silly schoolgirl grin crept over my face. I picked up the iPad and ran back up the stairs to his room. I wasn't shown the rest of the house, so I felt it was off limits. Plus, I wanted to find some sweatpants to snuggle into. I didn't want to be in my short skirt all day.

Walking into Caston's closet, I was amazed at the organization. I think it was bigger than my childhood home. The suits, jeans, crisp dress shirts, everything had its own spot. A dressing island with drawers sat in the middle of the closet. I opened a few drawers before I found a pair of sweat pants. After slipping out of my skirt, I slid on the pants. I felt naughty wearing them with no panties, but I'm not fond of wearing underwear more than a day. I walked out into the bedroom and noticed the sitting room off to the right.

I decided to relax in the sitting room. Sinking into the oversized chocolate chair, I pressed the power button. I noticed I had a few new emails. Cringing, I clicked on the icon. Beth, Professor Kim, and Caston Black. My heart fluttered with anticipation. I clicked Caston's email.

To: Sabrina Bennett
Date: April 24, 2012
From: Caston Black
Subject: Have I Told You

Sabrina,
I hope you are making yourself comfortable. Anything you need, feel free to ask Jules. I am trying to be home as soon as I can. Then we can get you over to pick up your things. I really hope you will stay with me again. I am sorry I rushed out on you this morning.
Caston

P.S. Have I told you how much I enjoyed sleeping with you last night? :)

To: Caston Black
Date: April, 24, 2012
From: Sabrina Bennett
Subject: Re: Have I Told You

You, sir, left me breathless and dazed. What will I do with you? However, you did mention you liked sleeping with me, so I will let it slide. I would love to stay again. I haven't slept that well in years. I've made myself very comfortable. I hope you won't mind. See you soon!
Bre

I smiled at my signature because I know he would rather me say my full name. I set the iPad on the side table. I looked around hoping I could find out more about him. There was a desk off to the side, books everywhere, and a large white lounge sofa with the comfiest looking blanket and pillows on it. I walked over to a stack of books and went through them. Nothing seemed to stand out, mostly classics. Sitting them down, I walked over to the window overlooking the pool and grounds.

The sun was bright today, but the breeze made it chilly. I stretched and yawned. I decided to grab a book, and curl up on the lounge chair to wait for him to come home. No sooner did I curl up under the blanket, I fell into the deepest sleep.

Chapter Five

Sabrina

I was sitting in the courtyard of my dorm. It was a beautiful fall day, the sun was shining and the air was crisp. I saw Beth coming out of the dorms. I waved, but she didn't see me. She was on her phone, and looked as though she has been crying. I stood up and made my way over to her. She almost ran into me. Something was definitely up.

Hanging up the phone, she looked into my eyes, and tears started streaming down her face again.

"Oh my God, Sabrina. I wish you had class with me today. Broc and I are fighting and I could really use some girl time."

"I can come after my class today, and we can go to lunch? Why is Broc mad at you?"

A smile finally graced her face, and she wiped the tears from her cheeks. "I would really like that, Bre. Oh stupid Broc, the quarterback just transferred into one of my classes, and Broc thinks I'm going to leave him for the quarterback."

Rolling my eyes, I respond by pulling her into a hug. "Broc's on the football team. Wouldn't he have faith that one of his fellow teammates won't steal his girl?"

She pulls back and shrugs her shoulders. "I don't know. You know how Broc can me sometimes. It's not like I haven't met him before… He's tall, blond, and oh so hunky."

I laughed. We started walking toward the buildings that our classes were in. "Can't say I've seen him before myself, but I'm not usually at the parties you go to. Plus, a jock? I don't know if I could deal with a jock."

"I've only talked to him a few times. Every time he's been with a different girl, but most of the players don't keep steady girlfriends."

Stopping in front of the building, I mumble, "I don't have time for guys."

She laughed. "If you met the right one you would. Now, promise me I'll see you after class. I don't want to get a text that says you decided to stay for extra practice." She sticks out her bottom lip, showing me her sad puppy dog face.

Placing my hand over my heart. "I promise, Beth. I'll be here."

She jumped up and down, then hugged me. "Oh, thank you! I'm already feeling better. I have to run. I'm going to be late."

I walked over to the next building and into my dance class. Since Beth and I have different majors, we usually didn't have classes together. All I could think about was what Beth said. Tall, blond, jock? Biting my lip, I felt a few butterflies in my stomach. Obviously, it has been so long since I've been on a date.

"Professor, I just wanted to come in before class to say I have to leave ten minutes early today. I apologize, and I'll do anything to make it up. Can I come in for a private lesson?"

Shaking her head at me and pouting her lips she responds with, "Sabrina, you're the most talented dancer in this class. You have a full scholarship, which they don't usually give out for dance. Please, tell me this won't happen again. I don't want to file a report to the scholarship committee."

"No, ma'am, this will not happen again. I have an appointment that I can't change. I feel awful about it." I really did feel awful lying to her.

"Fine. You can make up the class next week. Get with me tomorrow and we can set up a time."

"Thank you, Professor." With that I turned to walk to the locker room to change for class. Making sure I kept my watch on today so I could leave on time.

Arriving at Beth's classroom door, I tried to peek in to make sure I had the right room. The window was higher, so I stood on my tiptoes to peer in. Without any warning, the door flew open, and I was sprawled out on the floor.

"Oh my God, are you okay?" Someone was asking me in a deep voice. I felt a hand on my shoulder and one behind my neck, making my skin tingle with the touch. My eyes slowly opened to a concerned face hovering over me.

He had the most striking blond hair and blue eyes. He was wearing a grey t-shirt with an army green jacket. His bag was slung over his shoulder, and his smile was gleaming white.

I put my hand on my head and said, "I'm okay. I shouldn't have been standing that close to the door."

"You're right, you shouldn't have." Holding out his hand to help me up he continued, "Who stands peering into a classroom that close, anyways?"

Lowering my gaze I said, "I know. I'm supposed to meet a friend here after class, and I couldn't remember if this was her room."

"My name is Mark, by the way. Quarterback, if you don't know."

This was him, the guy Broc thought Beth was going to leave him for. What was he doing leaving so soon, class wasn't over for another few minutes?

Suddenly my head felt dizzy and I felt like my knees disappeared. "I'm... Oh I think I need to..."

"Oh shit."

I felt strong arms around me. A grumbling voice in my ear. I couldn't make out exactly what it was saying. I was being sat down on a chair, something cool was eventually placed on my neck.

"Hello, anyone home?" The knocking on my head made me cringe. If I passed out from my head hitting the ground, who in their right mind would knock on my head?

"Ouch. Really?" I slurred, as I opened my eyes. Mark was staring at me so closely I jumped.

"Oh good, I didn't kill you. Sometimes, I don't know my own strength," he grinned.

"Mark, get out of her face." Turning my head, Beth was now standing next to him. I smiled at her. She smiled and head nodded toward Mark, while wiggling her eyebrows up and down.

A blush crept up my face and my stomach was full of butterflies. He was beautiful for a jock. "I'm Sabrina, by the way. I kind of passed out before I was able to tell you."

"Cool. It's nice to meet you. I was just heading to lunch. I'm running late now because of you, but if you come with me I won't get harassed too much from the guys."

Was he asking me out? I cocked my eyebrow at him and turned toward Beth. "I have plans with Beth today for—"

"No, no, you go with Mark. We can catch up tomorrow or even later." Beth insisted, winking exaggeratedly.

My eyes widened in shock and I swallowed the big lump in my throat.

"Sweet, let's go." Mark grabs my hand and begins to drag me down the hall. I barely am able to grab my backpack. Looking over my shoulder, Beth is standing there giggling like an idiot, and holding her hand up to her head like a make-shift telephone.

We arrived at Kitty's Bar. Not the cleanest place to go and definitely not a place to take a girl, but I guess this wasn't really a date. I walked three steps behind him, because he of course had to make his entrance, and I didn't want to take away from that. Smacking backs and high fives proceeded all around.

"Yo, Bro, who's the chick?" Some guy in a baseball cap said, as he nodded his chin toward me.

"Oh, her? Some chick that made me late. I told her she needed to come with me so you guys wouldn't give me a hard time," Mark said to him.

"This chick's name is Sabrina," I said, walking up next to him and putting my arm through his. "He ran me over with a door and knocked me out. He should have brought me, anyways, to make up for it," I said, glancing upward toward him to see his reaction to my forward advance.

He scowled. Ooohs erupted from the guys. "Damn, she told you, son." Someone sang out to him. I could tell Mark wasn't happy, but all his guy friends seemed to take to me right away.

Lunch proceeded as normal, except when it came time to pay. Mark got up and stretched, then he proceeded to sling his arms over the shoulders of two of his buddies, he looked over to me and said, "You got this, baby? I need to talk with my boys outside." Then he walked out the door.

The waitress walked up to me with a look of disgust on her face. Handing me the check she said, "How can you stand them? I hate when they get seated at my table. They make crude comments, swat me on the ass, try to get me in their laps, and never pay me. The manager lets them get away with it because they're the football team."

I took the bill from her and made sure she was well compensated, but it pretty much left me broke for the rest of the month.

Arriving back at the car, Mark's face had the biggest scowl I'd ever seen. I sunk into the Chevelle, and he sped off before I even fully closed the door.

"What the fuck is your problem?" he screamed, making me jump.

"Excuse me?" I whispered.

"You heard me. I bring you to lunch and you undermine me to my friends. I could have told you to get the fuck out right then, but," he turns toward me, puts his hand on my thigh and slowly moves it up, "you look like a nice piece of ass and possibly someone to keep around."

Who treats people like this? I was about to tell him to fuck off, but when he turned toward me and put his hand on my knee my skin jumped at his touch. "Baby, I'm sorry, I shouldn't have yelled like that. I just don't like to have the guys think I can't handle my woman. Forgive me?"

I felt like he was truly sorry, so I smiled and nodded. He smiled and his hand started to move up my leg. Suddenly, feeling uncomfortable I shifted away from his touch. A growl sounded from deep in his throat, as he turned off the main highway onto a dirt road. The bumps and ruts bounced us around. He increased his speed, and I let out a shriek. "What the fuck are you doing? Let me out!"

Turning the car into a sliding halt we end up parked so far off the street no one would ever know we were there. I felt scared and panicked. Mark's face was dark and evil. "You are going to give me what I want."

"Really, and what would that be?" I snapped back, trying to reach for the door handle behind me.

"Your hot pussy wrapped around my cock. Here and now."

"You're full of shit if you think that is going to happen." My heart felt as though it was going to bust out of my chest.

"Oh, it's going to happen and you can't do anything to stop me."

He grabbed me, pulling me toward him. Once I was close enough, he shoved me over the front seat into the back. Landing on my back, I started to scream, but his hand covered my mouth as his face came to mine. He whispered in my ear, "No one is going to hear you. You should just stop screaming now."

I stopped, but tears were falling down my cheeks now. The bastard had the gall to lick my tears. He reached down, unbuttoned my pants, and drug them off. His free hand reached between my legs and he shoved his fingers into my unprepared body. The sharp pain shooting through my body sent another shriek escaping my lips.

"Tight little hole, isn't it. Don't worry, baby. I'll force it open with my huge cock."

"Please, don't." I whispered. "I'll do anything."

He shook his head as he removed himself from his pants, lining up. I squeezed my eyes shut in dread of what was to come. Then the sharp pinch and pull of his cock inside me sent an unimaginable hurt throughout my body. I just laid there, willing it to be over. It didn't last long, which I was thankful for. Right before he found his release he removed his cock from me and positioned himself over my face. Spraying his release all over me.

I felt disgusting. Like a whore. I was ruined.

Mark moved. Sitting back as he put himself back into his pants.

"Well, well, I see you were a virgin. Hope that was the first time you were always dreaming of." His evil laugh made me shiver and my words fail me.

I slowly sat up, wincing at the pain between my legs. I wiped my face off with my t-shirt. Mark crawled back into the front seat, starting the car.

"Get dressed. We're going back to my place. You won't tell anyone about this. Do you understand me?"

I could see him looking at me through the rearview mirror. His face was serious. I let a few tears escape and made a noise that I've never heard come out before.

"Good, now that we are on the same page..."

"What makes you think I won't turn you in?" Suddenly feeling my strength come back.

He turned around and smacked me across my face. "You won't tell anyone because no one will believe you. Telling someone you were raped by the quarterback? Please. Shit'll get swept under the rug, and you'll be the laughing stock of the university. Look you have two options. One, you'll be my girlfriend. Having a serious girlfriend with aspirations, even if they are as stupid as fucking dancing, will make me look good to the pro teams. Or two, you turn me in and become known for being the used, lying, whore that you that tried to slander the star quarterback. Your choice, baby."

He drives back down the dirt road. I pull my legs up to my chest and whimper softly into my knees. I have to stay with him. I can't lost my scholarship that I've worked so hard for. I thought I'd bear my future with him, until he got what he wanted and let me go. I had no idea the price I still had left to pay.

We pulled up in front of a frat house. I should have known. Getting out he said to me, "Let's go. I have half an hour before I have to be at practice." I slowly got out, trying not to fall once my legs hit the cement. Mark pulled me into his embrace and place a kiss on my lips.

A warm smile came over his face. Much different than he was a little while ago. "Baby, I'm sorry, but I just had to have you. You have to understand no one ever says no to me. Take that for what it is. I think we'll have a wonderful relationship."

I smiled tentatively as he turned and pulled me into the house and up to his room.

Chapter Six

Caston

I rushed out of the dining room, before I did anything I would regret. I had to clear my head. Why did I kiss her? How could I feel so deeply for her? I should never have brought her home. That was my first mistake. Dad would not be happy if he found out. He always warned me about innocent girls. *"Don't mess with the innocent ones, Cass. They'll take your heart and rip it to shreds faster than you can blink."*

Catching my breath in the kitchen, I placed the iPad I had my tech guy configure for her on the counter. I quickly jotted down a note to leave with it, and told Jules when I would be home. I fully intended on taking Miss Sabrina home tonight, and getting her to agree to the photo shoot I had originally planned for her, nothing more.

"Sir, where to this morning?" Terrance questioned.

Going through my phone I came to the security file on one Miss Sabrina Bennett sent from Will, my IT & background guy. I opened it immediately. Skipping over the early history, I went straight to the information regarding her and this Mark fellow. I could not believe what I was reading.

Gritting my teeth, I responded, "Terrance, take me to Mark Baker's frat house. He and I need to have a talk."

I pulled up my email to send Sabrina a quick note. My heart constricted. I decided right then I not only wanted her, but I needed her. I could not let her go on with the life she was headed towards with him. She needed me more than anything. I wanted to be the one to save her. My phone buzzed, telling me I had a new message, seeing how quick she had been to respond to me a smile crept up on my face.

She said I left her breathless and dazed. It seems as if she is falling as fast for me as I am for her. How anyone could treat her like Mark did is beyond my comprehension?

Pulling up in front of the frat house, I felt my blood boil. I had to calm myself down. I would surely be arrested if I did what I actually wanted to do to this so-called man. Terrance parked, and I got out before he was able to turn the car off. I reached the door and rang the bell. No one answered. I pressed and held it for a few minutes. Finally, there was someone on the other side, fumbling with some locks.

"Yo, dude do you even know what time it is? What the hell, man?" Surfer dude mumbled, as he rubbed his eyes and scratched his ass.

Nodding my head, I responded, "Yes, I do, thank you. I need to speak with Mark Baker." I pushed past surfer dude, stepping into the foyer, making him realize I would not be leaving until I saw Mark.

"Mark? Um, I think he's still sleeping." He laughed and continued, "He's probably still banging the shit outta that red headed chick he brought home last night."

I felt my blood begin to boil and my fists balled up. "Where is that son of a bitch?"

Surfer dude obviously recognized my anger and held his hands out to stop me from pinning him up against the wall. "Upstairs, third door on the right. Back off, man. Don't kill the messenger, dude."

I turned to head to the stairs and Terrance followed right on my heels. "Sir, please let me handle this. I don't want…"

"Fuck no, Terrance. I want this bastard's balls in my hand, and I want to squeeze them until they pop."

Coming to his door, I took a deep breath and raised my hand to pound, but I heard a giggle from inside. Oh hell no! I burst through the door.

"What the fuck?" Mark yelled, as the door flew open and a girl screamed. "You? What the fuck do you want?"

I crossed the short distance to the bed, grabbed Mark by his perfectly blond hair, and dragged him to a chair. He was grabbing my hand, trying to get away. I saw Terrance gather the girl up, get her some clothing, and help her out of the room. I shoved Mark's naked ass in his computer chair and pinned him up against his desk.

"I'm talking now. You do not talk, do you understand me, asshole?"

"Fuck you," Mark spit in my face.

"Really? Do you really want me to turn you in, and expose you to your coach, the school, and the media? I have that kind of power, Mr. Baker. You do not want to play with me. I want you to leave Sabrina alone. I saw her files. I know you beat the shit out of her, and she will not turn you in, because she thinks she cannot do better than you. I know you are the fucking asshole to put those ridiculous thoughts into her head. I know she is about to fail out of her classes, because you have hurt her so much physically and mentally that she cannot go to class. I know none of those good for nothing friends of yours would ever cross you and turn you in, but you better believe me when I say I will not hesitate if you come near her again. You told her you were done with her last night. You will not call her again. You will not see her again. If you see her on campus you will turn and walk the other direction. If you see her at a party you will leave the party. Do you understand me, Mr. Baker?"

"Who the fuck do you think you are to tell me what I can and can't do? That little bitch had it coming, fucking prick tease. She is nothing without me," Mark laughed.

I reached between his legs, grabbed his balls, and twisted. Out of the corner of my eye I saw Terrance start to head toward me. I shot him a look that made him stop in his tracks. Mark howled in excruciating pain. "Listen, you dumb, fucking jock. A man of my position knows a lot of people, if you ever want to play football again I would listen to me. Leave. Sabrina. Alone."

"Fine. Fine," Mark squeaked between clenched teeth. "Whatever, dude. She was getting old, anyways."

I pushed him away, and reached in my pocket for my handkerchief to wipe my hands off. Terrance threw clothes at Mark, and he quickly got dressed. Looking around his room I saw little bits of Sabrina scattered around. It made me sick thinking he was here fucking another girl and not thinking twice about her. Terrance walked toward Mark, found a box of his stuff, and dumped it on the ground.

"Hey, asshole. That's my stuff you are throwing around," Mark huffed. He really had no sense of self preservation.

"Honestly, I don't give a shit. Pack all of Sabrina's things in here, and do it now," Terrance said, shoving the box in Mark's hands.

I walked over to the closet to remove her clothes. I started removing them and suddenly got a whiff of her scent that lingered. Thinking about her made me want to touch her. I bent down to the closet floor and found her dance bag. I knew it had to be there somewhere. I walked back to Terrance, who was supervising Mark, and handed him the items. I sat in the chair and waited until the packing was done. I knew Terrance could handle it, but I wanted to make sure nothing was left behind.

Then something under the bed caught my eye. I stood up, walking over to the bed and pulled it out. It was box of toys. Sexual toys. My eyes narrowed, as I looked through the pitiful box. Mark saw me and immediately sputtered, "Those are mine. She could never handle that shit, anyways. I need someone who is more than a quick suck and fuck."

I turned around and swung, connecting with his jaw. His head snapped to the side and blood immediately flew out of his mouth. "That is for forcing these things on her. You're lucky I do not cut your balls off. I am taking them because obviously you are not trained to use them. Someone can get seriously hurt with these." Mark was whimpering on the ground, like he should be, the sick son of a bitch.

"Terrance, I will be in the car. Please, collect the rest of Sabrina's stuff, and meet me there."

I made my way back down the stairs. By now there was a fairly good crowd at the bottom, trying to figure out what was going on. I heard a few gasps when they saw me. I assumed they knew who I was. Good, maybe they would know I meant business then. Adjusting my coat when I got to the bottom step, I turned to the crowd of boys and said, "If any of you sorry excuses for men feel the need to hide in that asshole's shadow because you think he is a king, you have a big time wakeup call coming when you leave college."

Walking out to the car, I pulled out my phone and made a quick call. "He said he would stay away from her... Yes... You have the all the information you need if it becomes necessary... He is a sorry excuse for a man."

Checking my watch, I had just enough time to run to the office to approve the next magazine cover and run over some numbers with Ashton. I also need to discuss Vanessa's intrusion with Ashton, to see what we should do about that. It was never okay to come to my home unannounced.

Arriving home a few hours later, I could not wait to see the angel that is Sabrina waiting for me. Walking through the door, I could already smell her. How is that even possible? My skin tingled. I could not wait to get her in my arms, again. I left her much too quickly this morning. Now that I had cleared up the Mark ordeal, I was free to try to make her mine.

Jules met me at the closet to take my briefcase and coat. "Afternoon, sir, hope you had a lovely day."

"Today was especially lovely, thank you, Jules. Where is she? I cannot wait to see her."

"She went to your room after she collected her iPad, and I haven't seen her since. No lunch or snacks. Poor dear, I hope she is okay up there."

"I'm sure she is all right, Jules. Thank you. Can you start dinner for us? She will be staying, so make sure you have enough for her as well. I think we will take it on the balcony of my room."

"Very well, sir."

I turned and took the stairs two at a time. I had never felt this giddy before. Coming to my bedroom door, I opened it slowly, so I did not to startle her. My body stirred when I saw her clothing lying at the foot of my bed. I was excited to possibly have a naked Sabrina in my room somewhere. Looking over to the sitting room, I saw my angel sleeping on the lounge chair. She looked so peaceful with her hair spread out over the pillow and the blanket pulled up to her chin. I did not have the heart to wake her. I moved slowly to the connecting door and shut it, so I could change and get dinner set up for us outside.

When I was finished, I walked back to the sitting room. Feeling butterflies in my stomach was not something I was accustomed to. I sat on the chair by the doorway, watching her sleep. How can I explain to her that I did not happen to just run into her?

Chapter Seven

Sabrina

I woke with a start. Oh, dear Lord, how long was I asleep? I looked out the window and noticed that the sun was setting. I snuggled back under the blanket. Hearing a noise behind me, I jumped up and swung my head around.

"Oh my gosh, you scared the living crap out of me," I said to Caston, who was lurking in the doorway. "How long have you been home?"

"Oh, about an hour. I have been watching you sleep. You looked so peaceful, I did not want to wake you. "

I blushed and shook my head slightly. "I wish you would have. I was dreaming about Mark, and now my stomach is upset with the realization of how stupid I was to ever be with him. My mind is acknowledging things I couldn't before."

Walking over to me, he stroked the hair from my face. I turned my head and kissed his palm.

He cupped my cheek. "Sabrina, everyone makes mistakes in their life."

His hand slowly slid behind my neck and drew me in toward him. I licked my lips in anticipation of his kiss. My insides clenched. His lips slowly brushed mine, with the sweetest touch. I felt my lips tingle, as his tongue slowly parted them, seeking the warmth of my mouth. Slow and sensual, this kiss wasn't like the one from this morning. He slowed the kiss, pulling away.

He rested his forehead on mine, our noses touching, and he spoke the words I was thinking, "I hope you'll let me kiss you every day from now on." I nodded. I was at a loss for words. This man was becoming special to me, fast. It scared, and excited, me.

He backed away from me and looked at what I was wearing. I smiled and shrugged. "What can I say? I missed you, wanted to be comfortable, and I have no clothes here."

Laughing at my statement, he stood me up, made me stand in front of him, and spun me around slowly. "Well, if I do say so myself, my sweats have never looked so good." I giggled as he pulled me in for another kiss. Finally, he leaned back and said, "You must be hungry. You slept the day away, and Jules said you hardly ate breakfast after I left." I nodded with a silly smile on my face.

He grabbed my hand and led me through the main bedroom, out onto the balcony. He had a dinner set up on the table overlooking the pond on the side of the house. "Oh my, this smells delicious. I guess I'm hungrier than I thought." The candles flickered in the breeze and the sounds of the crickets started up as the sun sank slowly behind the horizon. "Why the change?" I asked.

Looking perplexed, Caston asked, "What do you mean?"

"This morning you were one hundred percent insistent that we wait until I've met and settled things with Mark and now…"

He sighed. Oh no. I wasn't going to like what he said, was I? "Well, I paid Mark a visit this morning after I left you. I hope you will not be mad at me for talking to him. I wanted to make sure I did not hurt him yesterday, and I wanted to see what his intentions were with you." I opened my mouth to speak, but he raised his hand to stop me. "I understand that I am not your keeper, and I hope you do not think I was intruding, but the feelings I have for you are so…"

My face softened. Interrupting him, I said, "I'm not mad. I'm relived, actually. To be honest, I was afraid to confront him."

"I would never let you do anything that would put you in danger. I would be with you the whole way." He reached across the table and grabbed my hand, stroking the back with his thumb.

"There's only one problem," I said, trying to hold back my smile.

"Oh, yeah? What would that be?"

"I have no clothes. We're supposed to get them from the house today."

Winking at me, he raised my hand up to his lips, and then peering up at me with his smoldering eyes he said, "Although, I do like to see you parading around in my clothing, Terrance and my other guys packed up all your belongings and brought them over this afternoon."

Giggling, I lunged out of my chair, catching him off guard. Straddling him, I grabbed his face and planted a huge, wet, sloppy kiss on his lips. When I pulled back, he laughed the most delicious laugh I've ever heard. "You, sir, are my knight in shining armor. You've saved me."

Picking me up, he carried me back into the room and laid me on the bed. His face grew serious. "I'm not as knightly as you might think, but I take care of those who mean something to me." Leaning over, he devoured my lips. His hands slowly made their way down my sides to the bottom of my shirt. He slid his hands under it, and his palms touched my bare belly. It felt like lightning bolts went straight to my core. He moved his kisses over to my ear and nibbled my earlobe, stroking with his tongue. His hot breath sent shivers down my spine. One hand slowly moved up to cup my breast, and the other slid under the band of the sweatpants. I felt a smile on my neck, as he realized I wasn't wearing anything under them.

"No panties, Sabrina. I approve." I moaned and arched my back to try to move his hand lower. His hand moved opposite of the way that I wanted it to, and I groaned. "All in good time. Enjoy the sensation."

He removed his hand from my pants and pulled the shirt over my head. Looking down at me there was a hunger in his eyes that made my juices flow. "Perfection only a dancer could have," he said, as he caressed my chest and took my nipples between his fingers. I moaned and let out a gasp when he squeezed them. Lowering his head, he took one in his mouth and nibbled. I'd never had anyone dote on me with such passion. These were all new feelings and sensations. I never wanted them to stop. His lips brushed light kisses down my body, stopping at my belly button, kissing from one side to the other. His hands kept my nipples in hard peaks, as he slowly furthered his descent. He stopped right above the waist of the pants. I ran my hands through his hair, wanting to grab on to anything. How could he make me reach my breaking point from just kissing me?

Looking up at me he says, "May I continue?"

As if he even had to ask. "Oh, God, yes," I panted. I smiled at the thought. Being asked was not only incredibly sexy, it was a nice change of pace.

He drew my pants down, as he slowly kissed his way down my legs. Moving back up to my hips he stopped when he came to the one thing I regretted in my rebellion stage. A small Tinkerbelle tattoo right below my left hip bone. Rubbing his finger over it, tickling, and he said, "Tinkerbelle?"

I blushed. Only one other person knew about this tattoo. I shrugged, "I was young and dumb. What can I say?"

He kissed it ever so lightly, making me shiver. "I love the way you smell. You're intoxicating." I shifted my hips under him, trying to make his mouth move closer to where I needed it. I wanted to feel his lips on me in my most private area.

"Bare, just the way I like it." With that he dove in, and I immediately felt myself build to climax. Everything he did was perfection. He licked and sucked my lips, nibbled my bud, then with a quick swirl of his tongue I went over the edge. He didn't let up, making me rise, again. Moving his fingers inside me, stretching me, I felt them curl up to touch my g-spot. I let out a yell I'd never heard myself make before. I came so hard I was twitching. I never wanted it to stop.

He slowly stroked me down from my high. Standing, he quickly discarded his pants and his glorious cock sprung free making me catch my breath. He was massive. I have never seen a cock that perfect before. He tore open a condom and slid it down his hard shaft before he leaned over to start moving up my body. I felt his tip wanting access.

Caston looked down at me with a fire in his eyes that made my breath catch. "Please, Caston...I need to feel you." I pleaded.

Hesitating briefly, he looked down at me, the hunger in his eyes made me gasp. Our eyes locked and with one quick movement he was inside me to the hilt. He stretched me more than I've ever been stretched before. I arched my back and grabbed on to his shoulders. The muscles twitched under my hands, and I dug my nails into his skin. He growled, as he started to move. The noises only made me reach my next climax that much faster. The feeling was so much deeper than I'd ever experienced. I could feel my muscles clench around him. Responding to me, he quickened his pace and moved my body so he was kneeling in front of me with my legs draped over his shoulders. His hands reached down and played with my bud until I was screaming out in ecstasy.

"Come for me, Sabrina," Caston growled. His words spun around in my head. The buildup was so intense. Within seconds of his request, I was screaming his name, and I felt him stiffen and clinch my legs.

We were both out of breath, as he withdrew from my body. He drew me close, so we were cuddling. He was stroking my arm whispering sweet nothings into my ear. I was just about to fall asleep when something hit me. "Caston, can I ask you something?"

"Anything, Sabrina."

"How did you know I was a dancer?"

Chapter Eight

Sabrina

I felt Caston's breath catch and his body stiffen around me after I asked that question. Why would that have affected him so much? He cleared his throat and said, "I helped clean out the closet in Mark's room. I was the one to come across your dance bag."

Oh how stupid could I be? Of course that's how he knew. "Caston?"

"Yes, Sabrina?"

"Thank you, again."

"Sleep now." He pulled me closer, and I drifted off into a peaceful sleep.

Mark and I'd been together for about a year. He was cute, if you only saw the surface. I felt the sideways glances from the girls who thought I must feel like a

queen, having snagged Mark Baker. On rare occasions, very rare, he could be nice and sweet, but most of the time he was frightening. He really wasn't too bad when I cooperated with him.

I laid back on his bed in the frat house and did some leg stretches, while I waited for him to come home from football practice. He had been in a mood lately and I was trying to surprise him and be there right when he got home to give him a massage and make him dinner. I closed my eyes and my mind wandered back to the last week of summer when Mark took me to a cabin on the lake for a last minute vacation before football season started up again. We were all alone. He was so attentive and even bought me flowers. It was almost as if this wasn't the Mark I was dating. Our last night there was the most amazing. A candle-light dinner out on the patio and Mark was fawning all over me. I felt so cherished. When we finished eating, he slowly leaned over, kissed my cheek, and whispered in my ear, "I have a surprise for you, baby." I turned to look him in the eye and smiled. I felt my cheeks getting hotter as he was looking into my eyes so deeply. "Wait right here."

Mark gave me another peck and walked inside. He was nervous. It was so unlike him. I started to fidget when I saw his shadow appear in the window of the cabin as he made his way back out to me. Then he appeared in the doorway. He was only a silhouette. What was he carrying? Oh wow, it was a guitar case. He could play? He walked over and pulled his chair right in front of me. "I didn't know you played the guitar."

"I never really told anyone before. None of the guys know."

He looked so cute when he blushed. He was opening up to me. All those harsh words he had said to me over this last year seemed to disappear. I reached forward and pushed the hair out of his eyes. He looked embarrassed. "What's that face for?" I asked.

He looked up at me and smiled. "I was afraid you would think I was stupid for playing the guitar."

"No way, Mark. Thank you for sharing this with me. I can't believe you're just now telling me this. Plus, guitar players are HOT."

He laughed. It made me smile to hear his laugh. "Can I play something for you?"

I nodded and leaned back in my chair. He got out his guitar adjusted it, so it was in tune. I couldn't help but notice how magnificent he looked in this dusk lighting. His hair was still a little damp from our swim earlier and he was wearing a white t-shirt and black jeans. Then he slowly started strumming, and my heart started to flutter. He was looking down at the guitar and wouldn't make eye contact with me. It was perfect. I was watching him in awe as he sang. His voice was amazing. Why wouldn't he share this with anyone else? When he finished he looked up at me. The look in his eyes made my knees quiver. He slowly put the guitar down to the side and ran his hands through his hair. I placed a hand on each side of his face and made him look at me. "That was truly beautiful. You're very talented and should share this gift with others. Thank you for sharing it with me. I didn't recognize the song though. Where is it from?"

"I wrote it." He whispered so quietly, I barely heard it.

I leaned forward and kissed him so lightly. He looked at me and scooped me up and carried me inside to the bedroom and we actually made love that night. The only time this year he actually seemed to care for me and take his time. I liked this new Mark.

Smiling to myself from this memory made me stroke my stomach as I thought about what happened that night, and what our life was going to be like now because of it.

I woke up to the door slamming. "Hey, baby. I was just dreaming about—"

"What's for dinner? You know I like my food ready when I get home from practice. I risk everything to have you here. You could at least do things right. Get it, now, and when you come back I need a release. Practice fucking sucked today."

I sighed. The peaceful, amazing memory was lost, again. I got up and picked up his bags where he dropped them on the floor and I gathered up the laundry to throw in as I walked to the kitchen in the frat house.

I stirred in my sleep. What time was it? My eyes slowly opened, as the sun was just starting to peek through the windows. I felt strong arms around me, and snuggled deeper into Caston's embrace. I could get used to this. I heard him moan, and I felt him rise up on his elbow and look over to me.

"Good morning, Bre."

I giggled and rolled over onto my back. He looked delicious. I snaked my fingers in his hair and pulled him in for a kiss.

"Mmmm, good morning to you. Bre, I thought you insisted on Sabrina, Cass?" I asked with a giggle.

"Cass?" he shook his head, "I changed my mind." I blushed, and leaned in to kiss him again. He deepened it this time, and I felt his erection pressing into my thigh.

"I could get used to waking up like this."

"Me too, Bre, me too."

He slowly let his hands travel down my body, and when he reached my sex, his finger slipped into my soft folds. His touch instantly made me wet. He played with my clit, while his lips were brushing my neck, the sensation made me shiver. I let out a moan, as he sheathed himself. I was so ready for him. When he pushed himself in, the stretching was mind blowing. He slowly started to move. I closed my eyes and arched my back into him. "Sabrina. Bre, please look at me."

I froze, Mark never wanted me to look at him when we were having sex. I would ask him to look at me, but he would scream, or just leave, if I did. Eventually, I stopped asking. I was ashamed that I wanted to feel that connection. How could I look Caston in the eyes after being told for so long that I shouldn't? I felt my eyes start to well up behind my lids, unsure of what to do.

I opened my eyes and stared deep into his soul. He was giving himself over to me with his eyes. Leaning over he kissed me tenderly, and I relaxed into his embrace. "There's my sweet girl," he whispered.

His movements sped up and I wasn't going to last much longer. "Oh, Caston, please. I want us to come together. I can't wait too much…" Suddenly, I felt him start to jerk, and it was my undoing. He yelled my name, and devoured my mouth as we finished.

We laid in each other's arms, and he stroked my arm gently. "Are you hungry, Sabrina?" he asked.

As if on cue my stomach growled. I giggled, "I guess I am."

"Let's get you up and get you something to eat then." He pulled away, and I longed for the return of his touch as soon as it was gone.

I rolled onto my stomach, looking over at Caston pulling on his sweatpants. I batted my eyes and said, "I'd rather have some more of you for breakfast."

Caston laughed. He reached over and smacked my ass. "Get up. As much as I'd love what you're offering, I need to get recharged too. You're wearing me out."

I smiled and blushed. My butt cheek stung where he smacked me, but it instantly made me wet and ready for him again. I could never tire of this man's touch.

Once I was decent, Caston took my hand and we walked together down the stairs to the breakfast bar. The sun was shining today, it reflected my mood. I was sure nothing could upset me. We sat down at the spots Jules had set out. I couldn't stop smiling. I hadn't felt this good since…since before I met Mark. It's amazing how I got so used to being unhappy, I developed a new definition of what happy means to fit my new reality. I guess I didn't realize it, until I was presented with a gift that brought to light what I'd have been missing.

I had the biggest smile on my face. I couldn't seem to stop staring at Caston as we ate breakfast.

"What?" he laughed. "Do I have something on my face?"

"No," I responded, giggling like a school girl. "I'm just so happy. I feel like a one-ton weight has been lifted off of my shoulders and I'm a new person."

A smile crept across Caston's face. He reached over to tuck a piece of hair behind my ear. "I'm glad to hear that, Bre. It's only going to get better. I promise, okay?"

I nodded and returned to my breakfast. When we were finished, I hopped up and gathered the dishes and started to clean the plates. Caston walked up behind me, snaked his hands around my waist, and kissed my neck. I shivered. "That tickles, but, please, don't stop."

I felt his smile on my skin, as he moved my hair and kept kissing along my upper back to my other shoulder. "You know I employ someone to clean the dishes, don't you?"

"Yes, but I don't want to be a burden on Jules, since she usually only takes care of you."

"Mmmm, you taste wonderful, Sabrina," he hummed, as he continued kissing me. I'm not sure how I didn't break any of the dishes in the sink...I could barely focus. "It's the weekend. What would you like to do? I'll take you any place you want to go."

He captured my mouth with his when I turned around to face him. My hands were wet from the dishes, but I couldn't resist pushing them through his hair. His hands grabbed my behind, raising me up, and I wrapped my legs around his waist. He walked me over to the breakfast bar and set me down. "Oh, that's so cold." I said, giggling through his kiss.

"I guess we need to heat it up then, don't we," Caston growled back.

As his hands started to push my shirt up, someone cleared their throat in the doorway. My head snapped up, and I started to turn around. I thought I heard Caston mumble 'fuck' into my chest.

"Well, I guess I won't be eating at your house ever again, unless I sanitize the countertop first. Caston, dear, where are your manners? How did I bring you up?"

"Mother, I am twenty-six, this is my house. I can damn well do as I please."

I wanted to die. I wouldn't turn around to see the women standing behind me, and wished I could just melt into the floor. Even Caston had yet to look at her. He brought his hands up to my face and kissed my nose. "I will be right back. Please, do not go anywhere."

Chapter Nine

Caston

Son of a fucking bitch! Beverly had the worst fucking timing in the world. I'm definitely talking to Terrance about changing the locks. I hoped she wouldn't scare Sabrina away. I kissed Sabrina's nose and asked her not to go anywhere. I wanted to continue this. I was sporting a full-on erection. I had to adjust myself before heading toward my mother. I walked around the breakfast bar, grabbed my mother by the elbow, and led her towards the front door. "What the fuck are you doing here?"

"Caston Holden, is that anyway to talk to your mother? Really, dear, I thought I brought you up better." She reached up and tried to fix my hair.

"Damn it, Mother, do not bullshit with me." My teeth clench. "My name isn't Holden, not anymore. How the fuck did you get in, anyway? The gate didn't buzz. What do you want? I have company."

"I see that, dear. Your newest slut can wait for you. They always do."

My anger was about to boil over. "She is not a slut."

"Oh, cut the crap, Caston. She's only with you for your money, or to be in the magazine. You'll never find true love, not when you're as rich and famous as you are. People will always use you. Don't trust anyone.

"As far as getting in, your landscaping crew was entering when I pulled up. They really should be reprimanded for allowing me to follow them in. I mean seriously, dear, they could just let anyone in."

She looks over behind me where Terrance has appeared. "You're really not doing your job very well. How can you keep my baby safe?"

"You're talking to me, not him. I'm sure you sweet talked those workers somehow. I know your M.O."

We reached the front door, and I wanted nothing more than to send her packing and tell her to have a good life, but she is my father's wife, after all. "What do you want?"

"Your father and I are hosting a party next week at the club for his birthday. You know the type. I thought I'd let you know, so you can prepare yourself and a date."

"Mother, I hate coming to your parties. I would rather not think about my parents that way."

"Oh, honey," she touched my cheek, "you owe us for your kinky background, or Black Hollywood might not exist, and then who would you be?"

I knew she was full of crap. I would be successful, no matter what, but Black Hollywood was my top grossing company. "I would still be successful, Mother."

Her hand moved from my cheek to my chest. It disgusted me when she looked at me with sexual appreciation. I removed her hand from my chest. "Please, show yourself out. Oh, and next time, call before coming over. I am planning on having company over permanently from now on."

Looking displeased, she spat out, "Fine. Do whatever you want. She will leave you high and dry, like the rest of them. Mark my words, Caston." She turned to walk out and stopped on the step and turned around. "I do hope you will be at the party, though. Your brother will be there."

I shut the door and leaned up against it. Parents and sex were two things that should never go together. I would admit I used to love their sex parties when I was younger, but lately I found myself wanting more than one night stands. My mind drifted back to the lovely goddess that was in my kitchen. Would she be up for a sex party? How would I even tell her about it? Ugh, I would think about it tomorrow. I rolled my head on my shoulders to relieve the stress of my mother barging in, then I pushed myself away from the door to walk back to the kitchen. "Bre, I'm so sor…Sabrina?" I hung my head. I knew she would freak out.

I made my way to the bedroom. That was the only place I could think she would be. I slowly pushed open the door and saw her sitting on the bed cross legged. Her face had a look of terror on it. I had to let out a small chuckle. "Oh Sabrina, please tell me you're not freaking out about someone walking in on us."

"Someone? Caston, really? It wasn't someone, someone I could be okay with, it was your mother! How am I supposed to look her in the face EVER?" Her adorable babbling ended with a high pitched squeal.

I walked over and sat next to her. "Well, just knowing you want to see her again makes me smile. Most women don't even want to meet my family."

She turned to look at me, still bug-eyed but with a look of longing. "Of course, I want to meet them." Then in a whisper that I almost didn't hear her say, "I think I'm falling for you.

"And who the hell is Caston Holden? I thought your name was Caston Black."

"I changed my name when I was old enough. I didn't want to be associated with them, anymore. It was my rebellion."

I saw the confusion on her face, but I wasn't sure how to explain my past to her, but I knew I had to try. I already knew I had fallen hard for her, dare I say loved her, but I had to show her exactly who I was. I didn't want any more surprises, but unfortunately being with me there would always be surprises. Could she handle them? I wrapped her in a big bear hug and kissed the top of her head. "Sabrina, honey, we need to talk."

Chapter Ten

Sabrina

As soon as Caston left the kitchen, I slid off the countertop and snuck upstairs. His mother? Oh my word, how am I ever going to face her again? She must think I'm a slut. Anyone else and I think I could have laughed it off. Caston Holden, who the hell was that? I thought his name was Caston Black. Maybe Holden was his middle name. Definitely something I need clear up.

I curled my feet under me and waited. I was sure it wasn't long before he came in, but I swear it felt like hours. My mind was scrambling, while he was talking to me. Why did he not want to be associated with his parents?

Then he did it. He said those dreaded four words that no one in any type of relationship wants to hear. 'We need to talk.' My body stiffened, and my heart felt like it was being ripped out of my chest. Oh, no, here it was. I wasn't good enough for him. I knew it. I shouldn't have gotten myself attached this quickly. My eyes started to burn with unshed tears. Mark was right, after all.

Noticing my tense body, Caston grabbed me by my shoulders and turned me, so I was forced to look into his eyes. "Sabrina, get those thoughts out of your head. They aren't true. " How did he know I what I was thinking?

"So are you a mind reader now?" I blushed, trying to look away.

"I tend to be sometimes, but, my dear, you are easy to read," he smiled, pulling my face, so I met his eyes. "Get dressed. I want to talk, and you dressed like this makes me want to do everything but talk."

I groaned. I just wanted to be in his arms all day, he made me feel safe, but he rolled me over and gave me a swift smack on the ass, again. That restarted my juices flowing. I got up and headed into the closet. I looked over my shoulder at him getting ready. He seemed happy, but nervous. I quickly got dressed in a yellow sundress. I pulled my hair up into a messy bun and slid on my brown heeled sandals that laced around my ankles. Even though, I had only taken a few minutes, Caston was already waiting for me.

"Ready?" he asked when I appeared from the closet.

"Ready for anything," I stated, trying to sound more confident than I was at that moment.

He smiled and stood up from where he was sitting on the edge of the bed. He held out his hand to me, I grabbed it, and we headed out. Holding his hand made me feel like I had strength I didn't possess on my own. Once we stepped outside, I saw Terrance standing by the Jeep. He opened the backseat and Caston helped me in. He said a few words to Terrance before getting in next to me.

"Where are we going?" I questioned.

He pulled me close and kissed the top of my head. "I want to show you my businesses. I need you to see who and what I really am."

I looked up at him terrified. "What does that mean?"

"Nothing, Sabrina, only that I'm a complicated man, and I need you to be fully aware of everything, before I take this any further with you. I can see myself with you forever, and I need to know if you can accept me."

He held me tighter, and I snuggled into the crook of his arm. We fit together perfectly. It was like I was made to be there. We drove in silence, but when I snuck a glance at him, he was chewing on the end of his thumb, so I could tell he was nervous. Wanting to calm him down and let him know I could handle what he had to show me, I turned my head and kissed the side of his chest. He smelled delicious. I rested my hand on his upper thigh and let it wander closer and closer to his manhood. When I finally reached it, I stoked it through his jeans. His breath hitched. I could feel him grow under my touch.

We suddenly came to a stop at a large building. Caston looked at me and asked, "Are you ready? We're here."

I nodded. Caston adjusted himself before getting out of the door Terrance opened for us. Once again, he held his hand out to me, and we walked up to the magnificent glass entryway. I looked up and saw Rose Builders over the door. "This is your building?"

He laughed lightly, as he opened the door for me, "One of them, Bre. We will go to the other one later."

The heels of my sandals made a clicking noise that echoed on the white marble tile as we walked in. I giggled when I saw all the employees scatter when Caston walked in. I guess they weren't expecting the boss in today.

"Good afternoon, Mr. Black. Didn't expect to see you today. Anything I can get for you, sir?" a beautiful blond, who was carrying a stack of files, addressed Caston.

I immediately didn't like her. She positioned herself between Caston and me, as we walked toward the elevators. This forced him to let go of my hand. I instantly felt insignificant, as I fell into step behind the couple. Wanting to crawl under a rock, I felt like I should turn and walk back out to the car. She was laughing and giggling at Caston's joke about the weather. Was she really flirting with him? How did he not see that?

"Oh, how rude of me, Nicole," Caston said, touching her on the arm. I thought he was going to introduce me to her. "Please, let me carry those heavy folders for you." I was mistaken. His behavior was a big letdown. I hadn't expected him to dismiss me when we were around other people.

Handing them over to him, she brushed away some hair on his shirt that wasn't even there. She spoke with him about emails and phone calls. She continued on, as if I wasn't even there, and it was starting to tick me off. When the elevator came to a stop, she filed out first, letting her ass sway to and fro in her shorter than necessary pencil shirt when she walked in front of Caston, leading him to her desk. I stayed behind a ways to see how long it would take for him to acknowledge me with Blondie talking his ear off. He set the files down and continued for a few more minutes when he suddenly snapped his head around, as he remembered why he was there.

Catching my eye, he held his hand out to me. I took it, but not without giving him the shittiest look I could muster. When my hand met his a spark of electricity ran up my arm, making me shiver. Looking confused, he pulled my hand up to his lips, never breaking eye contact with me, and pulled me into his arms. Turning toward Nicole he said, "Sabrina, I'd like you to meet Nicole. She is my PA. I couldn't get anything done if it wasn't for her keeping me in line." His voice changed slightly as he said, "Nicole, this is my Sabrina." I blushed at the way he described me. His Sabrina. Wow. How can I stay mad at him when he introduces me to her that way? Why hadn't I noticed the difference in how he spoke to everyone, but me? He sounded so controlled when he spoke to them. Every word was spoken and enunciated clearly.

Her mouth dropped open and then you would have thought she sucked on a lemon the way her face scrunched up. "Nice to meet you," she hissed.

"Nicole, could you, please, get Sabrina a new iPhone, and have Will set it up with her email and contacts? Have it delivered to my house tomorrow." He kissed my hand again and looked at me. "I'm sorry, Bre, but your phone is so old. I think it is time to get you in the 21st century. What do you think?"

I wanted to play it up in front of Blondie, so I giggled and put my hand on Caston's chest, and said with a sigh, "Oh, Caston, you're the most generous man. What did I do to deserve you?" I leaned up to give him a kiss on the cheek. I could see Blondie tense up out of the corner of my eye. That's right he is mine. Hands off.

Caston looked at me with a crooked smile, unsure of what he was witnessing, but kissed my head and said, "Okay, Sabrina, let's go. I want to show you my office, then we can go to the other building." He turned me toward a big wood door and started walking toward it.

I snuggled up next to him, but I wanted to rub it in Blondie's face one more time that he was mine, so I looked over my shoulder at her staring at us walk away. "It was so nice to meet you, Nicole. I hope to see you, again, soon." I giggled. Caston just shook his head.

Walking into his office, I was amazed at how big it was, floor to ceiling windows, black leather furniture, and a massive mahogany desk with a computer on the corner of it. It was a huge open space, but it felt warm. It definitely reflected Caston's style. In the corner of the room was a large table filled with blueprints and models. He let go of my hand and immediately walked over to that table. He turned around with a childish grin on his face. I, however, was still mad at him and wasn't going to let him get away with forgetting about me so quickly. So, I stood with my hands folded across my chest and didn't follow him. When he saw my look his eyes fell and his smile faded. "What's wrong?" he asked.

"Really, Caston? Do I really need to spell it out for you?"

He quickly walked back to me, wrapping me in his arms. "What, tell me, what did I do?"

I pursed my lips and hissed, "Blondie out there has a thing for you. Can't you see that? God, I wanted to puke with the way she was strutting around in front of you. And how did you forget I was with you?"

"Oh, Bre, please, please don't be upset. I'm sorry I didn't introduce you to her right away. I walked in here and my mind immediately went to work. It shouldn't be that way, but it's been my sole focus for years. I promise it won't happen again," he looked into my eyes. "Don't worry about Nicole. I only have eyes for you. Plus, she is my assistant, so there has never and would never be anything between us. Please, believe me."

He looked so sincere and sorry I couldn't stay mad at him. I leaned up on my toes and kissed him lightly. "I could never stay mad at you, but please don't leave me hanging anymore. You know I have self-esteem issues, and seeing Blondie out there only makes me feel more like an ugly duckling."

"An ugly duckling you aren't, my beautiful swan." He kissed me with so much passion my knees buckled. "Are we okay, now?"

I nodded. I knew he didn't do it on purpose.

Looking over to the table I said, "Show me what has you so excited over there."

His smile was bigger than a kid in a candy shop, and I could tell he really loved what he did. He led me over to the table and started explaining and showing me his projects. Everything seemed very foreign, but listening to him made me as giddy as he was. When he finished, I gazed at him in awe. He was out of breath from talking so fast.

"What?"

"You're just so cute. You really love what you do. That's so amazing to watch you."

He grabbed me in a big hug again, smiling from ear to ear. "I think I love you just as much."

I rested my cheek on his chest. I couldn't say it back. I wanted too. I needed too.

"Sabrina, you don't have to say it back. How about we get out of here and head to my other company? I wasn't worried about this one, it's the next one that has me worried."

Chapter Eleven

Caston

I sighed. This was going to be the hardest thing I've ever had to do. I held onto Sabrina so hard, never wanting to let her go. She snuggled up under my chin. My heart felt as if it was busting at the seams. I slowly pulled away, and lifted her chin so she would look into my eyes. They were a beautiful hazel color that sparkled with a fire that wasn't there a few days ago. "Are you ready, Bre?"

She nodded, and I grabbed her hand bringing it to my lips. She had the softest skin I'd ever felt. I opened my office door for her, thankful that Nicole was gone. I was definitely going to have to set a few more ground rules with her Monday morning. I caressed Sabrina's soft hand with my thumb as we waited in silence for the elevator. She was uncertain about what was going on and I wanted to ease her worries.

The elevator arrived with a ding that vibrated through my body. It was like an alarm clock awakening my desire for her. I looked over to her. She was so cute, twirling her long dark hair in one finger and chewing on her bottom lip. I could tell she was nervous about what I needed to talk to her about.

The doors opened and we stepped in. Typing in the code that made us bypass any floors waiting on the elevator, I needed to make this small space ours. I couldn't wait until the doors closed to get my hands on her. I stepped in front of her, took her face in my hands, and consumed her lips, like I was dependent on them for survival. Backing her up against the wall, I wrapped her hands around my waist. She pulled me even closer than I thought was possible. Breathless we finally parted and I rested my head on her forehead. "You do things to me, Sabrina. Things I've never felt before. Things I can't live without. Please, promise me something. Please, promise me to keep an open mind and let me explain everything when we get to my next stop?"

She gasped, but shook her head yes, while her eyes stayed closed. I wished she would look at me. Then I could tell if she would really let me explain. I had to believe that she would. Giving her a peck on the forehead, knowing our ride would soon be coming to an end. I pulled away from her body and grabbed her hand again. The doors opened, and we walked out to where Terrance had our car waiting.

The drive over to Black Hollywood wasn't a long one, but it was silent. I wasn't sure exactly where I was going to start. We pulled into the underground garage, so we could enter the building without being bombarded by paparazzi. They would just love to get a hold of her and smear her over all the tabloids. Once the car stopped, I turned to Sabrina and sighed. "This is it, Sabrina," I took both of her hands in mine, "this is my main company. Have you heard of Black Hollywood before?"

"Caston," she tried to talk, but I put a finger over her lips. I wanted to get everything out before I let her talk.

"Just listen Sabrina; please let me get this out." She nodded and let me continue. "Black Hollywood is a gentlemen's magazine. I spend a lot of time discussing sex, naked women, and everything pertaining to those things. It has been a source of tension between other women in the past, and I want to start this relationship out on the right foot and be one hundred percent honest with you. If you stay with me, you will be in the public eye and probably all over the tabloids. I need you to understand what you would be getting involved in. If you would like me to go on I will, but if not Terrance is prepared to take you to a hotel, and you can stay there at my expense until you can find a place of your own."

I paused waiting to see what she would say. It was only a few seconds, but the silence was like a knife slowly inching into my stomach. A smile inched onto her face, "Caston, I've known you were the Caston from Black Hollywood. Well, I didn't know that first night, but once Beth said something everything seemed to make sense. Your name is unusual. It is okay. I have an open mind. I won't go anywhere. I'm here for you, not your companies." Her hand was on my cheek, it made me feel a little better for the moment. I let out the breath I hadn't realized I was holding, and decided to take her into the building to continue with my confession.

I moved to open the door of the Jeep, but she stopped me. "Caston, look at me. Whatever it is, I'm a big girl and I can handle it."

"Follow me." I said, as I helped her out of the car, then held the door open to the back entrance. The walls were lined with half naked women, and for the first time ever I felt ashamed for what I did. I snaked my arm around her waist and pulled her close, to walk next to me. Really needing to get her into my office without any of my assistants seeing her until I finished my confession.

Chapter Twelve

Sabrina

I just don't understand why Caston is so tense. I already told him that I understood who he was, and that I could handle anything he told me. I wanted to stop and look at the beautiful pictures lining the walls, but Caston had me pulled into him and was almost running down the hall. Finally, stopping at a door he let out the biggest sigh I've ever heard. Looking over to him, and seeing the worry in his eyes suddenly made my stomach knot up.

Caston reached for the door and pushed it open, leading me in to the darkened room. I walked out of his embrace, making my way into the room a little further than he was and waited for him to turn on the lights. I could see pictures all around the walls, push pinned on boards and lying loosely on tables. Was this some sort of work room? This definitely wasn't like any office we saw at Rose Builders.

The lights went on, and I gasped and my eyes bugged out. I was staring at a bulletin board of snapshots. This couldn't be happening. My head spun around, and Caston wouldn't even make eye contact. "No," I said barely over a whisper.

Caston didn't respond. I walked over to the other board, scanning the other pictures. This couldn't be happening. I brought my hands up to my face and started to sob.

"Sabrina." Caston pleaded and tried to comfort me.

"Don't," I held out my hand to him, so he wouldn't come near me or continue his explanation just yet. I wasn't sure how I was going to deal with this. All these pictures were of me. How did he manage to get all of these? Why did he have them? I sank to the floor feeling very betrayed.

Caston gave me my space. He sat down on the edge of a chair that was close to me, but still far enough away. I could tell he wanted to explain. Do I let him? I said I could take whatever he had to tell me, but this was going too far. "You stalked me?" I said between sobs, looking up questioning him. "Why?"

"Sabrina," Caston tried to come near me, and I recoiled.

"Don't touch me."

"Sabrina, please, listen." He didn't listen. He sat in front of me and pulled me on to his lap. Not wanting to be there, I pushed at his strong arms wrapped around me and shoved at his chest, trying to escape his hold.

"Let me go, Caston. I don't want you to touch me. I hate you! You lied to me! I trusted you. How could you betray me like this?"

"This is my work, Sabrina. We do research on who we want to be our next featured Sweetheart. Collecting information and data. I saw you a few months ago at a performance at State, and I knew you had to be the next one. My employees have been getting pictures and information on you ever since."

I stopped struggling and turned to look at him. If my eyes could shoot daggers, I think they would have. Did he really think that was okay?

"How is this okay? How do you justify spying and collecting data on someone, without their knowing, as okay? Do you not see just how fucked up that is?"

I could tell my words stung him. Good. They should. I wasn't a piece of meat. His grip loosened on me, and I scrambled to stand up, leaving him kneeling on the ground staring at his hands in his lap. I stood and towered over him. "Everything you've said to me has been a lie. Why?"

He looked up at me with tears in his eyes. "Sabrina, please let me explain. No, I haven't told you the whole truth, but, please, let me explain."

I stepped away from him, shaking my head. "I think I want Terrance to take me to the hotel, now."

Caston's head whipped up when I asked to leave. His eyes pleading with me to stay and let him explain. My heart was breaking, but also melting, as I looked at him. "Please stay, Sabrina."

I suddenly froze. I had nowhere to go. A sob escaped me again.

I leaned on the edge of a work table trying to regain my senses. Taking a deep breath and closing my eyes, my heart was telling me to rush back into his arms. Steeling myself to his answer I asked, "Were you at the party stalking me?" I prayed he wouldn't say yes. I wouldn't be able to live with that. I wasn't sure I could forgive him now, I couldn't forgive him if it is true.

"No, Sabrina, I was not there to stalk you. Actually, I was shocked to see you there. I could not believe you were standing in front of me when I turned around. Then when you needed my help I could not help but rescue you. I felt you were a sign from God telling me you were the one. You are my other half. Why else would things fall into place the way they have?"

I wrapped my arms around my body. Tears were running down my cheeks. I shook my head. "I don't care. You betrayed me. I want to leave. I need to leave now." I walked over to the door. Thankfully, Terrance was standing on the outside of the door guarding it.

"I'd like to leave now, Terrance. Please, take me to Beth's house. I'll give you the address."

"Very well, Ms. Bennett."

I took one step out the door before I stopped and looked back over my shoulder. Caston was still on his knees with his head in his hands. I could tell he was crying. I wanted to run back to him and wrap myself in his arms.

Pausing, I tried to decide what the right decision was. No, I had to do this. I couldn't let another man hold me under his spell and manipulate me like Mark had. I straightened my back and turned around to leave him.

I followed Terrance back through the hallway and out into the garage that we had entered through. I crawled into the back of the Jeep and tried not to look back at the doorway. Telling Terrance where to go was so hard. I hoped Beth was home. I wanted to go to her apartment, instead of a hotel. Tears were still running down my cheeks, as I felt the car start to move. Looking back over to the door I saw Caston standing in the doorway with his hands in his pockets. I put my hand to the glass as if to touch him one last time. I left it there as we headed back out to the daylight. Out of Caston's life forever.

The ride to Beth's was long, even though, it was only a short distance away. I wanted to be anywhere else, but in the situation I was in. What was I going to do now? Spring break would be starting, and I had no one to be with and no place to go.

Terrance pulled up in front of a small apartment complex. My heart was breaking as I thought over all that has happened to me in the last few days. Had a boyfriend, lost a boyfriend, found a lover, lost a lover. What a mess. Now I only had Beth, if she would take me in. Looking up at the building in front of me I moved to step out of the car when Terrance appeared at the door.

"Sabrina, may I walk you up to your friend's door?"

"No, thank you, Terrance. I will be okay. Was that Caston you were on the phone with on the way over?" I knew I shouldn't ask questions I didn't want answers to, but I was just gluten for punishment, I guess.

"Yes, Ms. Bennett."

That was all he said to me. He handed me a bag that was worth more than the clothes I was wearing. I looked at him with a question showing on my face. "What's this?"

"Mr. Black made sure you had the things you needed in case this very thing transpired. He asked me to give them to you."

"Well, I can't accept these." I tried to hand the bag back to him, but his face told me if he was to come back with the bag he would be in trouble, so I pulled the bag to my chest to show him I was folding on this fight. His look of relief made me smile, just a bit.

"Is there anything else I can do for you, Ms. Bennett, before I leave?" I just shook my head to answer his question. "Very well. It was very nice to meet you Sabrina, and I do hope we cross paths again soon."

I smiled, weakly, at him. I would like to know all he has seen coming in and out of Caston's life. I bet he could write a book. I just added myself to that list and a new tear fell from my eye. I had to get inside before I lost it completely. "I'll miss you, Terrance."

I walked around him and ran up to Beth's door. Pounding on it, I prayed she was home. No one was answering, but I thought I heard noises coming from the inside, so I pounded again. "I'm coming, I'm coming. Don't get your panties in a twist." I heard Beth yell from inside. I looked back over my shoulder, Terrance was still standing by the Jeep, even though I told him to leave. I'm sure that was Caston's order, as well. I gave him a wave, and turned back around just as the door opened in front of me.

Beth's face was shocked to see me, but her smile quickly faded when she looked in my eyes. Quickly ushering me into the room before I broke down on her doorstep, she started the interrogations, "Bre, what's wrong? Oh my God, please tell me he didn't hurt you, again. Oh dear lord, honey."

I shook my head and sobbed, not able to talk to her at all. I struggled with Beth as she tried to remove the bag clutched to my chest. I slouched over it, smelling Caston. This only made me cry harder than I ever thought was possible. Beth being the friend that she always was just sat me down, helped me remove my shoes, and stroked my back and hair. She pulled me down over her lap and held me. "Well, I'm just glad you aren't with Mark anymore. I hate you're hurting, though." I drifted off to sleep on Beth's lap. I was so emotionally drained, I'm not sure how long I was out. Thankfully I didn't dream of Caston, or Mark.

When I started to wake up, I was sore from sleeping on the lumpy couch. I decided to lay still for a few more minutes. I heard Beth whispering into her phone. I struggled to hear her, while I remained still, so she wouldn't see I was awake and end her call.

"No, she is still asleep ... I don't think you should come over today ... God, I've never seen her like this before, Broc. I've seen her messed up from Mark, but this is worse ... No, I don't think it is a good idea for Mark to come over to see her ... Because he's an asshole that's why ... I don't care if he's your friend or not ... Broc, are you serious right now? ... No I'm not joking. ... He's a manipulative, abusive asshole. I can't believe you are defending him. ... I think we need a break. We obviously don't agree on this. You need to figure out your priorities. I'm done."

I closed my eyes to pretend I was still sleeping, so she wouldn't know I was listening to her. She slammed the phone down on the table, and I heard her walk toward the kitchen. I waited until she was out of the room before I sat up. My bag was gone. What happened to it? I started frantically looking for it. I was almost flipping the couch over when Beth ran out because she heard the commotion. "Where is it?" I screamed.

Shock flashed across Beth's face. She has never seen me like this before. "What? Sabrina what the fuck!"

"My bag, Beth. Where the hell did you put it? I need it!"

"Oh my God, Sabrina, chill the fuck out! It's in the spare room. What are you on? You have NEVER acted so crazy before!"

I sat on the edge of the couch and ran my hands through my hair. I was breathing so hard I was afraid I was going to pass out. What is wrong with me? "I just need the bag. Hell, I don't even know what's in it."

"Seriously? You almost tore my living room apart for a bag that you know nothing about! You're in need of mental help." She laughed, and sat down next to me. She flung her arm over my back squeezing me to her side. I gave her a sideways glare. "Look, I'll go get the bag, and we can go through it, okay? Are you sure you aren't on anything? I won't be mad if you are, just tell me."

"No, Beth, I'm not on anything. I feel like hell and my heart has been ripped out. My life is flipped upside down, and I'm not sure what

I'm going to do, or where I'm going to live. I'm sure I'm kicked out of school, since I haven't gone in over a week." I hung my head again and busted into more tears. How could I have any left?

"Honey, you can stay here as long as you want. You don't even have to pay me rent. You know that. I've told you this before." She hugged me, and popped up to go down the hall to retrieve my bag.

Breathe, Sabrina. I'm sure it is just clothes in the bag. You are a strong women and you will find a way to move on.

Beth came back holding onto the large coach bag. She set it on the table in front of the couch, then sat down next to me. We both stared at it like it was going to move on its own. I'm not sure how long I sat there. Finally, Beth broke the silence, "Well, are you going to open it or do you want me too?"

I looked at her and took a deep breath. Leaning over I unzipped the bag and spread it open. It looked to be clothes in the bag. My heart was beating out of my chest, as I started to pull things out. These were all new clothes. There was nothing in here that was mine. Beth's mouth was agape, watching as I removed one expensive thing after another. Trying to lighten the mood she quickly said, "Well, if you need any money you could always sell these clothes. They'd bring in a pretty penny." My eyes started to water again and she continued on. "Oh, honey, I'm sorry. I didn't mean to make you cry. I was just trying to lighten the mood. Please, don't cry." I straightened my back and shook my head to clear my tears away. When did he have a chance to pack this, or buy all these new clothes? Coming to the bottom of the bag I was in shock, the iPad was in there. My mouth fell open, and Beth spoke the words that I couldn't. "Holy shit, he gave you an iPad."

I knew this was the one I'd used when I was at his house. Without a word I got up, leaving Beth with unanswered questions, and walked to the spare room that I would be staying in. My heart was beating a million miles a minute, as I turned it on, and sat on the bed. Why was I so nervous? The telltale email arrival tone rang out. My heart was beating fast, and my hand trembled as I clicked mail icon. The top email was from him, Mr. Caston Black. I took a few deep breaths and closed my eyes. How had he gotten under my skin so fast? I clicked the email.

To: Sabrina Bennett
Date: April 25, 2012
From: Caston Black
Subject: Please

Sabrina

As I watched you leave today I was at a loss for words. I feel like my heart has been ripped out of my chest. I have fallen for you, Bre. Hard. I need you back in my life. My employees thought I was insane when I went into that room and started ripping pictures off the wall and tearing them up. I want you, and if you are not okay with being in my magazine, I am okay with that. I need you. Please, let me make this up to you. Please, let me try. I am not even sure where to start. I should have told you right away who I was and that I knew who you were. I never intended to meet you the way I did. It was supposed to happen 3 weeks from now, after my company sent you a formal letter asking for a meeting. I have never fallen so completely for anyone. You are special Sabrina. You are my other half. Please, give me a chance. It kills me that I no longer have your trust. I will spend my life making it up to you. I will give you all the time you need. Please, know you can ask me for anything, anytime.

I love you, Sabrina.

Caston

To: Caston Black

Date: April 25, 2012

From: Sabrina Bennett

Subject: re: Please

Caston

Please? Please, my ass. I trusted you. You knew everything about me already. What was the point? I still don't see how you justify spying on people as okay. I don't know if I can ever forgive you, or trust you again. I need time. Lots of time. Please, don't email me again. I will be returning all of the items to you. Please, send Terrance to pick them up. I don't want them.

Sabrina

I quickly hit send before I could rethink what I wrote. No sooner did the email disappear panic washed over me. How could I have actually sent him such a nasty email? I really wanted to take him in my arms and tell him I would forgive him and that all would be okay.

A light knock on my door pulled me out of my trance. Beth peeked in and saw my face. "What's wrong, Bre?"

"He sent me an email begging me to give him another chance. I replied to his email basically telling him to fuck off. What did I do?"

She crouched down next to me and pulled me into a hug. "Everything will be okay. You'll get another billionaire soon."

I hit her on the back. "Not funny, Beth," I said, with a slight giggle.

"Got you to smile and laugh, though. Didn't I? Let's get some ice cream, sit with the tub between us, and wallow over guys and how crappy they are."

I wiped at my eyes and nodded. I set the iPad down on the bed, and walked out of the room with Beth's arm around me.

"Looks like we both have guys to wallow over, huh?"

She looks at me surprised.

"I wasn't really asleep. Sorry for eavesdropping."

Wrapping her arms around me she squeezed me hard.

"Men just suck. Let's go get that ice cream."

Chapter Thirteen

Caston

I just stood there in the doorway and watched her go. I stood there until the tail lights were not visible anymore. I felt hollow. Turning to walk back into the building, I raked my fingers through my hair, pulling hard. Suddenly, all the breath was taken from my lungs, like I was punched in the gut. I bent over, resting my elbows on my knees, and took gasping breaths. Rage was building up in me. How could I be so stupid to let her go? I stood up and punched the first picture to my left. It came crashing down in a waterfall of glass around my feet.

I stormed down the hall and pulled out my phone to dial Terrance. "Terrance, please, tell me you are taking her to Beth's apartment... Good. How is she? No, don't answer that... Don't forget about the bag in the back. Walk her to the door, and if she won't let you, don't leave until she is in the apartment. Thank you, Terrance."

I gripped the phone until I heard it start to crack. I could hear her in the background crying, it was awful. Looking around the room, I saw her beautiful face smiling back at me. It tore me apart. I started racing around the room turning over tables, ripping down pictures, throwing bulletin boards.

A knock at the door pulled me out of my raged trance. "Hello?"

"FUCK!" I screamed to no one in particular.

The door cracked open and Luca my new intern said "Mr. Black, um, sir. I'm sorry, I didn't know you were in here. I heard the commotion as I, um, was coming to get things prepared to set up a..." He stopped when he saw the state of the room and his eyes immediately cast downward.

"It's okay, Luca. We are scrapping the Miss Bennett idea as my newest Sweetheart. Please, have someone come clear this room."

"Very well, sir," Luca muttered, as he quickly turned and ran back down the hall.

Damn, my hand hurt. I looked down at it, I was bleeding. Fuck. I wiped it on my shirt. So many thoughts were running through my head. I found my work laptop amongst the rubble of the office and quickly started writing to Sabrina. I have to get her back. I will do anything. I will do everything in my power to get her back.

I sat, staring at my screen, willing a response to my email to come through. I know she has the iPad, because Terrance had come back to get me at Black Hollywood. I sat staring at the screen overnight. I was not even sure what time it was anymore, and still, nothing. I got up, and started pacing again. The room was still a mess, no one on my staff wanted to come in here to clear it while I was still here. I looked down and saw a picture of Sabrina. Her long brunette locks were cascading down her back, and she was looking at the camera, as if she knew someone was taking her picture. Her creamy white skin was flawless, her smile barely there, her hazel eyes looked sad, even though she had a smile on her face. I touched the picture. I wanted to feel her again. Hold her in my arms.

I was ready to walk out of the room when my email pinged. I rushed over to the screen and looked at it. It was her. Quickly opening it, I read, and it felt like she ripped my heart out and stepped on it. I sat down at the desk and wept into my hands. I started typing my soul out to her. I have to get her to let me back in. Finally, I stopped and hit delete, she wanted time. I had to accept that. Looking down at the picture, I tucked it into my pocket, and headed out to the garage where Terrance was waiting.

"Sir, the iPhone came in. Should I deliver it to her in the morning?"

Looking up, I could see the pity in his eyes. He knew just as much as I did that she was a catch, and I had let her slip through my fingers.

"Please." I slid into the seat and laid my head back and closed my eyes, so I didn't have to think. My mind had other plans though and ran away with ideas on getting her back.

Chapter Fourteen

Sabrina

Beth was nice enough to let me stay in her apartment over spring break, the longest week of my life. Thankfully, it was rainy and gloomy, which reflected my mood perfectly. I slept for countless hours. The only time I got up was to go to keep my follow up appointment at the clinic from an earlier health problem. I didn't eat, who knows how much weight I lost in five days? I was miserable. Why was I doing this to myself? It was my choice to be away from him.

The doorbell rang twice every day while Beth was gone, but I didn't want to answer it.

I woke up on Monday to the sun shining. Any other day I would've been happy to see the sun, but not today. I still had nothing to be happy about. I had a massive headache, and I felt hung-over. Emotional hangovers are worse, I think. You cannot just get sick and make it go away. It stays with you.

I laid on the bed and pulled the covers up to my chin, squeezed my eyes shut, and tried to will myself back to sleep. Last week I was in the arms of the perfect man, today I'm waking up alone. Was I stupid for leaving him? The same internal fight brewed in my head and heart again this morning, just as it had every day for the last week.

I could hear Beth singing to the radio in the kitchen. I was thankful she was finally back. Like clockwork, the doorbell rang. I sat straight up in bed, with my eyes wide open. I nervously looked over at the bedroom door. Who was Beth talking too? I could hear her laughing and flirting. Ugh, the last thing I needed was to watch her and Broc be all lovey dovey. I sank back down in bed and pulled the covers over my head, trying to tune out any thoughts of love.

No sooner did the covers reach my face when my door flung open. "Good morning! How's my girl today? Did you miss me? I missed you! I wanted to talk to you last night when I got home, but you were already asleep," Beth sang.

I groaned, "Go away."

"Can't. I'm under strict orders to give you this."

I knew she was holding something out in front of me, but I refused to look. "Whatever it is I don't want it".

"Fuck that," she said, as she plopped down next to me. "If you don't want it, I'll take it."

She pulled the covers down and shoved a small box in my face. "What is it?"

"Don't know. Some guy named Terrance dropped it off. Um, you so need to introduce me. I'd love to get to know him better."

I glared at her like she had two heads. "Set it on the table and get out."

"Nope." She said, bouncing on the bed. "I want to see what it is. Plus, I need to get you moving. You have got to go to school today."

I groaned. "I'm sure Professor Lee has already filed my expulsion papers."

I sat up and took the box from her. She smiled, and got up to walk out. "I'll be leaving in a half hour, so get ready."

I stared at the box in my hands. In my heart I wanted to rip it open, but my head was telling me to throw it away. I took a deep breath, set it aside, and got up to shower. I hoped my extra shoes were still at school, since my dance bag was at Caston's house. Tears started to well up, again, but I shook them off and got ready.

When I was done I met Beth by the front door. She had a spring in her step and smiled when she saw me. "So glad you decided to come with me. It will be like old times, just you and me."

"Oh, sure. I don't think so Beth, sorry."

"Stop," she took my hands in hers, "you're a strong, confident, rather skinny person, did you lose weight?"

I just smiled and thanked God that she didn't mention the box sitting on my bedside table.

"Thanks, Beth, for everything."

Arriving at the dance studio, I took a deep breath to clear my head before I approached Professor Lee. I knew she was going to be very angry with me, and I prayed that she wouldn't kick me out. Straightening my spine, I walked in with my head held high. I spotted her across the room, helping out another girl with her turnout. My stomach was in knots, as I walked over to her. "Professor Lee, may I speak with you?"

"Ms. Bennett," Professor Lee stood up, with a big smile on her face, "I'm so happy to see you, again. Go, my dear, go get ready we have class to start." She hugged me, and scooted me off toward the locker rooms.

I'm not sure what just happened. I was ready to plead for my position in the dance program, and she was welcoming me back with open arms, no questions asked, or retribution for missing so many classes.

Arriving at the locker room the other girls seemed to be whispering among themselves. No sooner did I walk in they stopped, looked over at me, and quickly walked around me, before continuing what they were saying. It was very strange. What was going on?

Stripped down in the locker room, I was in my tiny v-string thong, looking through my locker for a leotard. I heard the door open, but didn't think anything of it because class should be starting soon and others had to get ready. I stopped digging in the bottom of the locker when I felt eyes on my backside. I felt a shiver run down my spine. I knew exactly who was standing behind me. Feeling that tingle in my lower regions, I stood up and slowly turned around. There he was, standing in front of me again. His eyes bore straight to my soul. He held out my dance bag. "Thought you might need this."

I wasn't going to cover up in front of him. "Thank you." I said, reaching forward to grab the bag from him. He caught my wrist, tugging me toward him. I gasped, as I crashed into his rock hard chest. I could smell his cologne and my legs felt weak.

"Why won't you let me explain? Give me a chance," he whispered into my ear, sounding so somber. His hot breath making me shiver.

I didn't know what to say. I wanted to forgive him. I wanted to make him pay. I wanted to lose myself in him. I had no idea what I wanted.

His thumb started to stroke my back, and a small whimper escaped my lips. I looked up at him, and put my hand to his face. Searching his eyes for the truth. I could see in his eyes he was sorry. He looked like a little puppy staring at me. Could I simply believe him? I could see deep into his soul that he would do anything in his power to get me back. We both sunk to our knees and I wrapped my arms around his neck. He pulled me onto his lap. His mouth sought mine, and my lips parted to let his eager tongue in. I pulled back, trying to catch my breath. His mouth found my neck and I closed my eyes and moaned. "Caston," I said breathless, "Please, don't ever lie to me, again. I can't take the lies, and I won't stay. I've been treated wrong for too long. I'm going to be a new stronger, confident woman."

"Sabrina, I'll never lie to you, again. I'm so sorry I lost your trust. I'll do everything in my power to get it back. I'll tell you anything you want to know, and answer any questions you have. Please, come back to me."

His mouth was all over my neck and shoulders, seeking comfort and asking for forgiveness. I wanted him so badly. The deep pull on my insides made me tighten my legs around him, looking for comfort. I could feel him growing underneath me. I wanted him. My hands twisted in his hair and pulled his head down to my chest. I needed him to kiss me there. We were getting lost in the moment when there was a knock on the door. "Hello?"

"Damn!" Caston said into my chest, making me giggle. He looked up at me and smiled. "That is the sound I love to hear. Please, forgive me?"

I nodded and gave him a peck on the lips before he stood us both up. He quickly straightened himself. I quickly grabbed my robe out of my bag, trying to hide my blush that was rising in my cheeks. I had to cover my mouth to hide my smile when I noticed what I had done to his hair. It usually looked perfectly messed up, but now it looks like we were up to no good in here.

"Mr. Black?" Professor Lee's voice echoed into the locker room. "Is everything okay in here?"

"Yes, Professor Lee. Ms. Bennett and I were just talking."

I had to cover my mouth to not laugh out loud.

"Please, hurry her up I'm ready to start class."

"Yes, ma'am. I will make sure she is out shortly."

I heard the door close upon her leaving, and Caston was back at my side in a nanosecond. His mouth engulfed mine as he stripped the robe off my shoulders, pushing it down to pool around my feet. He quickly lifted me up, I wrapped my legs around his waist, and he backed me into the row of lockers. His strong hands squeezed and kneaded my butt. His mouth quickly made its way down my neck, sucking a trail to my right nipple. My hands were pulling his shirt out of the back of his pants, and I wiggled my hips against the bulge in his pants to get more friction where I wanted it. His moan into my breast fueled my fire even more. I pulled the shirt over his head, then my hands roamed his hard muscles. My mouth sought skin, and tasted it magnificent, as my hands moved to the button of his jeans. Fumbling for a few seconds I finally felt the button pop and I slid my hands down to release his manhood. His mouth moved over to my other breast, and my head fell back slightly taking in a deep breath. His talented tongue did a dance over my nipple that sent shock waves through my body. "Caston, I need you. Please." I didn't need to ask twice. His finger slipped in me and he touched my core. I erupted in his hand and with a flick of his wrist my thong snapped. He quickly pulled out a condom and entered me, making me gasp at the fullness. My head rested into the crook of his neck and my hands tangled into his hair. His motions were fluid. I felt myself building again. I could tell by his grunts and clenched muscles he was almost there, too. I moved my head up to his ear and sucked on his lobe. The deep growl in his throat sent me over the edge, and he quickly followed me.

Our breaths were hot and heavy, our skin slick with sweat as we came down off of our high. God, I needed that. I needed him. "Thank you," I sighed into his neck.

He let a laugh escape him. "For what?"

I laughed. He slowly let himself fall from me. I unwrapped my legs from his waist. He set me down, and Caston's mouth found mine again, and he gave me a slow sensual kiss. "I should be thanking you. You're giving me a second chance. You have no idea what that means to me."

"Babe."

"Yes," he said.

"I need to get to class. As much as I'd rather stay with you for a repeat performance, Professor Lee is happy right now, and I need to stay out of trouble."

"I wouldn't worry about Professor Lee. She knows you're fabulous." He gave me a peck and smacked my ass, as I walked past him to clean up.

"Will you wait for me?"

"Always."

As promised, Caston was waiting for me outside of class. Sitting there on his phone, he looked like he fit in with the rest of the students. No one knew they were sitting next to the owner of multiple companies, with millions of dollars. I smiled with pride, knowing he was now mine. I walked up to him, with my shoes hanging over my shoulder. Once he saw my legs in front of him he looked up at me with hooded eyes. I could tell what he wanted, and I wanted him too, but not here. His hands grabbed my legs and pulled me onto his lap. I giggled, and he caught my mouth with his. Professor Lee cleared her throat when she walked out of the room. He quickly set me on my feet, and I ducked my face to hide my blush. He stood up next to me, kissed the top of my head, and turned me off toward the locker rooms. I peeked over my shoulder and saw Professor Lee and Caston talking. Then Caston placed his hand on Professor Lee's lower back and led her to her office. I froze in my tracks. What could they be talking about?

I walked out of the locker room a little later. Caston was standing in the empty waiting area alone with his hands in his pockets. Upon seeing me he held out his hand and said, "Let's go home, Bre. We'll stop by Beth's house, so you can get your bag." He pulled my hand up to his lips and I curled into the side of him as we walked out into the parking lot.

Should I move back in with him right away? Beth said I could stay with her as long as I needed. I felt conflicted.

"Bre, what's on your mind?"

I took a deep breath and spoke the truth. Promising myself I was going to be more confident I started with, "I'm not sure I want to move back in right away. I mean Cass do you think we are going to fast?"

He stopped walking and turned me to face him. I met his eyes, and he leaned down to place a chaste kiss on my lips. "Bre, I really want you to come home with me. I sleep so much better when you are in my arms. Last week was hell for me. I've never been in this situation before, but I love it. I know you are what I need to make my life whole. Please, move back in with me."

My heart sped up he was so sincere. I felt warmth spread through my body at his words, and I knew in my heart what I wanted. I wanted him. He's warm. Sincere. He's never pressured me. He is interested in me for me. He makes me feel safe, which I haven't felt since I lost my parents. Most importantly, his presence is calming to me.

Smiling I whisper, "I'll think about it."

"Okay, Bre. That's all I can ask for."

I linked my arm with his, and we continued on to the car in silence. When we reached the car Caston opened the door for me. I smiled and climbed into the SUV.

When he took his seat next to me I asked, "Caston, what were you talking to my professor about?" I knew it was none of my business but I had to know.

"Bre, I'm the main contributor to the arts for State. I wanted to make sure the department had everything it needed. In fact," he said looking over to me, "there were some things lacking, so I will be upping my contribution next Monday. Professor Lee almost fell out of her chair when I told her that." He laughed. It was heartwarming to hear him laugh.

"Nothing about me?"

A sly smile crept up on his face. "I might have mentioned that you're very special to me, and that should you want any extras to let me know and I would take care of everything." His face was serious now, "I want you to have the best of everything, Sabrina. I want you to do what you love, like I do."

"So you're the reason she took me back into the program with no questions asked?"

I saw him swallow hard, "I might have done a little persuading in that direction."

I nodded. I wasn't sure how I felt about that. "I appreciate it Cass, but next time please let me plead my own case." I turned around to look out the passenger side window. I've never been taken care of like this. It would definitely take some getting used to.

Chapter Fifteen

Sabrina

We pulled up in front of Beth's apartment. Caston parked, got out, and walked over to my door to help me out. He slipped me a warm kiss, as I stood next to him.

"I'm sorry I didn't talk to you before I talked to Professor Lee. I just wanted to make sure you can graduate. Forgive me?"

Even though he overstepped, I couldn't stay upset with him when he was only looking out for my best interest. "I forgive you, just please talk to be next time."

Smiling, I took his hand and led him to the apartment. I wanted to introduce him to Beth. After thinking about what he had done and how he had saved me, in more ways than one, I had decided on the way over I was going to go back to his house, but I hadn't told him yet.

Letting myself in with the key Beth had lent me, I could hear her singing in the kitchen. "Beth, we're here. I'm just going to get…"

"Bre! Thank goodness you're here. I..." Beth ran out of the kitchen and stopped dead in her tracks. Upon seeing Caston holding my hand, she dropped the bowl full of cookie dough she was holding.

Caston let out the biggest laugh, as I rushed to help Beth collect the broken bowl. "My God, Sabrina, you have to call me and warn me that a sex god is coming over. I would have looked presentable. You know in a garter belt and stockings, or something," Beth whispered, not so quietly, to me. "What the hell happened? I thought it was over between you guys?"

I stopped what I was doing, gaping at her in shock. She wasn't even helping me with the clean-up. She just sat on the ground drooling. "Earth to Beth." I said, knocking her over, as I stood up.

Caston was by my side, again. He had grabbed a towel from the kitchen and started wiping up the mess. "She couldn't have called you." Caston stated to Beth.

I looked over to him with confusion written all over my face. I tensed up at him answering for me like Mark had in the past. "And why is that, sir?"

Beth just giggled. I shot her a nasty look that made her suck her lips in to stifle her laugh. "Because, my dear," Caston said, as he took the broken pieces of bowl from my hands looking me in the eyes, "I assume you never opened the box I had delivered this morning, because you do not have a phone on you. I actually tried to have that package delivered every day for a week, but that's beside the point. So you don't have your new phone on you, do you, now?"

He had me there, and I had no comeback, so I flashed him my sassy smile instead. He kissed my forehead, knowing he had won, and Beth sighed. It felt good to be wanted, for a change. When he walked into the kitchen and out of our line of sight, I could see Beth snap back to reality. She was fluffing her hair and plumping up her breasts. She even pulled up her skirt, so it was shorter. "Really?" I questioned.

"What?" Beth spat out.

Rolling my eyes at her I said, "Primping, so you can look good for my..." My what...boyfriend?

"Sabrina, I need to look good. That is *the* Caston Black. Maybe he has a brother, or possibly that hot body guard, he can hook me up with?"

"Beth, he's just a man." I sighed, thinking about how wonderful he really was. "And what about Broc, have you made up with him, yet, or are you still split up?"

"No Broc and I are still split up. He hasn't come to his senses. So hook a sister up."

My eyes went wide as saucers.

"Oh, Bre, don't be so selfish..."

I shook my head at her, as I turned to walk down the hall to the bedroom I was staying in.

She was a piece of work. I quickly gathered my bag, iPad, and small box, which I now knew held my new phone. Walking back out into the living room, I could see Beth sitting on the couch, bending over to show her cleavage off to Caston. I scrunched my eyes closed, wishing she would, for once, not try to flaunt her body.

"Caston, are you ready?" I asked semi quietly when I reached the couch. Thankful Beth's over abundant cleavage didn't seem to draw his eye.

He stood up, and ever the gentleman, he collected the bag I was holding. He smiled at me, questioning my decision. My answer was the big smile split my face in two. He picked me up in his strong arms and kissed me. When we parted, he whispered in my ear "Thank you for trusting me enough to come home with me."

Beth sighed. He looked back over to her. "Thank you for taking Bre in last week. It was nice to meet you." He set me down and shook her hand before we turned to head for the front door.

Smiling at Beth, I mouthed, *I'll call you later.* I winked and bounced off to catch up to Caston.

Back at the Jeep he helped me in my seat and put my bag in the very back of the vehicle. I waved at Beth in the doorway, as we pulled out.

"Thank you," I said to Caston when he pulled out onto the road.

"For what, dear?"

"For not ogling Beth. She can be a bit much at times, but I love her like a sister."

He grabbed my hand and kissed it, "Honey, remember what I do? Beth was tame."

He set my hand on his thigh and returned his hands to the steering wheel. Feeling very brazen, I decided to move my hand up his leg. Coming into contact with his hardening length, I tightened my grip. His breath caught in the back of his throat and he stretched his neck. I unzipped his pants and slid my hand in, touching him skin to skin. Pulling him free, I slowly scooted over to take him in my mouth. The groan he let out was magnificent, and made me take him to the back of my throat. Working my tongue up and down I could taste his salty precum, I sucked harder. I wanted to taste more.

Suddenly, he pulled the car into the back of a gas station. I moved my mouth faster, and he growled, as his fingers tangled in my hair. The pleasure I was giving him made me smile around his cock.

"Bre, stop."

Not wanting to stop, I kept going. He pulled me up by my hair, and I winced, raising to relieve the pressure. A gush of wetness hit my panties. The thrill and pain of it excited me. He engulfed my mouth so intensely it took my breath away. His hands were all over my body, kneading my breasts, and gripping my ass. He quickly reached into his pocket and removed the condom to cover his cock, as I pulled my shorts down. Turning to look at me, the heat in his eyes made me moan. He leaned over the middle console, snaked his arm around my waist, and pulled me toward him, making me straddle his lap. Pushing my thong to the side, he plunged into my wetness, making me scream out in ecstasy. The feeling was overwhelming. He grabbed my arms and pinned my wrists together behind my back with one hand. I felt so helpless, but on fire. I could not believe we were doing this in broad daylight. The thrill of possibly getting caught had me worried. His mouth found my neck, and all thoughts and reservations left my head. My attention returned back to the sensation of him moving slowly inside of me. I could feel myself building to my climax, and I struggled against the restraint of his hands, trying to get him to let me go. I needed to touch him and push his head into my breasts. I wanted to feel his hot mouth on my nipples. I ground my hips deeper onto his lap, moving them in circles. I felt his stomach muscles tense under my movement. Abruptly, he let my hands go and wrapped his arms around my waist, burying his head into my neck. I wrapped my arms around his head, pulling him into me.

Caston growled into my neck, "Sabrina, oh my God," sending me over the edge. He followed right after me. We sat tangled in each other's arms breathing heavily.

"Wow," I huffed out between breaths.

"My God, you're perfect." Caston said, as he looked up into my eyes, moving the hair from my face.

"Take me home, Caston. I need you, again." Our mouths crashed onto each other, not wanting this moment to end just yet.

I'm not sure how we made it home without crashing. My hands were all over him, and he had one hand between my legs stroking my wet folds during the entire drive. Pulling up to the front door, Caston slammed the car into park and jumped out. Running to my side, he flung the door open, and scooped me up to carry me inside. We were so lost in each other, we forgot to shut the door to the Jeep. His mouth was on mine the entire time as he carried me over the threshold. Kicking the house door closed behind him, he pushed me up onto the wall, until I was straddling him with my legs over his shoulders and my exposed sex in his face. I let out a quick scream of elation, as he flicked his tongue on my clit. Folding myself down over him, I hugged his head. He alternated between sucking my lips and plunging his tongue deep inside me. Lapping up my juices, his tongue was doing things I had never felt before. I felt his hands on my ass, holding me up, and with one last flick of his tongue I was a convulsing mess. Blacking out, I felt like I'd lost my mind and all my ability to make any sound. I never thought seeing stars from an orgasm was possible before tonight. He slowly eased up on his licking to bring me back down to earth.

My arms went limp and I leaned my head back against the wall, too sated to support myself. Caston kissed the insides of each thigh and slowly lowered me off his shoulders, sliding me down the wall carefully, he asked with an evil grin, "Do you think you can stand?" I nodded, but he kept me pinned against the wall anyway. "Open your eyes." I did as I was told. "How was that?" His voice was smooth as silk. I shivered and took a deep breath. I smiled, but right as I was about to say something, he kissed me again, deep and hard. I could taste myself on his tongue, and I couldn't get enough. Still reeling with aftershocks from my last orgasm I suddenly burst again. I flipped my head back and screamed Caston's name, my legs gave out on me this time.

Caston scooped me up and carried me to the stairs. He set me on the steps and quickly discarded his clothing. His cock sprang out, throbbing, needing to be touched. I reached forward, but he stopped me. "Bre, I really want to be in your wet pussy right now, if you touch me I think it'll be the end for me." He reached forward, pulling me to his mouth, as he pulls my shirt over my head and unsnaps my bra. Cupping my breasts in his hands, he moved his mouth over my nipple, slowly sucking and toying with it until it was sharp as glass. His fingers squeezed my other nipple, until I gasped at slight pain. As he was playing, one hand grazed down my stomach and quickly made its way to my slit. Parting my lips, he pushed his fingers deep in me, again. I felt so helpless, wanting to touch his hard cock, but he asked me not to, so I raked my fingernails down his back. His head flung back, and he let out the deepest caveman grunt. It sent waves down my spine, flooding my already sopping pussy.

"Oh God, Caston, please. Please, God, I need to taste you, now." He removed his fingers and brought them to my mouth to suck. Without hesitation, I grabbed his hand and sucked his fingers clean, as if my life depended on it. Our eyes locked and I watched his breathing grow ragged and his muscles flex as he moved, making me want him more.

"Think we can make it to the bedroom?" His eyes looked into mine, already filled with promise of more.

"Oh, I think I can. But you…" I poked him in the chest. "I don't think you will be able to."

He laughed deeply and rolled off of me enough that I was able to hop up and turn to sprint up the stairs.

"Oh no, you don't," he calls out, laughing, jumping up to follow me.

I only made it to the top of the stairway before he caught me, and grabbed me around the waist, pulling me into him. I could feel how he was hard when he ground himself into my behind. His hands reached up to caress my breasts. I let out a moan, my head falling back onto his shoulder. Just as I started to get hot again, he lifted me up and flung me over his shoulder like a sack of potatoes and smacked my ass.

"Ouch," I laughed. "Put me down."

"Nope." He said, smacking me on the ass again. "You need to be spanked for trying to get away from me."

I heard a door open behind me and I froze.

"Jules, didn't know you were up here." Caston says cheerfully as if nothing is wrong. You'd never know he was standing there naked with me over his shoulder by the way he sounded.

"I'm so sorry, sir, I didn't hear you. I had my earphones on, while I was cleaning the room. Excuse me."

I covered my face and groaned into Caston's back. He laughed a deep, happy sound and started moving toward his room.

I squirmed in his arms, reaching down to smack him on the ass.

"Hold still woman, or I'll drop you." He said through his chuckle.

As we passed Jules, I covered my eyes and held up my hand for a slight wave. "Hi, Jules."

She giggled, "Welcome back, Ms. Bennett."

He carried me into the bedroom, and flipped me down on the bed.

"Cass, that was so not cool."

The smile engulfing his face was infectious. I'd never felt so happy. My heart felt like it was exploding in my chest. Crawling his way up to my face, I felt the light brush of his skin on mine and I shivered. Caston pushed my legs wide with his leg as he sheathed himself and positioned his cock at my entrance.

"Tell me what you want."

The deep, dark look in his eyes sent a rush of sexual butterflies through my body making my core ache for him.

"I need you, Caston, please."

He scoops my hips up, as he plunges into me hard and fast. The shock wave of pleasure that shot through me was like nothing I've ever experienced before. It didn't take long for us to come together.

Collapsing into each other's arms we drifted off into a peaceful sated sleep.

I woke sometime later to Caston stroking the hair from my face. I smiled up at him. Stretching and yawning, I placed a kiss on his chest over his heart.

He moaned lightly when my lips caressed his skin.

"Caston."

"Yes, Sabrina."

I bit my lip and looked up into his eyes. "You don't have to use a condom, if you don't want too."

"Bre, I don't think…"

"Cass, I was tested during our break." A blush rises in my cheeks. "I'm clean, and I'm on the pill."

His mouth devoured mine. "Oh, baby. I've been tested and I'm clean too. To feel you completely…" A growl escaped from his throat and he crashed his mouth to mine again. We just laid there making out on the bed feeling each other's bodies, memorizing every inch of each other.

My back arched, as his hand ran slowly from my leg up to my neck. Curving around my neck, his fingers entwined with my hair and he drew me in for another kiss. This was different feeling, this was controlled, needy even. His tongue swiped mine lightly, and the slowness of it made me tingle all over. My eyes shut and I let myself get lost in his kiss. His hand tightened in my hair, tilting my head to one side, so he would have better access to my neck. His lips made a light trail down my neck and I let out a whimper. I was sopping wet for him. "I need you, Caston."

"I want to make love to you, again. This time I want to take my time and enjoy every part of you."

"Please, I need to feel every part of you."

He wasted no time, as he positioned himself over me, rubbing his hard cock through my slit, making my juices flow harder. He looked down at me with hooded eyes. Not only was there love in them, there was compassion, there was need. I felt loved, wanted. Feeling like my old self. Whole again.

I watched him as he entered me. Slowly. When he was almost fully buried in me, his eyes closed and his head arched back. He made the most magnificent sound. I needed him closer. Reaching up, I slid my arms around his back and brought him down on top of me. He didn't protest. Wrapping his arms around me, we held on to each other, as if our lives depended on one another. We were connected. Our bodies fit together, like they were meant for each other. Feeling him bare inside me felt right and natural. His movements were slow and controlled. I could feel every ripple deep inside me. The need flowing between us was intense. His mouth was on my mine, tugging at my lip, and finally giving me the deepest kiss. I moaned into his mouth. I approached my breaking point. Reaching my climax, I broke my mouth away from his to let out a scream. Caston sped up slightly, reaching his climax soon after mine, collapsing on top of me. We were still holding onto each other, as we drifted peacefully into sleep.

I woke up, and the sun was shining, filling the room with warmth. Caston and I were still holding onto each other. It felt right being there with him. I let my eyes close, again, after I looked at my angel sleeping next to me.

I must have drifted back asleep, because I woke up again to movement next to me. A light kiss brushed my lips, and a smile crept up on my face. "Morning," I whispered with my eyes still shut.

"Good morning, my love," He kissed me, again, a little deeper.

"Mmmm, I could get used to this," I cooed.

"Me too, Bre." He brushed the hair from my face and leaned down to kiss my neck. "Ready to start the day?"

"Nah, let's stay in bed all day."

"I would love to stay in bed all day with you, but you have to get to class. I don't want Professor Lee on my bad side."

I stuck my lip out into a full pout. "But, Caston…"

He scrunched his face and closed his eyes. "Don't beg, please. I'm not strong enough to say no to you."

I snuggled up into his chest, hoping this would make him change his mind. To my shock, he moved quickly, scooping me up and carrying me to the shower. He stepped in with me and quickly turned on the water. Setting me down under the cascade of water, he grabbed one of the bottles off the seat. Pouring the gel in his hands, he lathered me up with the sweet smell of lavender.

I laugh at the lavender wash. "When did you start using lavender body wash? It wasn't here last time."

"I shopped for it one day last week when I was missing you. I wanted to find the scent that reminded me of you. I was hopeful that one day you would return to me, I wanted to be prepared."

The warmth of the water and the warmth of his hands moving along my body made me want him. As his hand slid and soaped up between my legs I let out a moan. His body was immediately pressed up against my back. I could feel he wanted me. I reached my hand around to his neck to pull him closer. His head leaned down to suck on my neck, as he cupped my sex with both hands. He used his fingers to spread me open. The water from the shower jet hit my clit, and I writhed in his arms from the sensation. As I was going to let go he moved his hands and bent me slightly forward. I placed my hands on the wall to steady myself, as he slammed into me from behind. He pumped into me hard. My moans echoed off the shower walls. His hands were gripping my hips, shoving me onto his cock, burying it so deep with each thrust. I wanted nothing more than to taste him in my mouth. "Tell me when you're coming, Caston. I need to know."

He rolled his head on his shoulders and grunted, "I'm so close, Bre."

I quickly spun around, before he could stop me, and dropped to my knees in front of him, taking him in my mouth to the back of my throat. I sucked, using my tongue to toy with his dick. I sucked harder, taking him deeper as I felt his first spurt in my mouth, so his thick cum would slide down. Looking up at him, while I was swallowing, seeing him brace himself on the walls made me grin inwardly. I didn't let up until he was done, not wanting to waste any of it. Licking my lips I stood up in front of him. He smiled and cupped my cheeks in his hands. "Bre,"

"Yes." I said when he paused.

"Have I told you lately how much I love you?"

Chapter Sixteen

Sabrina

Class seemed to fly by today. Knowing I had someone who loved me to come home to kept a smile plastered on my face all day. I gathered my bags, looked at myself in the mirror, and walked out of the locker room to the exit.

I was blinded when I steeped through the door. Flashes everywhere, I squinted and tried to cover my face. *What was going on?* Then the questions started all at once.

"What's your name?"

"Are you sleeping with Caston Black?"

"Are you the newest Black Hollywood Sweetheart?"

"What's your relationship with Mr. Black?"

All of a sudden I felt an arm around my shoulders, and I was being swept through the crowd. Terrance was ushering me into the back of the Jeep. The crowd followed us, and swarmed the car. Shutting the door, they started questioning him, since they knew they couldn't get to me anymore. He quickly moved around to the driver door and entered the vehicle.

"What the heck is going on, Terrance?"

He looked at me through the rearview mirror and smiled. "You didn't check your voicemail, did you?"

Crap. I forgot I had my phone on silent. Quickly grabbing my phone, I opened it up. Text messages from Beth and a voicemail from Caston were waiting for me. I hit the voicemail option, and my ears were filled with Caston's sweet voice.

"My dear Sabrina, someone has leaked to the press that we're a couple. There'll be a media frenzy waiting for you after class. I'm so sorry this happened. I'm sending Terrance to pick you up, so you will be safe. We'll address this tonight, or tomorrow. Again, I'm so sorry you're in the middle of this. I love you, Bre. See you when you get home."

I let my head fall back onto the headrest. Was this what my life would be like now? My phone beeped again. It was Beth.

~ *Call me. Mark did something stupid.*

Fuck! I knew who leaked my relationship now. Wonder how much money he was going to get for his 'story'? I squeezed my eyes shut and pinched the bridge of my nose. Caston wasn't going to be happy.

Terrance slowed to a stop in front of the house, and got out to open my door, but Caston beat him to it. I was startled at how fast the door opened and my face must have looked it. Caston asked full of concern, "Are you okay, what's wrong?"

"You startled me. I'm fine, really. I didn't listen to my messages before I left class, so the crowd took me by surprise, but I'm okay."

He helped me out of the car and immediately gathered me up in his arms for a passionate kiss. His tongue sweeping across mine made me weak in the knees. "I'm so sorry this happened. I didn't want it to be like this for you."

I snuggled deeper into his arms as we walked into the house. I kicked off my shoes and sunk onto the couch. "It's okay. I expected this eventually. Just didn't expect it so suddenly, but ..." I stopped, trying to think of the words.

"But...what?" Caston questioned, as he brought me something to drink. He sat down next to me and pulled me onto his lap.

He was wearing sweatpants, so I could feel his hard length through our clothing. I instantly lost my train of thought, and I moved my hips in his lap. His eyes hooded. Reaching up, he brushed some hair away from my face, and leaned forward to kiss my neck. I sighed, closed my eyes and tilted my head in the other direction to give him better access. He trailed kisses down my neck to my shoulder. Pulling the strap of my tank top down, he kissed me where it was previously laid. I shivered. Lifting myself up, I turned to straddle him. He continued kissing across the swell of my breasts, his hands squeezing my hips. Using his teeth, he pulled my tank top down to expose my bare breast. Taking my nipple in his mouth, he grazed it between his teeth. I let my head fall back, surrendering to the feeling. His hands made their way up my back. Cradling my head, he pulled me back in for another deep kiss. Finally, he pulled away, leaving me breathless, and he covered up my exposed breast.

I gave him a pouty face, and he laughed. "Sabrina, honey, I want you. Trust me. However, my parents are coming over for dinner. I don't want them to find us like my mother did last time."

I immediately covered my face, blushing horribly. "Oh, no. I can't face them."

"Yes, you can. Go change and come back down. We'll talk about this media frenzy later."

He stood me up and swatted me on the ass to get moving. Seeing the tent in his pants I gave him the pouty face, again, hoping he would change his mind. He laughed and swatted me, again. "Go."

"Okay, okay." I turned to walk away, but remembered what I was originally going to tell him.

"Caston, Mark was the one to leak our relationship."

His face reddened. "Fuck, I knew it. That son of a bitch. We'll deal with it, Bre. No worries."

He stood up, grabbing his cell phone, and headed toward the kitchen.

Chapter Seventeen

Caston

I cannot believe that asshole would talk to the tabloids and sell his story. Well, I guess I can, but not this fast. I punched a text out to Terrance and slammed my phone down on the counter.

"Honey, the anger, really?"

My back stiffened. "Mother, you always have the best timing." I adjusted myself, since I was still hard from Sabrina sitting in my lap, believe it or not, anger does not help it recede.

"Where's this new girl, Caston?" my dad questioned, as he came up behind Beverly, placing an arm around her waist.

"She's changing. She just got home from class. Can you, please, act normal around her?" I sighed.

My dad belly laughed and walked over to smack me on the back. "Son, I will. It's her you have to worry about," he said, nodding toward Beverly.

"Yeah, I know. That is what I'm worried about," I starred her down, "She already freaked Sabrina out the last time she popped in."

My dad and I just watch as my mother poured herself a glass of wine from the bottle Jules had left out on the counter. Without acknowledging that we were discussing her, she took the bottle with her into the living room. I shook my head and walked to the refrigerator to grab a beer for me and my dad.

As I handed it to him he asked, "So tell me, why her? What makes her different?"

We sat at the breakfast bar. I opened the bottle, starring off into the distance and took a long drink of the ale. "Dad, she is different. She is pure. I saw her dance a few months ago and her image was stuck in my head. Her smile melted me. I guess you could say it was love at first sight," I shrugged and continued on, "At first, I just wanted her for my magazine, but then I ran into her at a party and my world changed. She is everything that I need to make myself whole. Dad, she is my other half. My partner. I love her. I know it has only been a few weeks, but I have never, ever, felt like this before. She needs me, and I need her. I would do anything for her. Sabrina is not after my money. She sees the good in me. She needs me to protect her, and I want to do it. I would do anything for her. She fills something in me that's been missing for so long." I sighed and turned toward my dad, "I guess I sound ridiculous, right?"

Hanging my head, I waited for his response. I was sure he would say I was an idiot, and I needed to take a step back to clear my head. But to my surprise he grabbed my shoulder to make me look at him. He said, "Son, everything you've just said makes perfect sense. It looks like you have finally found love. I'm so happy for you. Take care of her and treat her like a princess. You know in your heart you have found the one. Don't let her get away, like I did." I saw his eyes well up, and he looked away before he continued. "I'll never forgive myself for letting her get away."

I wrapped my dad in the biggest hug I could. Thankful that he understood me and was on my side. In spite of everything, I love my dad. I heard a throat clear behind me, and I turned around to see Sabrina in the doorway. Pulling away from my dad, I walked over to her. She looked beautiful. Her hair was pulled up into a messy ponytail on the top of her head with tendrils falling down around her face. She changed into a white t-shirt that hugged her curves and showed just a bit of cleavage. Her jean skirt was short, but modest. My head fuzzed a little bit, wondering what she was wearing under it. Her bare legs and bare feet made me weak in the knees. Coming to a stop in front of her, I grabbed her face and gave her the biggest kiss I could. Talking to my dad made me realize, even more, how much I want her. I could feel her tense up, knowing my dad was watching, but she quickly relaxed into me wrapping her arms around my waist. Finally, pulling away, I looked her in the eyes and said, "I'm sorry, but you're so beautiful, I couldn't resist myself."

A shy smile and blush rose up on her cheeks. I loved that. I gave her another peck on the cheek before I turned around to walk her over to meet my dad. I wrapped my arm around her waist, pulling her into me as I introduced her. "Dad, I'd like you to meet my Sabrina. Sabrina, this is my dad, James Holden."

"The pleasure is all mine, Sabrina," my dad said in his smooth voice. "Please, call me James." He took her hand in his and leaned over to kiss the back of it.

Looking over to me he said, "You did good, son. She's a beauty. Keep this one to yourself."

Chapter Eighteen

Sabrina

His dad looked like an older version of Caston, a little more wear on his face and slightly more tan. His hands were strong. I could tell by his forearms, he must still work out. He was sweet. I gave him a nice smile, and a confident handshake.

Caston's face was beaming with his father's acceptance of me. Seeing it, I couldn't help, but feel the same happiness spread throughout my body. We made some small talk about weather and my schooling to fill the silence. Caston made me feel at ease with his arm around my waist. His thumb brushing my side made me warm and tingly.

Things were going smoothly when I felt Caston tense up next to me. I quickly looked up at him, his eyes were fixated on the door to the living room. Following his line of sight, I saw his mother standing there, glaring at us. "Well, well, I see I have missed proper introductions," she said, as she strolled to where we were standing.

Her high heels clicking on the tile floor was the only sound in the room. She held a wine glass in her left hand. I wondered how many glasses she had already. Edging her way in between Caston and James, I could feel her eyes roaming my body, judging. I felt like I should spin around in front of her, in order to get her approval.

"Well, Caston, where are your manners," she scolded.

I looked up at Caston to see his jaw clench, grinding his teeth. Why so much resentment toward her?

"Mother, this is Sabrina. Sabrina, please meet Mrs. Beverly Holden."

"Pleased to meet you, Mrs. Holden," I extended my hand and did a small curtsy. What the heck was that, I thought, laughing at myself for the curtsy. My smile seemed to sour her already pouty face, causing me to tense up like Caston had. I wanted to hide behind Caston to escape from the evil look she was bestowing on me.

"Well, it's finally good to place a face with your backside," she sneered shaking my hand. She then wiped her hand on her skirt like I had cooties.

"Really, Bev?" James snapped at her. "For fuck's sake." He turned and stormed off into the living room, leaving just the three of us.

I bit my lower lip and my eyes started to well up. I wouldn't cry in front of her, I didn't want to give her the satisfaction of knowing she got to me. I forced a smile on my face and said, "Excuse me while I see if Jules needs any help setting up the patio for dinner."

Caston leaned over to give me a peck on the cheek. He squeezed my hand before I left his side.

As I walked out of the room I heard his mother say to him, "So, when do we get to share her with you, Caston, dear?"

I froze in my steps. Did I just hear her right?

I quickly left the room, not wanting to hear anymore, and walked out onto the patio where Jules was setting dinner. I wiped at my eyes and took a deep breath.

Walking out a little further, I put on a happy face when Jules caught my eye. "Hey, Jules, can you use any help?"

"Oh, no, deary, I have it all taken care of."

"Oh, okay." I looked away, not wanting her to know anything was wrong.

I walked to the fire pit on the patio and sat down in one of the Adirondack chairs. The warm sun hitting my face felt good and made me forget what had just happened.

"Sabrina, dear, what's the matter?" Jules questioned, as she walked toward me.

"I don't think Caston's mother likes me."

"Oh, honey," Jules pats me on my knee, "she doesn't like anyone. She is an odd one, that's for sure. Don't worry, though, Caston loves you. He's never brought a girl home before..." She blushes and lets her sentence drift off. "Plus, I can see it in the way he looks at you. He won't let her hurt you." I could see the worry flash across her face as she said that.

"Why is she like that Jules?" I questioned.

"Honey, you'll have to talk to Caston about that. It isn't my place to say."

I nodded to show her I understood and that I wouldn't press her for information that would get her in trouble. "Thank you, Jules. Talking to you does make me feel a little better."

"Good." She patted the top of my head. The gesture made me smile, making me think of my mom.

"Are you sure I can't help with anything? I'd rather not go back in there just yet."

"Sure, come on. You can help me set out the glasses and napkins."

I sprang up, walked over to her, and I wrapped her in a big hug, catching her off guard. "Thanks, again, Jules."

"Anytime, deary, anytime."

Since it was a beautiful evening the doors to the house were open, and I could hear Caston and his mother talking quietly in the kitchen. I couldn't tell what they were saying because my back was to them. I felt as though the whispers were tense and very uneasy. I wanted to turn around to go back to Caston's side.

A short while later I heard glass break. I quickly turned around and saw Caston holding his mother's wrist. It was the hand that had been holding the wine glass, which was now shattered on the tile floor. His face was dark, furious. His dad still wasn't with them. What was going on?

Jules quickly rushed to the kitchen to tend to the mess. Beverly huffed and turned, leaving the room, most likely to clean herself up. I started toward Caston, but when he looked up and saw me he held his hand up to me. I stopped. He bent down to help Jules with the mess. I could tell he was apologizing to her.

Caston got up and ran his hands through his hair. His muscles rippled through his shirt when he did that. I couldn't help but stare. His shirt lifted slightly, showing the muscles at his hip. How I wanted to walk over to him and run my hand along that muscle. I wanted to follow it down into his pants. I bit my lip at the thought of taking his hard cock in my hand, stroking it, making him want me. Watching him enjoy himself and see that little liquid spot of pre-cum form at the tip of his head. I wanted to lick it, to taste him.

My cheeks blushed and I felt a hot wave of desire run through me. I pulled out a chair at the table and started to fan myself. Caston walked out onto the patio and witnessed me sitting down.

"Are you okay?"

Feeling embarrassed that he caught me day dreaming, I quickly responded, "Oh, yes, I think I'm a little faint because I'm hungry."

Concern swept over his face. "I think everything is ready. Let's get some food in you."

"I don't want to be any trouble, Caston. Really, I'm okay."

Taking the seat next to me, Caston immediately started shoveling food onto my plate. I let out a laugh and placed a hand on his shoulder. Leaning over, I kissed him on the cheek and threaded my fingers through the hair at the nape of his neck.

"You have to be famished after class. I'm sorry I didn't have us eat sooner. Please, eat." He turned toward me, handing me my fork.

"I want to wait for your parents. That would be rude of me to start without them."

As if on cue, his parents walked out hand in hand. Beverly had an evil smile on her face. I'm not sure what happened in that twenty minutes that they were missing, but the mood changed significantly.

Chapter Nineteen

Caston

I cringed inwardly when I saw my mother in the doorway. Why did I think dinner with them was a good idea? Then put wine in her hand...a recipe for disaster. I took a deep breath to try to clear my head as she walked toward us, preparing for whatever she would say. I saw the look she was giving me and it was making me uncomfortable. I know I will have to do damage control.

I tensed up as she wedged her way in between myself and my dad. "Well, Caston, where are your manners," she seethed.

I moved closer to Sabrina, as my mother snaked her hand down my backside and squeezed my buttocks. "Mother, this is Sabrina. Sabrina, please meet Mrs. Beverly Holden." I said though gritted teeth.

My God, she did not just say what I think she did. Why, oh why did she have to bring up walking in on us? Then to have wiped her fucking hands on her skirt, like Sabrina was trash. I could feel my jaw tense. I looked over at my dad, pleading for help but he had already left the room disgusted. Before I could say anything, Sabrina excused herself to see if Jules needed help. I could see the tears in her eyes. How dare that bitch do this to her!

I watched Sabrina walk toward the door, her ass swaying beautifully under her jean skirt. My thoughts were completely focused on her. I was snapped back to reality when my mother said, "So, when do we get to share her with you, Caston, dear?"

My head snapped back to her medically enhanced face. Her smug look was sickening. "Fuck off, Mother. I am not sharing her with you. EVER. Do not even try."

"Damn it. Please. Sabrina is special. I do not want you to fuck this up. You," I pointed at her, "leave Sabrina alone."

"Oh, honey," my mother started, her free hand resting on my hip. "Baby, I only want what is best for all of us. You know that. You have a reputation to live up to. You are a 'Sex God'. How would it look if you didn't have multiple partners? Your publication would take a nose dive. Women knowing you were off the market? Not a good thing. Now come to Mommy."

Her hand started to move up my shirt around to my neck. As she started to cup her hand around it I moved back quickly. This knocked her off balance. I am sure it was intentional, but she fell into me, and being the gentleman I am I was not going to let her fall to the ground. As I grabbed the hand with the wine glass, she twisted and the wine fell to the ground shattering everywhere. I looked up for my dad, but he was still nowhere to be found. I wanted to shove her into his arms and get her the fuck away from me. "Damn it, Beverly, get the fuck off of me, and leave me alone."

Her face was furious. I did not think she was capable of getting wrinkles anymore, with all the work she has had done, but I will be damned her forehead and eyes wrinkled like bad fruit. If daggers could have shot out of them, I would be dead. "You'll fucking regret this,

Caston. Mark my words. You call me Mother, NOT Beverly. I thought I made that clear years ago."

Through gritted teeth I replied, "Yes, Mother."

She was standing now, smoothing out her clothing to see if she had gotten any of the spilled wine on herself. Jules was at my feet, starting to clean up the mess. I could not let her do this by herself. I also felt eyes on me. Looking up I saw Sabrina looking back at me full of concern. God, how much has she seen? She started to move toward me, but she was barefoot and I did not want her cutting her beautiful feet. Thankfully, she stopped when I motioned for her to stop.

"Jules, I am so sorry for the mess. My damn clumsy mother." I gathered up the big shards of glass.

"Mr. Black, it is all right. Don't apologize. Just don't want the wine to stain the grout. I'll get this cleaned up in no time."

She looked up at me with concern. I am sure she saw what happened. She always does. I smiled the best I could and deposited the glass in the dust pan Jules had brought with her.

Standing up, I ran my hands through my hair and took a deep breath. I had to calm down. Out of the corner of my eye I saw Sabrina sit down and start fanning herself. Oh no, something is wrong with her. "Are you okay?" I questioned, as I went to my love.

Chapter Twenty

Sabrina

The meal went smoothly. It was almost as if I wasn't there. Beverly talked over me and never made eye contact, or acknowledge my presence. When I would catch James's eye, I would smile shyly at him and look away when he smiled back. Being by Caston made me feel somewhat at ease, I knew he would protect me. His hand on my thigh was rhythmically stroking my skin, letting me know he was near. I would flush when his hand would creep a little higher than it should on my inner thigh.

I felt the dampness pooling between my legs. I ached so badly for Caston's touch to slide between my legs. I needed his strong hands pulling me apart. Having him find my sensitive spot, making me come. It made me shiver at the thought. I wanted to come for him, and only for him. I squeezed my thighs together to keep the tingly feeling going. Out of the corner of my eye I could see Caston smirk at me. He knew exactly what he was doing to me, that bastard.

Finally, the time came to see his parents out. Caston hugged his dad and whispered something in his ear. It made his dad belly laugh.

James stepped over to me and wrapped me in a big hug, too. It caught me off guard and I gasped as his arms wrapped around me. "Good night, dear Sabrina. I'm so happy my son has met such a beauty. I can't wait to see more of you." He said to me.

"Let her go, James." Beverly snipped.

He released me and patted my cheek. He turned to walk out the door, but stopped to grab Beverly's arm. He pulled her into him and wrapped his other hand behind her neck, pulling her into a deep kiss. My eyes were as wide as silver dollars. Was I really seeing this? I quickly looked away, feeling like I was witnessing something I shouldn't be. Caston cleared his throat. His mother was the first to pull away. Her gaze into her husband's eyes was intense. "Let's go home, Bev," James growled.

"God, no, take me to the club. I need it." Beverly said just above a whisper.

What the fuck am I seeing? Turning to Caston James said, "You sure you don't want to come? Ha! What am I saying you'll come, but are you sure you don't want it to be at the club?"

"Dad, I told you..."

"Yeah, yeah I know. Just thought I would see if you changed your mind. Evening, dear," James said with a head nod to me, as he led Beverly out the door without so much as an acknowledgement from her.

As soon as the door shut on them I let out the biggest sigh of relief. That last few minutes were the strangest of my life.

"Was it really that bad?" Caston laughed, pulling me into him by my waist.

"Yes." I rested my forehead on his shoulder.

"I'm sorry, she is a bit much. I never know what is going to come out of her mouth." He kissed the top of my head while his thumbs stoked my back.

"A bit?" I questioned as looked up at him. "What happened with the wine glass? And what in God's name just happened between them before they left. Caston, that was, honestly, the weirdest thing I've ever witnessed."

Caston lifted me up to wrap my legs around his waist. I held on to his neck and leaned back to look into his eyes. His hands had a firm grip on my ass. "Do you really want to know what was going on there? I know we need to discuss it, but right now?"

His hands were distracting me, and I really didn't even hear him ask the questions, much less have the wits about me to insist on getting the answers to them. Instead I leaned forward to take his mouth in mine. "I've wanted to do that all evening." I said.

He moaned deep in his throat. "Oh my God, Sabrina, you have no idea how hard it has been to keep my hands to myself."

"Well, sir, you didn't do that good of a job, but I'm glad you didn't. Your touch was the only thing keeping me from running away"

His grip on my ass tightened and his fingers inched their way under my panties. "I love this ass." His head nuzzled into my neck nipping at my collarbone. My panties were instantly soaked.

I ran my hands through his hair and pulled his head back. I had to have him. I captured his mouth with mine. I tightened my legs around his waist, grinding myself into him. I needed relief. He moaned and quickly spun me around and carried me up the stairs. I nibbled his ears and neck the whole way.

He carried me into the bedroom and, much to my surprise, out onto the balcony. He walked over to the large lounge chair and laid me down. Standing up he removed his shirt and leaned over to crawl up my body. His hands started at my waist. They pushed my white shirt up over my head. He cupped my breasts through my bra and sucked on the cleavage spilling out of them. His mouth moved up to my neck and I fell back onto the cushion. Caston's mouth followed me down, never letting up his assault. He slowly made his way down, kissing between my swells. When he got to my belly button, he stopped and kissed in a circle around it. Then he dipped his tongue in making me shiver. All the while his hands were kneading and playing with my nipples though my thin lace bra.

The sun was warm on my skin, but the air was brisk. Between the pleasures Caston was giving me and the outside air, goose bumps raised on my skin. His mouth moved further south and I gave a moan, as he pulled my skirt down exposing my thong to him. It was a small light pink mesh thong with black polka dots on it. The front had a small bow with crystals hanging from it. Caston took the material in between his teeth and pulled it down my legs. He stood over me and placed his hands on his hips. I looked at him and I bit my lower lip. I took my hands and started caressing my stomach, then moved them down to cover my sex. I felt too exposed on the patio. His eyes were roaming my body. "Do you trust me?"

I looked at Caston with trepidation. I've only known abuse. Can I give myself over to him? My face must have looked unsure because Caston ran his fingertips down my cheek soothing me.

"Sabrina, I would never hurt you. All you have to say is stop. I will always protect you. That is my solemn vow."

Swallowing hard I whisper, "I trust you, Cass."

He removed his belt from his shorts. "Move your hands away from your pussy."

I did as I was told, moving them to rest on my hips. He walked to my right side and let a fingertip trace up my arm as he did. Without warning the tip of his belt struck me between my legs. It was unexpected and stung, but felt amazing. I gasped and rolled my head back, taking in the feeling. I was panting when his thumb plunged into my mouth, commanding me to suck it. As soon as I was focused on that he snapped at my pussy again. My heart raced. I was soaking down there. He took my wrists and flipped me so I was kneeling toward the back of the chair. The belt was lightly smacked across my ass. I was squirming, needing to be touched. "Please, Caston, touch me," I pleaded.

Right then my arms were bound behind my back and I was pulled backwards. I was panting as I let myself adjust to the new position. His breath in my ear was exhilarating. "Don't think," he growled, "just feel."

I closed my eyes. One of Caston's arms snaked its way around my body from behind, cupping my breast. I leaned my head back on his shoulder and turned toward his neck. I kissed him lightly, as he began to play with my nipples. As the torment got harder I returned my own assault with bites to his neck and collarbone. I stretched my bound hands lower, reaching out to try to touch him. Finally, I was rewarded with a large mound pressing into my hands. Caston's breath caught in his throat when I squeezed, letting him know what I wanted.

He got up and removed his shorts. Upon returning to the chaise lounge he used my helplessness to push me forward slightly. Positioning himself behind me he pushed his hard cock into me. I instantly felt my juices run down his length.

"Oh God, Sabrina, you're so wet."

Words escaped me as the feeling of being stretched took over. I turned to speak, but he started to move. My mouth opened with a gasp, and he took my mouth in a hungry kiss all while pumping in and out of me. His tongue danced over mine, swirling deep, getting to know every part of it.

I couldn't believe how I felt. Feeling helpless, because I had no use of my hands to support myself, but somehow it made me feel secure. It made absolutely no sense. In Caston's capable hands, I knew I wouldn't be harmed and that he would never take advantage of me.

Pulling on the belt he held my bound hands tightly, while the other hand snaked around my neck, pulling me back into him. I wanted his hands all over me. I craved his touch. His tongue licked me behind my ear and he nibbled on my lobe. His cock was still pushing inside me. I arched my back pushing my breasts out, begging him silently to grab and pinch my nipples. I wanted his hand to reach lower and play with my clit while he was inside me. "Caston, touch me."

He nibbled across the back of my neck. Slowly his hand traveled down my abs to the top of my sex. The slowness of his hand was a sharp contradiction to his fast paced thrusting. It was driving me to the brink. I knew as soon as he touched me I would explode. His hand did not proceed lower, though. It rested just above where I needed it. I arched into him again, grunting my frustration.

He flipped me over to my back without warning. He kept my hands bound, so I couldn't touch him. Dropping down between my legs, he started sucking and playing with my lips. Oh.My.God. I couldn't hold on much longer. I tried to buck my hips up to get him to kiss me, so I could taste myself on his lips. He teased my clit with his tongue, circled my clit and bit down. That was my undoing. I gushed, coming all over him and the lounge chair. I was bucking and my mind felt like it had exploded. Just when I thought I could not take anymore, Caston moved up my body, swung my legs over his shoulders and pushed into me again. He was relentless. His hands loosened on my bound hands, and I was able to free them. I reached around to grab his ass. Perfectly hard and round, I squeezed it to force him into me harder. "Caston, harder. Please, harder. Make me come, again."

Pushing my legs to the side he smashed onto my body and took my mouth with as much force as his cock thrusting into me. I grabbed his head and kept him close to me.

"Sabrina, come, now."

I didn't hold back. Another wave flowed through me and we came together gloriously. He kept pushing in me until he was done filling me.

I wrapped my legs around his back and kept a hold on his neck. He rested his head in the crook of my neck. Our breathing was ragged. We were still connected. This was the best feeling, being one with the person you love. I had to tell him, but the words caught in my throat. "Cass?"

I felt his mouth turn up in a smile. "Hum?" he mumbled.

"That was magnificent. Mind-blowing."

"You were just as magnificent." He laughed and then kissed my neck before pushing off of me and letting his manhood slip from my body. He stood over me looking down at my body spread open. "My God, that's the most beautiful thing I've ever seen."

"What is?" I smiled.

"You spread out, open with the glistening of sweat over your rosy, flushed skin. My fluids falling from your body. Your brunette hair fanned out above you. Your chest, with your pebbled nipples rising and falling deeply from trying to catch your breath. Your muscles rippling from the aftershocks of your orgasms. Your smile. Your eyes. Everything about you, Sabrina. Everything is beautiful."

A tear fell from the corner of my eye. He reached down and cupped my cheek wiping away that tear with his thumb. *I love you,*

Caston, I said in my head and heart, but the words wouldn't form on my tongue.

"I didn't scare you did I?" His face was full of concern.

"Scare me, what would scare me?" My face scrunched, and I draped an arm over my head. "I was anything but scared. Exhilarated and excited, yes. Scared, no way."

He sat down next to me and brought his face to mine. Hovering just above my lips, as if waiting for an okay. His eyes were searching mine. My breath caught.

"Caston, I..." His mouth covered mine, not allowing me to finish my words. His tongue swept over mine. He stopped kissing me and rested his lips on mine. I could feel him smiling.

Chapter Twenty-One

Caston

After I brought her inside, we laid on bed in each other's arms and talked for hours. We talked about his work, my classes, TV shows that we liked, jokes we've heard, and anything that came to mind. I was feeling full of life and free. Laughing and enjoying myself more than I had in years. The last time I felt so free was when I met Sara. In the wee hours of the morning Sabrina eventually fell asleep in my arms.

I stayed awake after Sabrina, not wanting to let her go, because I was afraid this was a dream. I knew she was going to tell me she loved me when we were outside. However, I did not want her to say it yet. I knew she wasn't quite ready. I didn't want her to second guess herself and her feelings.

She looked so peaceful curled into me. Her skin as soft as velvet; I could spend all day touching her. Watching her sleep was peaceful for me. I stroked her cheek. Her eyes fluttered a bit.

"Mmm ... is it morning already?" Sabrina questioned groggily.

"No, Bre. Not even close. Go back to sleep."

"Okay."

She snuggled deeper into me, and my heart felt like it was going to explode. I wasn't sure what the future was going to hold for me, but I sure as hell hoped it included Sabrina. That thought calmed me and I drifted into a peaceful sleep.

The warm sun drifting into the room stirred me awake. I smiled before I even opened my eyes. My girl was still wrapped around me, sleeping soundly. I kissed her forehead, her nose, her temples, and finally I lightly kissed her lips. A deep intake of breath filled her lungs and a smile spread across her face. I hovered my mouth above hers and I waited until she was awake before I kissed her again. This time I wanted the kiss to wake her up. "Good morning, sweetheart."

She blushed. I loved that rosy color on her cheeks. "What a good morning it is." Sabrina said.

"What would you like to do today, Bre? The day is ours. No school, no work. You name it, and we'll do it."

"Well..." she bit her lip as she thought about what she wanted to do. She also snuggled closer. This was getting a rise out of me. I tried to will myself down. I wanted her to know I wanted more than just sex from her. She was different. "Can't we just stay like this all day?"

"Is that what you want? I can make that happen."

She was so cute when she was thinking. I kissed the worry lines out of her forehead. "For now, yes." Her hand moved from around my waist and ran its way across my hip down to my manhood. She wrapped her hand around it. "I also want this."

I inhaled deeply. Knowing that she is saying this honestly made me pin her to the bed. She didn't want my money or in my magazine; she wanted me for me.

Her smile beamed up at me. I leaned over and kissed her tenderly. Her arms snaked around my back and pulled me closer. I deepened my kiss. My tongue searched her mouth. I sucked and nibbled her bottom lip. The lightest groan escaped her and I could feel her hip muscles flex below me, inviting me into her.

Not wanting to take her immediately, my tongue grazed her jaw up to her ear. I brushed a piece of her hair away to give me better access to her neck. I nuzzled and nibbled her collarbone. She was squirming beneath me, trying to get some relief. I palmed her breast, as I moved to the other side of her neck, nibbling her skin as I went. She was perfect in every way.

I rolled over, making her straddle me. I wanted to watch her, give her the control. Her hands rested on my chest. I held onto her hips and lifted her up to slowly sit on my cock. Taking it in slowly inch by inch, her warm core felt magnificent as it spread open for me. She was so wet and ready.

Her eyes locked with mine as she slowly started to move her hips. Rocking back and forth, I sucked in my lower lip, the feeling was magnificent. There was no rush, we were both savoring the feeling. Her hips swirled and my breath caught. Her sly smile made my heart swell. She knew what she was doing to me. I reached between us and found her clit, rubbing it in small circles to bring her closer to her release. Her breathing increased as her excitement rose. Watching her made me so hot. She was close to coming. I watched as she ground her hips harder into me, making my cock hit her special spot. She reached up and caressed her breasts, pinching her nipples. I needed to be closer to her, moving my hands up her back as I sat up, pulling her into me. My hands tangled in her hair, bringing her mouth to mine engulfing it. Her arms hugged me close. We started moving faster in perfect sync. I wouldn't last much longer.

"Sabrina, I'm so close. You feel so good."

"Me too, Caston. Oh, God."

She arched her back laying back onto the bed, as she ran her hands through her hair. Watching her ride my cock as she stretched out over me was my undoing. I grunted and slammed my cock into the soft folds of her pussy, letting my release coat the inside of her walls. I ran my hand from her neck down her chest and stomach. As I pumped my last few drops into her I reached for her clit. Flicking it once she came over my cock.

I removed myself from her warm depths, pulling her limp body into me until her convulsing subsided. Stroking her hair and kissing her lightly to bring her back down to earth.

"If this is how you want to spend the day, Bre, I'm going to have to get something to eat soon. You're draining me." I whispered.

"Me too, Cass. Are we alone in the house today?"

I propped myself up on my arm to look over her. "What do you mean, love?"

"Is Jules working today? What about Terrance?" She blushed and looked away as she asked. It was precious.

I cupped her face and kissed her lips. "We're alone. Jules has weekends off, and well, Terrance is here, but he'll leave us alone. Why, are you worried about someone seeing you naked? You have a beautiful body. You should share it with the world."

She shook her head and covered her eyes.

"Promise me something." I said, as I pulled her hands away from her face and kissed her palms.

I could tell she was unsure, but showing that she trusted me she said, "Anything."

A smile spread across my face. "One day, let me take pictures of you to show you just how beautiful you are. Let me show you how I see you."

Her natural response to shake her head no took over, but I could tell she was thinking about it. "One day. One day, I might."

I kissed her again, my way of thanking her for trusting me.

Chapter Twenty-Two

Sabrina

I wiped the mirror clear and smiled at my reflection. I had a look of bliss plastered all over my face. As I brushed out the tangles in my wet hair, I blushed thinking about what we'd done in the shower. I could feel myself getting wet again. Caston really was a sex god, he knew how to please every surface of my body.

I heard the phone ring out in the room. Caston answered it. I went to the door of the bathroom to try to listen to what he was saying.

"Really? Now? Can't Sam take care... Okay, I understand... We'll be there tonight."

I was excited. Where were we going? At least, I hoped I got to go. I slipped the fluffy white robe on that had been hanging on the hook by the door. It was so soft. I snuggled it up around my neck and tied the front shut. Pulling my hair out from the collar, I gave it a scrunch and walked out into the room.

Caston was standing by the window, running his hand through his hair. He looked delicious in his jeans, his naked chiseled chest, and bare feet. He was so in deep thought he didn't hear me walk up behind him. I snaked my arms around his waist, and kissed his muscular back. His muscles twitched under my lips. Taking a deep breath, he rested his hands over mine. We stood there for just a few seconds before he turned around and caught my face in his hands. Looking deep into my eyes, he leaned forward and took my mouth in his. I stroked his lower back with my thumbs, and rose on my tiptoes to deepen the kiss. Tongues moving about, searching and learning each other. When we finally parted he didn't move far. He was still hovering above my lips. "I've got some bad news, Bre."

I pulled back a little, trying to get a better look at his face. "Oh?"

His thumbs stroked my cheeks. He had a worried line between his eyes. He took a deep breath and gave me a peck. "I have to go into the club, tonight. There's a problem with some of the members, and I'm the only one that is allowed, per the rules, to dismiss them and revoke their membership."

What was so wrong with a club? I loved clubs. "Okay... I could be up for some dancing. Can I come to the club with you?"

He reached behind his back, and took my hands from where they were resting. Bringing them up to his lips, he kissed the backs of my hands and squeezed them. "Sabrina, it isn't that kind of club. Well, there is dancing, but it isn't a dance club."

"What kind of..." My mouth fell open as realization hit me. "Oh my God. Caston!"

I pulled my hands from his grip. His face scrunched up, like he had eaten something sour. "Sabrina, it's who I am. It's something I enjoy."

I turned to walk toward the bed. It was still rumpled from our earlier romp. I rested one arm across my waist, my other hand cupped over my mouth. Shaking my head, I took a deep breath. My eyes were shut, so I could to collect my thoughts, not knowing how I felt about this. I soon laughed at myself. *My God, Bre, he is the owner of Black Hollywood, it makes sense that he has a sex club.*

"What is so funny?" Caston asked in a voice that sounded hurt, barely above a whisper.

I turned to sit on the edge of the bed. "I just realized how stupid it is for me to be surprised. I mean, I know who you are and what you do. But I feel so very out of place in your life."

"Oh my God, Sabrina," He rushed over, and knelt in front of me. "Don't you ever think that. Ever. You're the single best thing that has ever happened to me."

He rested his head on my lap, wrapping his arms around my hips. I ran my hands through his damp hair. We sat like this for a long time.

Realization hit as I thought about the night before. "Caston. Your parents. The club. Were they going to your club?"

I felt him cringe as soon as I asked the question. He looked up at me and his eyes said it all. He didn't even have to answer. Sitting back on his heels he nodded.

My eyes went wide in horror. I don't have my parents anymore, but to think of ones parents having sex wasn't the most pleasant picture.

"Are you at the club often? Are they? I just want to know what I'm getting into."

"Bre, honey, it is part of the image. I used to be promiscuous, but I'm not that man anymore. Ever since I saw you dance at the Winter Gala. Honey, you have to believe me, I haven't been with anyone since then. I couldn't get you out of my mind. Before you, well," he looked away embarrassed, "I was there almost every night."

My mouth fell open in disbelief. "Every night?" "

"I didn't have sex every night. Most nights, yes, but it is my club. I had to be there, even if it was only to show my face."

I nodded.

"Please, say something."

I wasn't sure what exactly to say. I had so many questions, but I didn't know where to start. So I said the first thing that came out of my mouth, "How often are your parents there?"

"My parents?"

"Yes, I'm assuming that's the club they were referring too last night?"

"Ya, well. My parents are complicated. I will tell you everything, but I need you to do something for me."

"What's that?" I asked.

His panty dropping smile snaked across his lips. I felt the heat in my stomach start to dip lower again. This man would be the death of me, if he could make me feel like this just from a smile.

"You, either need to get out of this robe and dressed, or I'm going to rip it off of you and have my way with you, again."

I took a deep breath and bit my lower lip. I crossed my arms across my chest and brought one hand up to my chin, as if I was seriously considering what to do.

"Hmm, decisions," I said, as I tapped my chin. Two can play at this game. "Well, I guess I better get ready then."

I moved to stand up, but Caston let out a laugh, and tackled me back onto the bed. He slowly leaned down and lightly kissed my neck, while his hand parted the robe to allow himself in, slowly palming my breast. I licked my lips, concentrating on every feeling.

His hand moved away from my breast. I whimpered at the loss. He used his finger to turn my head back toward him. His crystal blue eyes looked deep into my hazel eyes. I could feel his hot bulge, begging to be released. His hand returned to the robe, this time undoing the bow that was holding it closed. Leaning forward, he lightly kissed my lips, as the robe fell open. My skin instantly dotted with goose bumps. His fingers trailed lightly from my belly button to the top on my sex. Still lightly kissing me, his finger slowly dipped into my soft folds. Stroking me. My breath quickened, I bucked my hips trying to get him to move faster. My body ached to come.

Suddenly there was a commotion outside the door. Both of our heads snapped to the door, and Caston covered me up with the robe.

"Mrs. Holden! Mrs. Holden, you can't go in there."

"Fuck off, Terrance!"

"Mrs. Holden, stop."

I rolled to the side covering my face. Is this happening, again? Seriously? Caston was almost to the door when it burst open.

"Caston, I demand you fire Terrance. He said you told him no visitors." She walked over to him, put her hands on his chest, and got really close to his face. What the hell? Almost like a lover, not a mother...

He tensed up when his mother's hands landed on him, roaming his bare chest. I felt nauseated. I looked away, feeling like I was seeing something that I shouldn't be seeing.

"That is right, Mother. I said NO visitors, and I specifically mentioned you. What the fuck are you doing here? Again? Busting into my house unannounced." I looked up at Terrance with a questioning eye.

"Oh, baby, I'm so distraught."

He took her hands and removed them from his chest, like they were slimy. I had to put a hand over my mouth to stop from laughing out loud. I guess a little sound escaped. Her head flew over to where I was sitting on the bed in the robe.

"You, again?" she huffed. "Caston, I can't believe you are..."

"Shut the fuck up, Mother. I know why you are here. It is exactly why I am being called into the club tonight. Get the hell out of my house, and never come over unannounced, again. Do you understand me?"

"She is not like us, Caston. She can't be what you need."

"But see, that's what you do not understand, she is what I need."

Am I still in the room? She is talking like I'm not here. What is she talking about? What does he need that I'm not capable of giving him?

Caston looked over her shoulder. "Terrance, please remove Mrs. Beverly Holden, and if she ever shows up unannounced, you have my permission to call the police."

She looked back toward him shocked. "Oh, honey, please, I'm so sorry." She reached to touch his face. He recoiled, and nodded for her to be taken out of the room.

"Damn it, Caston," she said, as she was being led off by the elbow, "What are you going to do with Anthony and Allie?"

Caston's face reddened. He balled his hands into fists so tight his knuckles where white.

He followed Terrance and his mother down the hall, screaming. "You know very well I have to dismiss them. Damn it, Mother! I should be dismissing you and Dad, too, but I can't do that! I should, but the fucking drama that would cause...damn it, Mother!"

I quickly got off the bed and headed to the closet to get dressed. I still heard yelling, as I was getting ready, but I couldn't make out what they were saying.

I put on a little sundress and my hair up in a messy ponytail on top of my head. I stepped back out in room. Caston was still nowhere to be found. I sat on the bed, waiting for him, again, same as I did the last time his mom busted in on us having sex. I had to find out what her deal was.

Finally, he walked into room. "What the fuck, Caston?"

He stopped dead in his tracks, looking at me, like a deer caught in the headlights of a car.

"Last time I brought up your parents, you distracted me. Then your mom walks in on us, AGAIN. Seriously, if I am going to be in a relationship with you, and trust me I want to be, you have to tell me what is going on!" I got up and walked over to him. I poked him in the chest. "I love you, Caston. Damn it, I want to be there for you, but I can't do that when you're keeping things from me." I turned around to walk back to the bed. "I want nothing more than for us to be honest with each other."

He walked over to me. I fully expected him to tell me to get the hell out of his life. Instead he stood in front of me, took my face in his hands, and laid the biggest kiss on me. I felt my body melt into his, I started to forget everything I had just said. Suddenly, my wits returned and I pushed him away. "No, no. You won't distract me, again."

He dropped to his knees and pulled me down to him. "You said you love me."

Surprised, I looked down at him. "Oh, Caston, I do, I really do love you." I sunk to the floor searching his face for answers. "Is that a shock to you?"

He nodded slowly. "No one has ever loved me for who I really am." His voice was filled with wonder and disbelief.

I pulled him to my chest and held him close to me, stroking his hair. "I'll tell you every minute of every day if I have to, Cass."

We sat on the floor wrapped up in each other's arms for so long my legs started to fall asleep. I didn't want to be the one to break our embrace. Caston needed me. I wasn't sure why, but I wasn't going to let him down.

Finally, he started to move back. Looking incredibly worried and slightly ill he said, "I'll tell you about my parents, but I won't be able to finish it before we have to leave for tonight. Are you sure you want to attend with me? "

"You couldn't stop me if you tried," I smiled.

The smile that spread across his face was so childlike it warmed my heart. He stood up and reached his hand out to help me up.

I smiled and took it, saying, "This is familiar."

Chapter Twenty-Three

Caston

She'd just told me she loves me and agreed to put herself out to the world as my other half. Floating on cloud nine, I pulled her up and into my arms. I pushed a tendril of hair that had escaped her ponytail behind her ear and brushed her cheek with my thumb. "You're risking so much by being with me. Are you crazy?"

"Crazy for you," she replied with a light kiss.

Holding her, I nuzzled my face in her neck. She smelled so good. I felt myself getting hard for her. I couldn't get enough of my sweet girl. And just like that I felt like someone punched me in the gut. What had I done promising to tell her about my parent's history and my past? Where was I going to start? It was so complicated...and fucked up.

Backing out of her embrace, I needed to take a breather. "Let me get a shirt on, so we can leave."

A sly smile crept onto my face, as I pictured her in a sexy outfit tonight and my cock started to defy me, again.

"What?" she asked tentatively.

"Nothing, I'm picturing you in all the naughty stuff I'm going to buy you."

She blushed and looked away. "Caston, you're bad."

I walked to the closet to get a t-shirt, my heart was beating a million miles a minute. I couldn't keep her in the dark. I had to be honest with her. I had to figure out the easiest way, so I wouldn't scare her away.

Once inside my closet, I took a deep breath, removed my cell phone from the pocket of my jeans, and quickly dialed the store attached to the Sweetheart Club.

"Caston, darling, how are you?" the sweet voice cooed when she saw my number on the caller ID.

I didn't have time for small talk, so I got straight to my point. "Hey, Sara, I am going to need you to clear out the upstairs in about an hour. I am bringing my new girl in, and I want it all to ourselves."

"Sure. I'll work on that right now."

"We will be coming in the back, so we can have the car ready in the garage for the club tonight."

"Gotcha. So how have you been? Your brother misses you. He said the club was crazy last night."

"I know. Mother causing problems, again. I am so pissed at her. I actually threw her out of my house this morning for walking in on us unannounced, again."

"Not, again. Oh my word. Will you be here tonight? Masquerade night is always a huge hit!"

"Yes. I have to clean up the shit Mother caused last night. Plus, I can't wait to see Sabrina in a mask."

"Oh, the mystery girl has a name." I could hear her heels, as she walked through the store. "Is this the same Sabrina from the gala? I can't wait to meet her, Cass."

"Very funny, Sara. Be nice, okay? I think she is the one." I said, as I pulled my shirt over my head.

"No! Mr. Most Eligible Bachelor, off the market, for 'The One'?" she gasped and laughed.

I had to laugh with her. It sounded weird, but it didn't feel weird. The thought made a smile spread across my face.

"I know. I can't wait for you to meet her. See you in an hour."

"See ya, Cass."

Looking in the mirror I rumpled my hair, grabbed my keys, and headed back out to the room. She was sitting on the bed cross legged, looking through her phone. I stopped. She was so perfect. She must have felt me staring, because she looked up into my eyes and smiled.

"Ready?"

"Yup."

She climbed off the bed and slid on her heeled sandals. Her legs looked magnificent. Shaking my head, I said, "Let's get out of here before I throw you on the bed and never let you go."

She laughed. I grabbed her hand and we headed down the stairs to the garage.

It was a beautiful day, but we needed to talk, so I decided on the Jeep. Opening her door and helping her in, I took a deep breath. This is it, I thought to myself, my biggest, deepest secret.

"Lunch, then shopping, since we skipped breakfast. Sound like a plan?"

"Lunch with talking, and then shopping with talking." She corrected me.

"Yes, Bre," I said, leaning over to kiss her cheek, "No worries. I plan on telling you everything, but when we're shopping I want you to just enjoy. Okay?"

She turned toward me and nodded with a big smile on her face.

I patted her on the knee and pulled out onto the road. I could tell she was nervous about what I was going to say. Hell, I was nervous. Only a few people knew my secret.

We drove for a little while in silence. I wasn't sure exactly where to start.

"Okay, Sabrina, what I am about to tell you, I trust you to never reveal this to anyone. In all honesty, if my lawyer found out I was telling you this without signing a NDA, he would have my head on a platter."

She shifted to turn herself toward me, so that I knew I had her undivided attention. "Caston, I would never tell anyone."

Taking a deep breath, I started. "My parents have an open marriage. I was brought up in that lifestyle. They had parties, and people over all the time. Ever since I was a young teenager I have been attending these parties. I mean, like starting at about thirteen, maybe? I don't know, it's been a long time."

I sneaked a quick glance to see how she was handling this so far. Now she was the one looking like a deer in the headlights, but when she saw me looking at her, she gave me a reassuring smile.

"My brother, Jon, is five years older than me. He was already attending them. I didn't want to be cooped up by myself anymore, so one night I snuck downstairs. To say I was shocked would be an understatement. I hid in the corner and watched everything. I felt so many things I'd never felt before. It scared and excited me to watch all the couples. When I went back up to bed that night, I laid in bed staring at the ceiling with the biggest hard on."

I let out a small nervous chuckle. "I think that is the first time I masturbated."

Thankfully, she thought that was funny, too, because she let out a chuckle before she covered her mouth to hide her smile.

"Glad you find that funny."

"I'm so sorry," she reached over to touch my forearm, "I didn't mean to laugh."

I smiled and laughed. "I'm messing with you. I know it's funny."

"Jerk."

"Ha! Anyway, my brother came in to check on me that night. He knew what was up. Poor guy, trying to be the parent when he was only a few years older. He gave me the sex talk and told me about how wonderful it was."

"Really?" she asked astonished. "So, you had sex when you were thirteen?"

"Oh, no, probably fifteen. I just went to the parties and watched, then went upstairs and jerked off. When I was fifteen, I was tall enough to pass for eighteen, so the couples that wanted threesomes felt that it was okay to include me, because they thought I was older, or at least that's how they justified it to themselves."

"Oh, well then..."

"I can't believe that you're being so okay with this."

"Caston, I love you. I'm trying to be open minded. You are being truthful with me. What more can I ask for? But I don't think that was right for a young boy."

"Say it again." I looked over to her and grabbed her hand.

"What?" she looked confused.

"Say it again, say you love me."

"I love you," she sighed and smiled.

I brought her hand to my lips and kissed the back of her hand lightly.

"We're here."

She turned to look out the window. "Here?"

I brought her to the Little Grass Shack. It was a little hole in the wall restaurant with must have fabulous to-die-for food. I nodded. "Best food on the east coast."

I got out of the car and walked to her side to open the door. I saw her put her sunglasses on before she got out of the vehicle.

It was a beautiful spring day, the sun was shining, the flowers were in bloom, and it was unseasonably warm. I couldn't wait to eat outside with her while we looked over the beautiful state park.

I took her hand and led her to the outdoor seating. "Do you think this will be okay?" She sounded nervous.

"Sabrina, trust me, no one will look for us here. Ed has never called me out to the paparazzi. He is a good guy, we can trust him."

I saw her visibly relax the moment I said we were in the clear.

Pulling out her chair, I kissed her neck as she sat down.

"Caston! My man! I haven't seen you in a few months. Where the fuck have you been?" Ed yelled when he stepped out onto the patio.

He was a burly, hefty man, with greasy black hair that was slicked back. The tattoos up and down each arm were intimidating and he had a slight limp in his walk. He wasn't someone you would want to meet in a dark alley if you didn't know who he was, but in all honestly Ed was the biggest teddy bear you would ever meet.

"Ed, long time, no see." I met him when he was almost to the table and gave him a big slap-on-the-back hug.

"You son of a bitch, I thought you forgot about us."

"Never. Ed, I'd like you to meet someone."

I turned to walk him over to the table. "Ed, this is Sabrina Bennett. Sabrina this is Ed, owner of this shack."

She reached out her hand and tried to stand up. Ed, the gentleman that he is, stopped her. "The pleasure is all mine, ma'am. Please, don't get up on my account."

She smiled.

I sat down next to her and took her hands in mine. "Ed, we would like whatever is on special and some privacy."

"Sure thing, man. It was a pleasure to meet you, honey. Hope this a-hole brings you by to visit us again."

She squeezed my hand. "I hope so, too," she responded.

Ed walked off and I looked over at her and smiled. I was so ridiculously happy.

"So..."

Looking perplexed I asked, "So, what?"

"So, keep going with the story."

Chapter Twenty-Four

Sabrina

My heart felt so warm and fuzzy, since I told him I love him. It was the truth and I couldn't deny it anymore. I wanted to find out everything about him, good, bad, and ugly. It didn't matter, though, I would be with him no matter what. He made me understand what it was to truly love someone.

I'd thought I had loved before, but this love with Caston was different, honest, and pure. Mark had never loved me, as a matter of fact, I don't think he ever said it to me. I would say it to him all the time, but he never reciprocated.

Coming back from my daydream, I sat there listening to his story of his parents. Thirteen? He was a baby still.

The little restaurant Caston brought me to for lunch shocked me. It was a little nothing, hole in the wall place, but Ed, was super friendly and Caston seemed to be very comfortable here.

I wanted him to continue. "So?" I urged.

He looked at me as if he was not sure what I was talking about. "So, what?" I had to laugh at him.

"So, keep going with the story."

He squeezed my hands and smiled. "So eager for information, aren't we."

I leaned over and kissed him, holding his gaze when I backed away. "When it has to do with you, I'll take anything I can get."

"Let's just enjoy lunch and not ruin it with my fucked up childhood."

I nodded, frustrated that he was stalling but I couldn't judge. I had secrets of my own that I wasn't telling him.

Lunch was fabulous. We had homemade barbeque burgers with sharp cheddar cheese and bacon, potato pancakes, and fabulously sweet homemade cinnamon applesauce. We laughed the whole meal. Ed even came by when we were finished eating and talked business with Caston. It was nice to see him so relaxed.

The sun started to set and Caston finally hinted that we should get going. I was starting to get nervous now.

Sensing something was up with me while we walked to the Jeep, Caston asked, "Is everything okay?"

"Just nervous."

When we got back to the Jeep he pinned me up against the Jeep. "You only have to say the word and I'll take you home."

He leaned forward and pressed his hardening length into me. My insides heated. I leaned in close to his ear. "What would you do if I asked you to take me right here against the car?"

His breath caught and he made the most glorious noise deep in his throat. I leaned back, seeing his eyes were closed and that he was trying to regain control. I opened the door and slunk down into the seat. I pulled him forward at the hips and undid his pants. We were in the corner of the lot, facing a privacy fence, so no one could really see us. I released his cock into my hands. I ran my hands up and down the impressive length. Seeing a clear drip form at the tip, I leaned forward and took the tip in my mouth, swirling my tongue around. The salty drop of pre-cum hit the back of my tongue and it was as if I was starved. I sucked his cock into my mouth. I could feel his muscles tighten as I continued the assault with my tongue. I cupped his balls with one hand, while my other hand followed my mouth to make it more intense. I felt so wild. Ever so carefully, I dragged my teeth along his shaft. That is what sent him over the edge. I immediately started to feel the squirts of cum splashing into my mouth. I sucked him deeper, so I wouldn't drop any and make a mess. As the last of the hot, sticky liquid released into my mouth I let him fall from my mouth with a pop. Kissing the tip of his massive cock, I tucked it nicely into his pants and buttoned them back up.

Turning in my seat, I reached for the seatbelt, and waited for him to join me. Oh God, I was so wet and horny, but I was also proud of myself. Caston finally shut my door and joined me in the car. "My God, woman. That was unexpected. Holy shit!" He ran his hands through his hair and tried to regain his composure. I had the biggest, goofiest grin on my face.

Finally able to pull out of the parking lot, he said to me, "Don't you worry, Sabrina. I'll make that up to you tonight."

I was so wound up, I almost came at the words of his promise.

We started to head into town and were soon hit rush hour traffic. Caston's hands were gripping the steering wheel so hard his knuckles were white. "Is everything okay?" I questioned.

He looked at me and half smiled. "Just thinking about tonight. When we get to the shop, I'm going to go around back. We'll meet Sara at her office before we head upstairs to shop."

"Who is Sara?"

"Sara? She is my brother's wife. Jon, remember? You'll meet them tonight. He runs my club, and she runs my shop. "

I swallowed hard. "Wonderful, I'll meet them for the first time at a sex club. I met your mother for the first time naked on the counter of your kitchen. Could I be more mortified?"

His smile made me melt. It also made me forget my worries. How did he do that?

I noticed we were in an industrial park that had been turned into retail shops and bars. "Oh, I know this area. We're in Kinley Park." I turned to look at him. "Is this where your club is? I never knew there was a sex club on this strip."

He smirked. "Exactly."

"Ah, I see."

"Let's go get you stripped down and fancied up for tonight. Should be a lot of fun, it's our masquerade event, so you even get to wear a mask."

I felt so giddy. Shopping. What girl doesn't love to shop?

We pulled into an underground garage that had a door on it. "Every member gets a door opener," Caston said, answering my unasked question, "people can enter the club privately. Membership is very exclusive, and highly vetted. Every member signs a confidentiality agreement. The shop has two entrances, one from the street and one from the garage. The club is only accessible from the garage."

"Interesting. Explains why I never knew there was club here."

Upon parking, I quickly exited the car.

Caston gave me a look of disappointment. "Please let me get your door for you next time. I like taking care of you."

I took Caston's outreached hand, and he guided me to the elevator. My panties were soaked through from taking Caston in the parking lot and a drip is running down my inner thigh. The anticipation of what lay ahead had me more excited than I'd ever been.

We were greeted at the elevator door by a tall, dark-haired woman. Her skin was the most beautiful color of ivory and her hair was down past her shoulders with a light wave to it. She looked prim and proper in her gray pencil skirt suit, not someone you would expect to see in a sex shop.

"Caston, dear." She took him in a big hug.

"Sara," He kissed her on both cheeks, "Thank you for clearing the VIP floor. I know it was short notice.

"For you, Caston, anything. You know that."

She motioned to me. "Oh, yes, Sara, please meet my Sabrina. Sabrina, this is my sister-in-law, Sara."

I stepped forward, taking her hand in mine. She pulled me into a hug. "Oh, Sabrina, it's good to see someone finally snag Caston's heart."

I laughed. I wasn't sure how to respond to that.

When she finally released me, Caston reclaimed my hand, my insides melted and I blushed.

"I'll leave you two alone. Caston, you know where everything is. If you need anything at all, just holler." With that she patted him on the shoulder and walked down the hall, through a door out of sight.

Caston turned toward me and made me look up at him with his finger. "You sure you want to do this?"

I nodded. I was terrified, but so very excited.

"Okay. Let's go upstairs. That is where the good stuff is."

"Good stuff?" I questioned.

"More expensive, quality items."

"Ahh, should I be concerned my, uh—" I paused, not exactly sure what to call him.

"Lover? Boyfriend is too childish. Guy friend is too informal." I could tell he was struggling with our status, too.

"Anyway," I spoke to get rid of the tension, "should I be concerned that you know more about sex toys and lingerie than I do?"

He swept me into his arms, bringing his lips down to mine. His tongue licked my lips, seeking entrance into my mouth. I obliged parting them, letting our tongues dance together. Breathless, we finally parted.

"You should be honored." He whispered close to my ear. The feeling of his breath on my neck made me weak in the knees. My heart started to pound in my chest. I wanted him to take me right here against the wall. I moaned a little, and he leaned back and snickered.

He led me up a curved stairway. Reaching the top my mouth hung open. Beautiful garments were hung up and displayed. Items so sexy I blurted out, "How will I choose?"

Caston stopped and looked at me with a raised eyebrow. "Choose? Baby, you don't have to choose."

I dropped my eyes to the floor, still unsure.

"I'll buy you all of it and more. Now let's go pick out an outfit for tonight, and then we can work on getting the rest of it."

Caston led me by the small of my back into the boutique. There were a few large, cushy chairs facing a three-way mirror. He pushed me a little further, while he stayed back. "Go find some outfits, and bring them back here to model for me. We'll find the perfect one for tonight."

Suddenly feeling like a kid in a candy shop, I hopped up and down and clapped my hands. I took off into the racks of satin and lace. Caston just laughed and shook his head at me.

Walking through, I ran my hands over all the materials. Bows, lace, satin, leather. My heart was fluttering. I grabbed a few items and kept looking. Then that I saw it. A smile spread across my face, I knew this was the outfit. Thinking of myself in it and Caston's reaction, I felt myself getting damper between my legs. I quickly looked over my shoulder and saw Caston checking his phone. I grabbed the slinky material and took off in the direction we came from.

Making my way back downstairs, I sought out Sara. I started to walk down the hall when she emerged from one of the rooms. "Sabrina, can I help you?"

I smiled, suddenly blushing. "I need your help. I want to surprise Caston with my outfit tonight. Can you help me?"

"Of course I can!" She linked her arm in mine, dragging me off down the hall.

We stopped in front of a door, and she turned to look at me. She brushed a hair from my face, tucking it behind my ear. I leaned my head into her hand, feeling a little flushed. I'd never had a reaction like this to a woman before. She reached back and took my hair out of its holder. "You're really beautiful. Caston is a very lucky man. You head on in there and start getting ready. I'm going to go tell him he needs to get ready himself, and that you will meet him in the Presidential room at the club. I'll be right back."

Chapter Twenty-Five

Caston

I'd fallen hard and fast for Sabrina. What the fuck kind of spell was I under? I wanted her to be mine. My mind dreamed about dropping to one knee and asking her to marry me earlier when we were talking about what we were to each other. I needed her to wake up next to me every day.

Feeling myself start to panic slightly at the thought, I sent her off to pick out outfits and sat down to check emails. Trying to keep focused on anything that didn't involve her was a hard task. I had to collect my wits and shake the spell she had over me.

Out of the corner of my eye, I saw Sara walking up to me. Sitting forward slightly I said, "Sara, we are fine. You don't need to check up on us." I slouched back down into my chair suddenly exhausted.

"Babe, your girl isn't even up here anymore." She laughed, as she strode over to me.

I stood up and looked around. "Damn it, Damn it, Damn it." I kicked the chair. She left. I knew she would.

"Relax, Hollywood. She sought me out, because she wanted to surprise you. You have a good one there. Why is she with you?" She sat down on the coffee table in front of the chair I was just sitting in.

"Oh, ha ha," I turned back around and looked at Sara.

"Seriously, Cass. I remember when you first saw her at the gala. You were so wound up that night. I know she's the one," she sighed. "However, have you told her about Beverly, yet?"

I hung my head and sat back down. "Getting there. It takes more than a few hours to explain that."

She took my hands in hers and stroked her thumbs over the back of my hands. "Get to it. Don't lose this one. Okay?"

I pulled her into a hug. "Thanks, Sara. You really are too good for my brother."

She laughed so hard she had to cover her mouth.

"She will be waiting for you in the Presidential suite, Hollywood. Go...get yourself ready for her."

I kissed her cheek and stood up to go to the club to get ready. Looking back over my shoulder at her sitting on the table, I whispered, "Thank you." She nodded at me. "You really are a good person, Sara. I'm sorry it didn't work out between us."

She smiled her sad smile. "Cass, if it did I wouldn't have my wonderful husband or my babies."

I nodded, turned around and made my way back down the stairway.

Chapter Twenty-Six

Sabrina

I walked into the Presidential suite. I was so nervous, not sure what to expect. Did I make the right decision to surprise Caston? I had no idea what I was doing, or what to expect.

The astonishing room was dimly lit by a crystal chandelier that hung from the middle of the room. The red walls were erotic. The four poster king size bed fit perfectly in the room. I walked over to the bed and ran my hand over the sheets, they were a cool black satin. A shiver ran down my spine, as I thought of how they would feel on my naked skin. The room smelled sweet from the dozens of red rose vases that lined the room. A soft music played overhead. I assumed it was music from the iPod dock on the bar across from the bed.

My skin got goose bumps, as I thought about what we could do in here, a pool of liquid was forming between my legs at the naughty thoughts going through my mind. I closed my eyes behind the cat-like mask that obscured my face and took a deep breath. With my eyes shut, my other senses were on high alert. I knew by the hairs that rose on the back of my neck that Caston had entered the room. I could feel the electricity that flowed between us.

"How do I look?" I said, slowly turning around.

My breath hitched, as I laid eyes on Caston. He was dressed in a 20's zoot suit, accented by a white silk hankie, pearl gray spats, and diamond studded platinum watch chain. He looked as though he stepped through a time machine. His hair was slicked back, he looked like a gangster.

I had on a red and black lace corset with red fringe accents. The corset showed off my hourglass figure perfectly, and pushed up my breasts creating two beautiful milky white mounds. The fabric barely covered my nipples. My black silk thong was microscopic and it had a big black bow adorning my ass. The fishnet stockings were held up by rhinestone garter clips. My favorite part of the outfit, because of the red soles that pulled together the entire outfit, where my simple five inch black heels.

His eyes caught mine. "Wow, you look breathtaking, Sabrina." I blushed, feeling his eyes roam my body.

I laughed nervously, as I played with the red fringe on my corset. Walking over to me, he played with my black wig. "This could be interesting tonight, Ms. Bennett." I instantly felt flush, and wet between my thighs.

"Only if you play your cards right, Mr. Black" I said, as I brushed past him to the long mirror on the wall behind him.

He let out a laugh and grabbed my elbow, as he drew me back into him. I could feel his arousal pressing into my back. He leaned down to kiss my neck on the spot that makes my knees give out. Leaning forward, he snaked his hands down and reached further to touch the outsides of my knees. They slowly traveled up my thighs slowly, stopping briefly to toy with my black and red lace garters, and he nibbled my neck. He whispered in my ear, "I. Always. Play. My. Cards. Right. Miss. Bennett." His hot breath sent a shiver down my spine. I let out a slight whimper at his words that were so full of promises. Closing my eyes, I let my head fall back onto his shoulder. His hands continued up and cupped my hot sex. I could feel him grow harder at my back. Reaching my arms behind me, I slid them between our bodies. Grabbing him through his pants, I stroked his hard cock. Letting out a deep throaty moan, he turned me around and his lips quickly found mine. Devouring each other's mouth, I started to undo his pants and reach in for his cock. Backing away from our kiss, I bit my lip and held him with my gaze, as I ran my hand from the base to tip of his granite shaft. Reaching down he lifted me up, I wrapped my legs around his waist and he walked us toward the bed. I thought he was going to put me on it, but he passed it and sat me on the dresser on the opposite side of the room.

Sliding between my legs, he grabbed my black satin thong and, with one quick tug, ripped it apart. "We won't need these tonight," he growled. "However, that big bow on your ass is very inviting."

Two fingers plunged into me, working their way in and out, spreading my folds open, and hitting my special spot.

"Holy shit, Caston, right there," I screamed, as my first orgasm hit me unexpectedly.

I arched my back, trying to get him to pay attention to my breasts. My nipples tingled, needing to be touched.

I whispered breathlessly, "Oh, Caston, please."

Leaning down, his mouth bit the cleavage that was spilling out the top of my corset. I let out a loud scream, as his bite sent me over the edge yet again. I wrapped my arms around his head and weaved my fingers through his hair, pulling him into my chest, as my insides rippled around his fingers.

169

His teeth grabbed the fabric of the top and pulled it down. His mouth found my hardened nipple. Flicking his tongue over the hard point, his fingers continued their assault on my pussy, I was approaching the edge again.

Before I could come he withdrew his fingers and took them into his mouth. "I love the way you taste, Sabrina."

I whimpered at the loss, but my eyes hooded in ecstasy, as I stared at him sucking my juices off his fingers.

He slid me to the edge of the dresser and stepped back. He looked me over, spread open, waiting, aching for him. Removing his belt, he threw it on the bed, letting his pants fall to his ankles. His steel cock sprang free, causing me to lick my lips. With one quick move, he entered me. The feeling was magnificent. Wrapping his arms around me, he started to move. His fingers dug into my hips, as he eagerly slid in and out of my sopping pussy. "God, Bre, you feel so good. I'm going to explode."

My hands intertwined around his neck as I brought his mouth to mine, exploring it ruthlessly. Digging my new, red soled, fuck me heels into his rear I pushed him into me harder.

"My God, Caston, I love you." I yelled as my orgasm shook me. Caston's head tilted back and he gasped in ecstasy as he came, pumping everything into me.

There was nothing sexier than watching him come. I loved it. We stilled as our orgasms subsided. He lightly kissed my lips. I nuzzled into his neck, taking in Caston's manly scent.

"Sabrina, you're perfect in every way. I love you."

He withdrew and walked over to the adjoining bathroom to get a washcloth. When he returned, he gently wiped me clean. His soft touch was making me want him again. When he was satisfied he took me by the waist, lowering me to the floor.

"Let's finish getting cleaned up, so I can show you the rest of the club. I'll call down to have another thong brought up," he said, flashing me his fabulous smile.

Half an hour later Caston took my hand and asked, "Are you ready for this?" Leaning over, he kissed the top of my head.

"I'm not sure. I thought I was, but my stomach feels like it's going drop out."

He pulled me in, hooking my arms around his waist. I looked up at him. His eyes were full of concern. "Oh, I almost forgot," he reached into the pocket of his suit coat and pulled out a long velvet black box. "This is to show everyone you're mine, and they aren't to approach you without me around."

I took the box from him and opened it. "Oh my God, Caston, it's beautiful."

Inside the box was a black diamond choker. It had a pendant hanging down that was a beautiful platinum heart. The heart had a filigree design, but as I looked closer to it I realized it was our initials laced together. My heart melted knowing he had to have had this designed just for me. "This had to have cost a fortune. When did you have this done?"

"Bre, you're worth way more than this silly necklace. You're mine, our hearts are one."

He took the box and removed the necklace. Stepping behind me he held it in front of me, slipping it around my neck. It was heavy and cold. My hand went up to touch it. My heart felt heavy, like the necklace around my neck. Taking my hand he led me over to the mirror by the door. He stood behind me again and held me around my waist.

"It looks magnificent on you."

I caught his eyes in the mirror. "Thank you." I turned around in his arms, leaning up on my tiptoes to lay a kiss on him. "Not just for this. For everything."

I couldn't be sure, but it looked like he wanted to say something to me. Instead he swept me into the deepest kiss; my knees gave out. He caught me, holding me up in his strong arms.

Feeling his strength flow through me, I broke the kiss and led him to the door.

"I'm ready," I said, "With you by my side, I'm ready for anything."

Opening the door for me, he placed his hand on the small of my back and led me out into the hallway. Deep bass music filled my ears and hammered in my chest. I looked around, taking in the sights around me.

It was the inside of a large warehouse that had been renovated to fulfill the needs of the club. The middle of the building was open, the lights and music filtered up from the ground floor. There were two floors of rooms lining the walls. People were scattered around the floors. Some talking, some dancing, and some were making out.

Caston led me down the hall, acknowledging people, as we made our way to the grand staircase. I was being looked over from head to toe, judged, as if making sure I was good enough for the company I was in. Feeling extremely self-conscious, I pulled Caston in a little closer. He snaked his arm around my waist, as we walked down the stairs.

Reaching the bottom floor, Caston was met by a group of women fawning for his attention. He dismissed them with a wave of his hand, but then a taller gentleman walked up to Caston and leaned in to whisper into his ear. Possibly security, but I wasn't sure. Caston gave a curt nod and turned toward me. Leaning over he kissed me on my forehead.

"Honey, I have to take care of a few things. Do you want me to take you to our VIP room?"

I shook my head. I wanted to seem confident to him, even though, I felt like I could throw up at any time.

He smiled at me, and gave my hand a squeeze, before he headed off in the other direction.

I felt alone and scared. I was just about to turn and run back up the stairs when a warm hand was placed on my lower back. I stiffened not knowing who it could be.

"Bre, where is Caston?"

I let out a deep breath. "Sara. Oh, thank God, it's you. He had to go take care of something."

"Already? Damn, well let's get you up to the VIP room." She grabbed my hand.

I stopped her. *Sail* by AWOLNATION began and I was feeling a little brave. Wanting to have some fun, I smiled at Sara. "Let's go dance. Caston has work to do. He'll come find me when he is ready."

It was dark in there, but I think she blushed. She reached up and ran her hand across my collarbone, along the necklace. She reached the pendant and took it in her hand. Her face seemed melancholy. "I see he gave you the choker."

I smiled, but felt butterflies in my stomach at her touch. Smiling, I took her hand and led her into the middle of the dance floor. The music took over and I started dancing. Everyone around us was grinding up against each other. Men on women, men on men, women on women. We were moving as one. I felt free on the dance floor. This is who I am. I felt sexy and confident.

Sara was dancing with me. Her hands were on my hips, moving them to the music. She walked around behind me, still moving with me. We were flush against each other. Her hand snaked around my stomach and pulled me closer. Closing my eyes, I leaned up against her. My skin heated. I felt myself becoming aroused. Her lips brushed up against my shoulder, causing a shiver ran down my spine. I suddenly felt her hand on my breast, kneading it though my corset. Her kisses and nibbles became deeper. The music still possessed me, and I turned to face her. Her hands slid around me to grab my ass. I rested my elbows on her shoulders and ran my hands through her long flowing hair. Our eyes locked, and I was transported to another place. It felt like it was just us on the floor, as if we were in our own world. I bit my lip. We leaned toward each other. Microseconds away from kissing; our lips a mere millimeter from touching, and all of a sudden, I was spun away from Sara, and my lips were being taken by my love. His hands were all over me, just as Sara's were minutes before. I looked behind him, seeing Sara was grinding up against another man. Turning my attention back to Caston, I turned around, pressing my ass into his crotch. His hands roamed all over my body and his lips sucked along my neck. Breathing into my ear he said, "That was hot."

I let my laugh take over my body and laid my head back to rest on his shoulder, while I continued to grind into him. Caston growled, turned me around, and lifted me up by my ass. I instantly wrapped my legs around his waist, and he walked us off the dance floor. My heart was still thumping with excitement, and I was out of breath.

He set me down in a room with one wall open, overlooking the dance floor. It had white walls with a black marble floor. The furniture was white leather couches and chairs, with black and red throws and pillows strewn about. This particular room had its own small bar in the corner with a personal bartender.

Caston walked over to the bar, while I walked over to look at the dance floor. The main room was packed with people. Looking from this perspective, I was able to see there were a few poles with some very talented women on them. There was also a few large square beds off to the side, with about four, or five, couples going at it on the beds. I rubbed my thighs together. Watching the spectacle in front of me, after what nearly happened on the dance floor, I was soaked and thoroughly excited.

Coming up behind me, he wrapped his arm around my waist and offered me a glass of water. I accepted it. My small sip turned into me downing the entire glass.

"See anything you like?" Caston's hot breath was on my neck, his voice so full of promise. He leaned down to kiss me. His tongue was cold from the drink he just took. Goose bumps raised on my skin from the temperature difference.

I could still see Sara on the dance floor. She was with the man who swept her away from me, and another was now grinding behind her. I watched as they kissed, sucked, and toyed with her. She looked up toward our balcony and caught my eye. Leaning back into the gentleman behind her, she wrapped her arms around his head. Her eyes were hooded as the other man worked his way down her front, reaching her pussy. She never broke eye contact with me, she wanted me to watch. I wanted to look away, but I was so turned on. The guy lifted up one of her legs, hooking it over his shoulder and moved her thong to the side. The instant his head made contact with her hot flesh her head fell back onto the man holding her up. Her long fishnet stocking leg moved, and I saw the spike of her heal dig into the back of the man lapping at her juices. The man holding her up cupped her breasts and pinched her nipples.

I suddenly felt a pinch on my nipples. Caston had noticed my stare and started mimicking what was happening on the dance floor. "You like watching her?"

"Oh, yes, yes I do." I sighed breathlessly.

"Don't take your eyes off her."

His other hand slid down, moving my thong away from my pussy, exposing my soaked flesh to the spectators below. I rested my foot on a small stool to my side, giving him better access just like her leg that was over the man's shoulder. His mouth was on my neck sucking. "Oh, Caston."

He had an ice cube in his mouth; the mix of sensations on my hot skin almost made me come on the spot.

I continued to watch Sara being taken on the dance floor. Caston moved his fingers in and out of me as the man was licking her. We seemed to be connected by a jolt of electricity. I clenched Caston's head and let my orgasm take over. She seemed to do the same to the man below. As we both came down from the aftershocks she caught my eye again and blew me a kiss. Still spread open to the crowd below I suddenly felt flush, coming back to the reality that everyone just saw what we did.

I turned around burying my head in Caston's chest. "Don't do that," he took my chin in between his finger and thumb, raising my head up so I looked at him.

His big blue silver eyes were so full of love. I could see to his soul. I smiled shyly. He walked me back to the couches at the back of the overlook and helped me sit. My body was still shaking, with embarrassment, with aftershocks of the amazing orgasm I just had, and with fear of what is to come. I took a deep breath and shook my shoulders getting rid of all those feelings.

I smiled at Caston. "I'm okay."

He slouched down and looked me in the eye. "Yup, there's my girl."

He leaned forward to kiss me, but there was a racket in the stairway. We both looked over toward the doorway to find Sara and the man who was just between her legs were laughing and carrying on as they walked in.

They stopped in their tracks when they saw us staring at them. "What?" they said in unison.

Sara bounded over to me and plopped down right next to me. Almost sitting on my lap. I giggled when she grabbed my hands. "That was so amazing, thanks for sharing that with me."

I blushed at her reference to what just happened on the dance floor.

Caston got up, walked over to the man, and smacked him on the back. He talked close to the man's ear, so I couldn't hear what he was saying. Sara was saying something to me, but it was going in one ear and out the other, since I was straining to hear Caston.

Their conversation was very serious. Caston's and the man's faces were very hard and etched with concern. I finally couldn't take it anymore. Turning to face Sara a little more, I interrupted, "Sara..."

"Ya."

"Who is that man with, Caston? The one you came up with."

"Oh God," she jumped up, pulling me with her. "We're such idiots. I'm so sorry."

We walked the few steps toward the men. She wrapped her arm around the man's waist. "Jon, honey, we never introduced you to Sabrina."

I saw Caston mentally scold himself. "I'm so sorry, Sabrina. This is Jon, my brother. Jon, this is my girl, Sabrina."

Jon was slightly taller than Caston and older. He didn't look anything like Caston, which I thought was very strange. Usually siblings look a little alike. Jon had chocolate brown eyes and his shorter hair was so blond it was almost white. He flashed his 100-megawatt smile at me, as he reached for my hand. The smile was the only thing that linked him with Caston.

"Pleasure is all mine. Finally, I get to meet the famous Ms. Bennett. Cass hasn't stopped talking about you since we saw you dance. You're a beautiful dancer, my dear."

His smile made me blush. I felt like he was looking through me, as if he had x-ray vision. I put my hand in his. He brought it up to his mouth and kissed the back of my hand, letting his lips linger.

"Thank you."

I reached for Caston, letting him pull me into his arms. I looked up at him. "You sure do talk about me a lot."

"How could I not? You're my everything."

I let out a big sigh. He always says the most perfect things. I let myself zone out to the music as Caston and Jon talked. I was brought back to reality when Caston kissed the top of my head. "Bre, I've got to go deal with the fallout from last night. Make yourself comfortable here. Don't go down to the dance floor without me." I stuck my lip out in a full on pout. "Oh, Sabrina, don't give me that face." He leaned down and sucked my lip into his mouth. The dampness between my legs grew. "Things get out of control down there. I don't want you getting into something that you aren't comfortable with, or expecting." He held my face in his hands. "Promise me?"

"Promise." I smiled.

"I'll be right back. I'll make up my leaving to you then."

I slid my hand down between us, massaging his cock. "I can't wait," I purred.

I watched Caston, Jon, and Sara walk down the stairway. Turning around, I walked back to the small bar and poured myself another glass of ice cold water, since the bartender seemed to be missing as well. The liquid cooled my burning throat. I was all alone in this suite.

The music changed. A little slower. Letting the rhythm flow through me. Letting the music take over, I started to dance. Running my hands over my body and moving my feet, the world around me disappeared.

Suddenly there was a crash, and I spun around. Tripping over my feet, I almost fell off my five inch heels.

"Better watch your step there."

I covered my mouth. My other hand went across my stomach. I felt sick. Beverly was standing there. She'd knocked over a chair just to get my attention.

"Beverly," my voice was barely above a whisper.

"Mrs. Holden," she corrected me through a sneer.

"Mrs. Holden."

Backing up, trying to get the most space between us, the back of my legs hit the couch, and I fell back onto the cool leather. If I could have crawled into the wall and hid, I would have.

She had on a black leather leotard and heeled boots that went up to her thighs. How she walked in them, I had no idea. She had little black cat ears on her head and a long whip in her hand. The eyes behind her cat mask were cold and vacant. I was terrified.

She snapped her whip onto the marble floor. The crack made me jump. She laughed. Evil bitch.

Her red hair was an unnatural color. It seemed to glow in this lighting. She started to walk toward me, and I started to tremble.

"Listen up, you little whore. I don't think you understand the magnitude of my power. I can make your life a living hell, and if you stay with Caston, understand that it will be hell. I can't believe he has fallen under your spell, you money hungry bitch. What did you do, brainwash him to believe you cared about him? You aren't right for him."

She was in my face now, with her finger poking into my chest. Her red nails were sharp and they felt as though they were cutting into my skin. I winced at the pain.

"Stay. Away. Leave him now. Before he even comes back here. I'll relay the message."

She stood up and walked over to the bar, pouring herself a drink of something strong. I could smell it all the way from where I was sitting. She acted as if she had no doubt I would follow her edict.

I pulled my legs up on to the couch and hugged my knees into my chest. Rocking myself, I closed my eyes. Mark was all that came to my mind. This is how Mark treated me. Why do I let people walk all over me? I had vowed myself that I would change. *Caston, please God, if you can hear me, please come save me.* I knew it would never work, but a girl could wish, right?

Almost, as if on cue, I heard noise on the stairs. Caston appeared at the top. I rushed into his arms almost in tears. He stumbled back slightly when my body hit his. "What's wrong Sabrina?"

Wrapping me in his arms he cuddled me. Safety. "She is what's wrong," I mumble into his chest.

Chapter Twenty-Seven

Sabrina

Sabrina is beside herself. I left her and she was fine. What could have...
HER! Damn it! I cradle Sabrina to my chest. Comforting her fears.

"Beverly, I am not doing this anymore. No more lies. No more
threats. No more, Beverly!" I screamed.

"Caston, if you know what is best for you and your dear little
whore. You'll continue to call me Mother, and you'll get rid of her
once and for all. She has already cost you more than you know." She
walks toward us much too calm. I brace myself, covering Sabrina's
head, so she doesn't have to hear all the yelling.

"No, no fucking way! Your threats will NOT run my life
anymore. Sabrina is my everything. She made me realize that you are a
piece of shit, trying to ruin my life. Oh, and Beverly..." I laugh, "trust
me, I can ruin you so fast your head will spin."

Just as I moved Sabrina behind me to protect her, a hard smack
lands across my face. I could feel the sting rise to the surface. I was
afraid Beverly would lay her hands on her and hurt my beautiful girl.

Beverly's boney finger was in my face, "You will call me Mother, or you'll regret it. Mark my words, Caston."

"GET. THE. FUCK. OUT. OF. MY. CLUB!" Thankfully security was bounding up the stairway, as I finished saying that. They drug her away from Sabrina and me.

Sabrina's legs gave out from under her. I sunk to the floor with her, cradling her to my chest. All the commotion had made people on the dance floor and the music come to a halt. Everyone was staring up here. Sara, thankfully, was right there to draw the curtains to shut us off from the rest of the club.

"Sabrina, please settle down. Shhh, baby, please." I stroked her head, trying to calm my hysterical girl.

Sara fetched a glass of water and knelt down to hand it to her. She laid her hand on Sabrina's shoulder and kissed her ivory skin.

Sara looked up and caught my eye. Her look was pure resentment. She had almost the same experience with me and Beverly.

"You have to get her out of here, Cass," Sara spoke in a hushed tone.

"I know." I mouthed back. Tears were burning my eyes, but I couldn't let them fall. I had to be strong for her.

Sara slid her hand down Sabrina's legs and moved to unbuckle her shoes. She was so tender about it. I knew Sara still loved me in a way that was unsaid. She was always there to pick up the pieces of my life, when they would tumble down.

Sabrina was still trembling and sobbing into my chest. I shrugged off my jacket and draped it around her shoulders. "Where are her clothes, Sara?"

"My office. I'll come with you."

I picked her up. "Bre, honey, just keep your head in my chest. I'm getting you out of here."

I descended the stairs and thanked God that there were strict confidentiality and no cell phone policies in the club, or this would be already hitting the tabloids. Sara walked a few steps in front of me and shooed people back onto the dance floor. I turned the corner to head to Jon's office. I stopped and looked behind me. The red and blue lights of the police were flashing through the open doorway at the back door of the club. I leaned over and kissed Sabrina's hair. Jon walked out of the main office and flashed me a small smile. I took it as his sign that everything is in order with Beverly.

Sara had already made it to his office and was waiting at the doorway to help me. Walking in, I set Sabrina on a small pink couch at the far end of the room. She was in shock. All she did was stare off into space. I cradled her face in my hands and kissed her.

I stepped back to give Sara room. She had Sabrina's clothes. "Go make sure everything is settled with Jon. I'll get her ready to go."

"Thank you, Sara."

Turning to walk out of the room, I grabbed my phone from my pocket and dialed Terrance.

"Terrance, have you heard?"

"Yes, sir, what are the next steps?"

"Police are here now. I am going to meet up with Jon. I am filing a restraining order against her for Sabrina and myself. I want all of the locks changed on everything of mine."

"Yes, sir." I heard him scribbling notes down as he was driving.

"Has Dad called yet?"

"No, sir, he hasn't."

Jon walked up to me. I held out my hand for him to hold his thought.

"Ugh, I do not want to hear him fly off the handle about this. Anyway, please call all security personnel at my companies to update them on the events of tonight and a little background on why we are taking such serious measures."

"On it. I'm also on my way to come pick you and Ms. Bennett up."

"Thank you, Terrance."

Ending my call, I turn to Jon.

"Police are ready for you to sign the paperwork," he said.

I squeezed his arm. "Thanks. Is she still fuming from her ears?"

"Oh God, she is flipping out in the back of that squad car."

"Dad?"

"He didn't even know she was here. He is furious. After the other incident, she wasn't supposed to come here for a few weeks." Jon said as we walked to the front entrance. "At least, that is what she promised me, anyways." He added under his breath.

Signing all the paperwork took longer than I wanted to be away from Sabrina, but I needed to assure her security.

"Are we done yet?" I asked, annoyed.

The police officer nodded, and I spun on my heels to run back to her.

Sara was just closing the door to the office, as I made my way down the hall. "What's wrong?" I yelled.

She put her finger up to her lips to quiet me. "She fell asleep on the couch. You have to tell her, Cass. If she really is the one, she needs to know."

I squeezed my eyes shut and pinched the bridge of my nose. "I know, I know."

Sara grabbed my other hand and gave it a squeeze. "Everything will be okay. You'll see."

"I sure hope so. I can't lose her."

She stood with me and a few tears fell from my eyes. I took a deep breath. Squeezing Sara's hand again, I let myself into the office. I had to get away from her before I really lost it.

Shutting the door behind me, I slid to the floor with my knees up and ran my hands through my hair. The flood gates burst, I cried like I haven't done since I was a child, since the day I was taken from my mom.

Chapter Twenty-Eight

Sabrina

I'm so comfy that I don't want to wake up. Stretching out in bed, I feel around and Caston isn't with me. Panicking, I sit straight up in bed, immediately awake. An instant migraine hits me, and I fall back to the pillow clutching my head. "Oh my God, what did I do last night?" I say out loud to no one in particular.

I feel the bed dip next to me, and I peak through one eye to see Caston, holding out a glass of water and some pills. "Take these," he says quietly, so not to irritate my headache.

I reach out to grab the items and my hand brushes Caston's in the process. The tingle that goes up my arm, sends a shiver down my spine. The spark between us is undeniable, but if Beverly cannot leave me alone I won't be able to stay.

Caston moves closer to me and pulls me into his lap. His rhythmic stroking of my hair behind my ear slowly eases my pain, taking it away. Having him close makes me fall into a deep sleep.

SMACK. My head flings to the side, spinning me around. "You fucking bitch. I told you, I wanted my laundry done."

I catch myself on the bed. Damn. I overslept and forgot to get the chores done, again. Slowly turning around, I sit down casting my eyes downward, trying to not provoke him anymore than he already is. "I'm sorry, Mark." I whisper.

He throws the laundry basket at me. I catch it just before it hits me in the face. I see him coming at me and before I can move he kicks me in both shins. I fall off the bed over the basket. The pain. I whimper.

"Fucking bitch, get up!"

I try to stand, but immediately fall again. The pain is awful. I glance down to my legs. The bruises are already showing. How long will these last? I've already missed school for other injuries. I close my eyes and will myself to stand. The pain is excruciating. I pick up the basket, holding it in front of me to protect my stomach, since I haven't told him about the baby yet. I have to wait for the right moment, when Mark isn't this worked up.

"What the fuck is wrong with you, anyway?" he screams. "Do you have the fucking flu? You have been sick for weeks, and look like shit. How am I supposed to take you places?"

A tear runs down my cheek as I think about the ultrasound picture in my purse. I just shake my head. "I'm not sure. I guess just sick. I'm sorry."

I try to get by him to go do the laundry, so he does not see me break down. Thankfully, he lets me pass. As soon as I reach the hall, I sink to the floor and burst into tears. Oh God, why?

Finally, composing myself, I hobble to the laundry room in the basement. Broc is sitting on the folding table with his headphones on. I try to sneak past him, so he doesn't notice me.

"Hey, Bre!" he yells over the music in his ears.

Not making eye contact, I raise my hand to acknowledge him. My eyes would show that I've been crying, and who knows what kind of shiner I have on my face right now. Thankfully, he goes back to reading his magazine. Black Hollywood. Of course. I roll my eyes. Men's eye candy.

Finishing what I can, I drag myself back up the stairs, and I start to feel woozy. I pause, putting my hand over my stomach. Breathe, Bre. It will pass. This morning/ all day sickness is for the birds. I'll never be able to finish school now.

After a few deep breaths, it finally passes. I quickly hurry back to the room in case it returns.

As soon as I shut the door, a punch lands in my side and I fall to the floor. My hair falls over my face. Moving it out of the way I look up. Mark is glaring down at me. He has my ultrasound picture. Our baby.

"WHAT THE FUCK IS THIS?"

"It's our baby," I begin to sob.

Mark freezes. His shoulders square off. "YOU FUCKING WHORE! Who are you cheating on me with?"

"What?" Oh God, how can he think that? I'm never out of his sight.

"Who the fuck is the father!" The look on Mark's face terrifies me. I have seen him mad before, but this is a whole new level.

I open my mouth to answer. That is when I see it. I foot coming toward me. It connects right in my stomach. "NO!" I scream, clutching myself.

Repeated kicks all over my body. I try to curl up into a tight fetal position. I have to protect my baby. Please, God, if I get out of this, I'll get away from this man. Two last kicks do me in and I black out. One to my back to make me uncurl and one devastating kick to my stomach.

"Bre, Bre, oh my God, call 911." I hear through the fog, then nothing.

I slowly wake up. I'm in the hospital hooked to monitors and IVs. Beth and Broc are seated next to me. Beth's head is rested on the side of the bed, while she is holding my hand.

"What is going on? Where is Mark?" I whisper. Everything hurts so badly.

Beth sits up looking at me in shock. Broc runs out of the room to get a nurse. "Oh my God, honey. I'm so happy you're awake. I've been so worried about you."

"Worried, why?"

"Honey, you have been in a coma for two weeks. Broc found you at the bottom of a staircase. You're so bruised and broken. Honey, we weren't sure if the brain swelling would go down."

Fear runs through my bones, as realization of the severity of my injuries sinks in. "The baby," I whisper.

Tears fall down her cheeks. I know what that means.

I lost it. Oh God, my baby. He made me lose my baby.

Caston is gently shaking me, trying to wake me. "Bre, what's the matter? Honey, you're crying and yelling out in your sleep. Tell me"

I clutch to him tighter, I cannot show my face. The memory of losing my baby is still so fresh in my mind. The memories of the hospital and recovery still hurt. My heart still hurts. I thought I was over this.

"Caston, I lost a baby about six months ago." I whispered into his chest. "I'm so embarrassed that I went back to that piece of shit. I thought I was finally turning a corner, but I guess everything with Beverly coming after me brought it back to the surface."

He tenses as he tightens his hold on me. "Oh, Sabrina. Cry all you need. You'll never forget and you shouldn't. The baby was a part of you."

I cry harder. "I'm an idiot. Broc and Beth knew what happened. They tried to get me to turn him in. Mark came to see me in the hospital. I'm not sure why I listened to him, or even gave him a chance to talk to me. He reminded me of all the pictures and videos he had of me that would immediately get me kicked out of school. He also reminded me that no one would believe that he was to blame since he was the one grieving because of my infidelity. I knew it wasn't true as much as he did but I couldn't risk anything. When I took him back he changed his tune and convinced me that he was sorry. That he would spend his life making it up to me. I told the police that I fell down the stairs, because my morning sickness had made me so weak. I could tell they didn't believe me, but they couldn't press charges if I wouldn't corroborate the story. I'm so fucking stupid." I sob harder into his chest. He sits, stroking my back trying to calm me down. I feel as though I could throw up.

"Beth, wouldn't talk to me for a month. She stayed her distance from me. That's actually why she wasn't with me the night I met you."

I look up at him to see him looking down at me. His eyes were so warm and full of love. "Why didn't you tell me this before?" he asks.

"Oh, Caston, I'm so embarrassed that I'm one of those stupid women. I was so scared. I couldn't risk my reputation." I also didn't want to say because the doctors told me this might affect my ability to have children in the future.

I look away ashamed of my past. I should have told him before he fell in love with me. Being with someone who may not be able to have a child is a big deal.

He leaned down and kissed me tenderly. The kiss started out light, but quickly deepened. "You aren't stupid, and I don't love you any less," he said when he pulled back. Another peck and he added, "Bre, you're all I need."

I squeeze my eyes shut as more tears stream down my cheeks. He said exactly what I needed to hear. *You're all I need.* This time I'm the one to lean forward to kiss him.

Not letting his lips leave mine, I move up and straddle his lap. His warm hands grip my hips. I can feel him under me. Our tongues dance over each other and his hard cock presses up against my slit, making me wet. I rotate my hips, making us both moan. His hard chest is pressing up against my breasts. I run my hands through his hair, kissing down his neck and along his jaw. Nibbling at his earlobe, I kiss him right behind the ear. A shiver goes down his spine and his breath catches.

His hands reach around and grip my ass, hard. Kneading and pulling it. I need to be filled. I continue my decent down his neck while I'm still grinding in his lap. Slowly moving down his body I reach his belly button, looking up at Caston I dipped my tongue into it. His eyes darken with desire. He stared directly at me, he looked as though he wanted to eat me alive. Not breaking eye contact, I moved further down noticing my large wet spot on his crotch. A sly smile crept across my face when I saw it. I moved my mouth over that spot and took it into my mouth sucking up my fluids and him through his shorts. He took in a deep breath and tangled his hands in my hair, holding me in place.

I need him in my mouth, now. Pushing up, just far enough to be able to pull his pants down, to free his magnificent, smooth cock, I take him in my mouth. I open my throat and push his cock all the way down. I want it all. Feeling his head hit the back of my throat, he groaned and let his head fall back. The grip on my hair tightened, which made me want to speed up. I sucked and teased him, popping him out as I reach the head of his cock. Using the tip of my tongue I play with the vein that runs along the underside. I wrap my hand around his girth and stroke him base to tip, as I suck his ball sack into my mouth and move it around with my tongue. I feel them suck up to his body, and I know a drip of pre-cum has formed on the head of his cock.

I lick my lips and move back to suck it up. The salty fluid tastes magnificent. Taking him deep in my mouth, again, Caston lets out a loud growl, pushing me off of him, onto my back. He kicks off his shorts and moves to crawl up over me. Taking one of my legs in his hands he moves his mouth from my foot to my center, nibbling as he goes along. I toyed and squeezed my nipples.

Reaching my pussy, he hooks his arms around my hips, pulling me apart with his long fingers. Slowly he takes his tongue and dips it into my velvety folds. He exposes my clit and lightly blows on it.. Shivers of pleasure run through me. I grab his head and push it deeper, he devours me. Sucking my sides and licking. His finger rubs circles as his mouth sucks on my lips. "You're driving me insane, Caston." I tug and pull on his head, moving it exactly where I need him most.

He groans into me and the vibration makes me quiver. Laughing at my reaction he looks up and smirks at me. Just then his cell phone rings. Looking defeated he sighed and dropped his forehead to rest on my pelvic bone. "Fuck me."

"With pleasure, let it ring." I try to persuade him to come up and sink into my wet hole. "Please, Cass?"

"I can't. Just a minute, I won't be long."

He hops up and goes to his phone. I laugh at his hard cock bouncing as he walks over there. Licking my lips I let my hands roam and take over my own pleasure. I tune him out and continue but I never take my eyes off of him.

He reaches down and plays with his cock, while he is on the phone. I can tell he is distracted from watching me and his own pleasure. As I sink two fingers into myself, Caston hangs up and bounds over to me.

He scoops me up onto his lap, one push he is in me to the hilt. I gasp at the extremely full feeling. His beast stretches me. "Sabrina, you feel so good." He says into my neck.

We move together. My soul feeling free, since I have told him about my dark past. My hidden secret that only a few knew about. I wrap my legs around him and hold on. Rocking on his lap we're one. One soul. Our orgasms take us at the same time. We hold on to each other until our breathing calms.

Pulling back, I take his head in my hands, lightly kissing his lips. "Caston, you're my other half." I rest my forehead on his. A tear drips from my eye. Still connected he kisses my tears away.

More tears fall from my eyes, because Caston doesn't say it back. His eyes don't have the same twinkle they did just a few minutes ago. I pull him closer, while my heart breaks.

Chapter Twenty-Nine

Caston

Sabrina told me I was her other half. So many thoughts were going through my head. My love for her, the bitch, Beverly, her lost baby, marriage. I could only hold her tight. It was the only thing my mind would let me do, because I couldn't think straight.

Her tears were falling down my chest, making small rivers that tickled as they fell to my stomach. I wanted to take away her pain, but I couldn't do that until I shared my secret with her. "Bre, baby," I pull her back a little, trying to make her look at me, "I love you more than words can describe. I want to take your pain away, but you need to understand my secrets, too. I won't feel right until you know."

"Tell me then, Caston. Please," she sobs. The look on her face breaks my heart in two. My poor girl, the feelings in her are tearing her apart. I needed to calm her down before she had a full blown panic attack.

I pick her up and carry her to the shower. There is no sound except the water. I set her on the bench, her shoulders were arched forward, shaking as her tears still fall from her eyes. She was broken, and I needed to fix her. Taking the sponge, I washed her. Starting at her neck the bubbles slid down between her breasts. My touch was soft. I wanted to feel every part of her body. I slowly moved down to her breasts, caressingly passed under each round globe. As I grazed over her nipples she let her head fall back, turning herself over to my touch.

Moving my hand lower between her breasts, I stopped just below her belly button. I watched her breathing change. It was now slow and controlled deep breaths. Her eyes were shut and occasionally her tongue would dart out to lick up some of the mist from the steam the shower was producing. Unconsciously, her legs parted.

Acknowledging her need, I slid the sponge lower between her legs. Her breath caught as I washed her; removing all the stickiness of our last love making. I kept running it slowly up and down her slit. Occasionally, I would let one of my fingers graze between her swollen lips. Her hips tilted into my hand. Leaning over a little further, I took her upturned mouth in mine, hungrily kissing her.

Shutting off the water I quickly grabbed the robe off the hook and wrapped her in it, so she would not chill. Taking a towel I blotted her hair and combed it out. She watched me intently as I dried off. Her pink swollen eyes never left me. I picked her up and carried her back to bed. It was only mid-day, but after her confession, our love making, and the events from last night as soon as her head hit the pillow she was fast asleep. I brushed the hair off her face and covered her up. I sat next to her, watching her sleep for hours.

Chapter Thirty

Sabrina

I'm not sure of the time when I wake up again. It's dark outside. Caston is sitting next to me staring down at me. I smile and reach up to touch his cheek. "Hi," I whisper.

"Hey," he responds leaning into my hand. His eyes look so pained.

"Why so gloomy?"

"What is your earliest memory?"

The question catches me off guard, "What?"

"Your earliest memory? What is it?" He takes my hand in his, cradling it in his lap.

"Well, I guess it would be my first dance recital. I was wearing a green leotard with hideous gold sequins. A green tutu with sequins on the edges. I had white tights and white shoes. A little gold crown over a braided bun on the top of my head. My mom had caked my make-up on, and I had the brightest red lipstick on my lips," I laughed at the memory, happy I was smiling again. "I had the skinniest legs. I was thankful, because my song was about teddy bears, so I got to dance with my favorite bear." The memory made my heart jump. That was a happy time.

Caston's eyes looked misty. "I would love to see pictures of that." His hand brushed some hair out of my face. He looked so lost.

"No way. I have those hidden away really well."

He laughed out loud and finally smiled.

Sitting up, I asked, "And yours?"

He looked up at the ceiling and took a deep breath. I could almost swear he was fighting off tears. "I was four. It was Christmas, I'd asked Santa for a camera. I'd just gotten into taking pictures. I was using an old camera my mom had. I loved showing her my art, as she called it. It always made her smile. Anyways, my mom was doing her best to try to talk me out of the camera. I remember going to bed on Christmas Eve so excited, because I knew Santa would come through for me. I was cold, but I never complained, because Mom worked so hard to keep food on the table for us. I remember waking up in the middle of the night and sneaking out to catch Santa. Instead, I found my mom crying. I watched her for a little bit, but I knew she needed me. Crawling over to her, I pushed my way onto her lap. She gladly accepted me and rocked us gently. She said to me, 'Baby, Santa can't bring you that camera. Money is tight this year for him.' I told her I understood. I know you're thinking this is his happy memory? It's so depressing. Honestly, though, the love from my mom that night still warms my heart. I remember how beautiful she was in the glow of the Christmas tree. The twinkling lights reflecting in her eyes. That is why it is my happiest moment."

I understood. I leaned forward and lightly kissed him. "I understand. But I don't under..." He put a finger over my lips to quiet me. I sat back again knowing he had more that he needed to get off his chest.

"What is your saddest memory?" he asked.

Tears suddenly filled my eyes. My heart broke. "Besides losing my baby... When the police came to tell me my parents were dead. It's all my fault they're dead. I was so selfish. Please, I can't talk about this right now."

I didn't want to elaborate anymore. It was still too fresh for me. "And yours?" I asked wanting to change the subject.

"When I was taken away from my mom."

"What? But I thought..."

He shook his head. "Beverly is not my mother."

"But..."

Caston got up and walked away from me. Sitting straight up in bed I folded my legs under me. "Please, come back, Caston."

He pinched the bridge of his nose and faced the fireplace. "James is my dad, but Beverly is not my mother, she's my aunt."

I sat up in shock. "What?" I sputtered out.

"I don't want to talk about that right now."

How can he just skip over that piece of information like it isn't important?

He turned around and started to walk back to me, "It was just after that happy Christmas. The school bus had dropped me off outside of my apartment, and there was a fancy car out front. All the hoodlums in the area where swarming it, but the security guard kept shooing them away. I was four, so I thought it was cool to see such a shiny car. Then I saw Mom in the doorway with a big man. Mom never told me anything about my dad. I didn't even know he was alive. When I saw this man I had a feeling he was my dad. I was so mad at the man, because she was crying so hard. She turned to look at me and bent down, welcoming me home into her embrace. I asked her why she was crying. She didn't answer me. Stroking my hair she picked me up, hugging me hard. The big man behind me said 'Rose, we have to go. Please, don't make this harder than it has to be.' She just cried harder."

I patted the bed next to me, so he would come to sit by me. He needed me to give him strength.

"I asked her what was going on. Who that big man was? She walked me into the vestibule and sat on the stairs with me. She looked at me and brushed the hair out of my eyes. Her eyes were the most beautiful sparkling emerald green. I'll never forget them. I've never seen anyone with eyes that color since."

He looked away from me, as if he were reliving that very scene in front of him. A few tears fell from his eyes. Still he continued, "Anyway, she took my little hands in hers and told me that the big man was my dad. His name was James and he was going to be taking me to live with him. I asked if she was coming with me. More tears ran down her cheeks, and she told me no. She said that my dad could take care of me better. He had more money and it was the best for me. I begged her not to send me away. I told her I wouldn't eat so much. I sobbed. She pulled me into her lap and cuddled me for the last time. James was getting frustrated in the doorway, obviously annoyed for having to wait. She told me that it wasn't my fault that she couldn't take care of me anymore. She told me she failed me."

I pulled his head down on to my lap. He was crying so hard. My heart was breaking for him. I stroked his hair and wiped his tears as they fell. "I begged and begged her not to send me away. I could barely see her anymore, I was crying so hard. James came over and scooped me off my mom's lap. I screamed for her. He carried me over his shoulder, kicking and screaming, I stretched behind him to try to reach her. She just watched me go. Tears were streaming down her face, too. I'll never forget her face when James put me in the car. She just stood there."

His sobs were shaking through his whole body. I did not even know what to say to him. "I'm so sorry, Caston," I whispered, "Where is she now?"

I did not know it would be possible for him to cry harder, but he did. "She's dead. Dad told me when I was about six. He told me she was in an accident. I felt so lost. I always held out hope that when I was older I would find her and take care of her, but when he told me she died..." He trailed off, stopping what he was saying.

"Oh, Cass." He held on to me like his life depended on it. His head buried deep in my lap. My heart was breaking for him. I knew what it was like to lose a parent.

Suddenly, he sat up, taking deep breaths and wiping at his tears with the backs of his hands. "I'm sorry," he said, "God, what is wrong with me blubbering like a baby."

"Caston, it's a normal response to cry when you're sad."

He looked at me. "That is not how I was brought up."

I nodded, "I know, but that isn't how it should be."

His look was intense. I got up and walked to the closet and put on some shorts and a t-shirt. Pulling my hair up into a ponytail, I walked back over to him and took his hands in mine. His eyes never left me. I eased him up off the bed and wrapped my arms around his waist. Leaning my head on his chest I could hear his heartbeat. It was still a little fast. He finally put his arms around me and he started to calm down.

"Have I told you that I love you, today?" I asked.

He sighed and squeezed me. "How did you know I needed that?"

"Just figured," I shrugged.

We stood holding on to each other for a little while longer. Finally, I turned my head and kissed his chest. "I'm starving. Let's get out of here and get a bite to eat."

"Bre, it is eleven thirty at night."

Leaning back to try to look him in the eyes, "So, is that supposed to mean that I can't be hungry?"

He leaned over laughing and kissed me hard making my knees weak. "Okay, okay, let's go get you something to eat."

Caston took the black convertible Jag this time. I was in heaven, watching the stars pass above me as we drove.

"So, what do you want to eat?"

Never taking my eyes off the stars, I responded, "Surprise me."

Caston stepped on the gas to go faster and I let off a little shriek along with a laugh. My smile was splitting my face in two. I was so happy and carefree, since I told him my secret. It felt as if a ten ton weight was off my chest. What made things even better was when I looked over at Caston his smile was also carefree.

Driving along for about a half an hour, we pulled into a small 24-hour café and I looked at him puzzled.

"Trust me," he said, "Stay here, I'll be right back."

Quickly, Caston returned, putting a few bags in the backseat. He pulled back out onto the road and we drove for a few more minutes. It was quiet, we didn't speak. It wasn't an awkward silence though, it was calming.

I was surprised when we finally turned on to a road that was hidden among some trees. The road was unpaved and bumpy. When the road ended, I looked over at him and I raised my eyebrows.

"Come on," he said, as he got out of the car. He walked to the trunk and grabbed a blanket and then returned to grab the bags from the back seat. He came around to my door opened in waiting for me to get out. Deciding he was serious I got out slowly. He was yards ahead of me already. So, I shut my door and quickened my step to catch up to him.

A few feet into the woods we came upon an opening among the trees. There was no wind and the moon and stars lit up the area in the most romantic lighting.

Even though, it was a balmy night, I got a slight chill. I wrapped my arms around myself as I took in the beautiful surroundings. I removed my flip flops, holding them in my hand. I wanted to feel the grass between my toes. The fireflies in the trees made it look like twinkling lights, the crickets were nature's symphony, and the owl in the distance hooting every so often put me into a trance.

Caston snuck up behind me and wrapped his arms around my waist. "What are you thinking about?"

I snuggle into him. Finally, looking up at him, his eyes melt my insides. I turn around in his arms and slide my arms around his neck still holding onto my flip flops. Leaning up on my toes I kiss his soft lips. "You're my world. I'm so thankful you came into my life."

My lips find his again, and we're lost in each other. When we finally separate, I notice the candles and the blanket in the middle of the opening. The food is sitting on the blanket with an open bottle of wine. My mouth dropped open in shock. "You got all of this at the little café?"

"What can I say, I can be very persuasive," he winked and took my hand to walk me over to the blanket.

Helping me sit down he sat across from me. He unbuttoned his shirt just enough to make my heart race. I could not take my eyes off his forearms when he poured the wine for us.

"This smells delicious, Caston."

"Soup and sandwiches. Nothing fancy, but a good late night dinner."

I smiled and dug into the food. We talked and laughed, enjoying the amazing starry night. When we finish the meal, he refilled my wine glass and cleared the food containers.

"I'll be right back."

"Okay." I smile and lean back on to the blanket.

I heard Caston return, but I was mesmerized by the night sky. I was pulled out of my trance when I heard a click, click, click. I panicked that the paparazzi had found us until I turned over on my stomach, but it was Caston standing a few feet behind me with a camera in front of him.

I smiled up at him. "You scared me."

A few more clicks of me on my stomach with my feet in the air. He dropped the camera to his waist. "I'm sorry, you're too beautiful and this lighting is amazing."

He knelt down in front of me, taking the wine glass from my hands. Licking his lips he leans in for another kiss. A pool of liquid drips into my panties. Leaning further, he kisses that spot on my neck that makes me shiver. I let out made a soft moan. "Strip for me," he whispers in my ear.

My breath hitches. I sit back on my heels, looking at him. My nipples are pebbled and poking through my thin shirt. I take my hand and remove my ponytail. He picks up his camera and starts snapping away, as I shake my hair out. It falls over my shoulders. I look up at him with hooded eyes and bite my lip. More clicking, but I heard a moan come from behind that camera. I smiled ever so slightly, knowing I was turning him on.

I cross my arms in front of me, grabbing the hem of my shirt, and start to pull it up slowly. Teasing him, I pulled it up and bunched it in my hands between my breasts, showing my stomach. I placed a flat hand on my abs and moved it south. After a few more shots, I removed my shirt. The air on my nipples made them hard as rocks. I pinched and rolled them between my fingers.

I rose up on my knees, spreading my legs slightly. I unbuttoned my jean shorts, pulling them apart slightly, so he could see my light purple G-string. Hooking my thumbs in the loops of my shorts, I leaned forward, pushing my breasts out toward Caston. He kept snapping away.

I could see the bulge in his pants, with the anticipation of taking him in my mouth, I licked my lips. Standing up, I pushed my shorts down and kicked them toward him. Hitting him exactly where I wanted. He pulled the camera away from his face and started laughing. "You're doing great, Bre. So sexy."

I turned around and ran my hands through my hair and spread my legs. I did feel sexy for once. Caston made me feel wonderfully full of love. I pulled on one of the sides of my thong and untied it. Holding on to the other side, I faced Caston once again. I was almost fully exposed. Taking the other side in my fingers I slowly let it untie. Letting it fall to the ground, I stood there naked. For him. I was so turned on. I was a slick mess between my legs.

The energy going through my body was electrifying. My heart was beating a million miles a minute from nerves, but everything was so erotic. I moved slowly dipping my fingers between my wet folds to feel my wetness. Bringing my fingers up to my mouth, I sucked it clean. My eyes shut and I felt like I was floating.

Laying down on the red plaid blanket, I rolled onto my back. Caston walked over and took some pictures from above me. I started to run my hands over my breasts and pinched my nipples, making them stand up asking for attention. I moaned, as I continued sliding my hands down my belly.

"Oh my God, Sabrina," Caston groaned, "I think I'm going to blow in my pants." He kept clicking away, though.

My body was trembling, needing relief. "Caston, please, put the camera down."

He let the camera fall to the ground and crawled over to me. His hot hands were suddenly all over me, his tongue licking the salty sweat off my collarbone. My orgasm was on the edge, I needed…

As if he could read my mind he leaned over and devoured my lips. Sliding his hand down ever so lightly, he flicked my swollen clit. I ripped my lips from his, throwing my head back and arching my back off the ground, letting my body ripple through the waves of my release.

Coming back to reality, I rolled over and undid his shorts, making him pop free. I took his cock in my mouth and sucked. Rolling my tongue around his hard shaft I felt him throbbing, wanting to burst. His hands were in my hair pulling my mouth from his cock. Guiding me up by the hair, he once again caught me in a passionate kiss that took my breath away.

Moments later he pushed me down, so I was on all fours, presenting my ass to him. He positioned himself behind me. Teasing me with his tip at my opening. Leaning over my back, he reached around to grab my breasts, kissing between my shoulder blades.

As he pushed into me, I let out a throaty moan. He felt so magnificent. I needed him to fill me and use me hard. Being outside the sounds of our love making echoed among the trees, mingling with nature's sounds. Our moans and slick skin slapping against one another added to the spring night. Falling into a quick pattern, I felt like I needed more. I swiveled my hips into him. My juices were dripping between my legs. He pulled me up by my hair and I reached my arms around him, winding my hands in the hair at the nape of his neck. He bit my neck, which sent me into a spiral. "Caston, I want more. I need more." He picked up his pace and I groaned deeper.

The sound that came out of Caston was like the growl of a wild animal. He pushed me down onto the blanket and lifted my hips to give him the proper depth. Reaching between my legs, he drew up the moist liquid that has been dripping like a faucet from my pussy. Spreading it over my rosebud, he dipped a couple fingers in my tight hole. Just from his fingers, I felt my legs spasm.

He began to move them, stretching my ass, sending sparks of ecstasy through my body, blowing my mind. Every nerve in my body was on high alert. He withdrew slowly and pushed them back in a little faster, taking my breath away. I knew I was going to come soon. I felt my liquid pooling, ready to burst. "I love you, so much, Cass. I'm going to explode."

Without much warning, he withdrew his fingers and fell over my back, driving his cock in to me harder than before. I felt the hot liquid of his release being emptied into my pussy. His cock rippling in me, making me come harder than I ever had before. That was something new, and I was already aching for it again.

He circled his arms around my waist and rolled to the side, pulling me into him. Not breaking our contact we laid on the ground a jumble of legs and arms. Connected in the most intimate way. My head felt fuzzy with sexual endorphins. We drifted off to sleep in each other's arms.

Waking up I wasn't sure what time it was. It was still dark and the candles were still lit, so I knew we couldn't have been asleep for long. Caston was still wrapped around me.

"Cass," I said lightly, shaking his arm, "we should get up and get dressed in case someone finds us."

"Mmm," he mumbled into my back. The vibration tickled.

He loosened his grip, and I searched around for my clothing. "What time is it, anyway?"

"Dunno," he turned onto his stomach, mumbling into the blanket.

"Worn out?" I said laughing.

He nodded his head. Collecting his clothing I smacked his fine round ass nice and hard, sending echoes through the early morning quietness.

Back in the car, the dawn was breaking in the east. The sky was an orangey, pink color. It was going to be another beautiful day. Caston slid on his sunglasses. I felt so calm. Everything was falling into place, my life, my love, and school finishing up. I couldn't be happier. Looking over at him, I reached over and grabbed his hand. I brought it up to my lips and brushed a light kiss on the back of his hand. He gave my hand a squeeze. Looking over at me, a smile crept onto his face.

"I'm so happy," I said with the goofiest smile on my face.

"Bre, you have no idea how happy I am."

Giving my hand another squeeze, he turned back to watch the road. I could tell something was still on his mind, but I knew he would tell me when the time was right.

Chapter Thirty-One

Sabrina

Rolling over in bed I felt Caston's warm body next to mine. I cracked open my eyes to the sun was pouring into the room. "Don't you have to go to work?" I said, as I brushed my hand over his chest.

A small groan came from his throat. "Don't you have to go to school?"

"Ugh, don't remind me," I said, rolling onto my back, resting an arm over my head.

He leaned over and plopped a big wet kiss onto my mouth before heading to the bathroom.

My cell phone started to ring. It brought me back to reality. I haven't heard it ring in so long I almost didn't realize it was my phone. I popped out of bed to find it.

It was a number I did not recognize.

"Hello?" I asked tentatively.

"Sabrina, its Sara. How are you?"

"Sara, I'm okay now. Thank you for checking."

"I was worried about you."

I paused, not knowing how to respond exactly. My stomach clenched when I remembered our sexually charged interactions at the club a few days ago.

"Anyways, I'm also calling because Caston's birthday is in a few days. Jon and I wanted to do something special for him, and we would like you to be a part of it."

"His birthday? I didn't realize."

I walked out on patio, so Caston wouldn't hear me if he came out of the bathroom.

"I figured he wouldn't tell you. He's such a party pooper. We have a party planned in Las Vegas next weekend. We were all going, anyways. He wants to check out the new club. Jon and I went behind his back, though, to plan a whole bash. It'll be great. I'll email you the details, if you can keep it a secret."

"What can I do to help?" Feeling out of the loop. I sat down on the patio furniture and bit my thumbnail.

"Nothing, hun, just wanted to make sure you were in the know. Didn't want two people to be surprised next weekend."

"He hasn't even mentioned Vegas to me. I'm not even sure I'm invited."

Sara let out the loudest laugh. "Oh, honey, I'm surprised Caston isn't following you to class. He would never go away for the weekend without you."

I smiled, thinking about that.

Hearing her giggle lightly, I listened a little more closely. I could hear Jon in the background whispering something. I wondered what they were doing.

"Anyway, I'll see you in a few days. Jon is trying to get my attention, so I have to go. If you have any questions give me a call."

I hung up the phone and peered out over the grounds. What do I get the guy who has every material thing he could want?

Hearing soft footsteps padding towards me, I looked over my shoulder. Caston was wrapped in a towel, his hair wet and messed up. He looked delicious.

"What's wrong?" He looked concerned.

"Why didn't you tell me you were going out of town this weekend?"

He paused in his tracks, looking caught. "I... I was..."

My eyes started to well up. His look said it all. He was not planning on taking me.

I got up and walked past him quickly, so he wouldn't see me cry. Taking off to the bathroom I locked myself in.

A light knock sounded on the door. "Bre, what's the matter?"

"Nothing," I let some tears leak down my cheeks.

"Sabrina, I didn't say anything because I was going to cancel it. I wouldn't go without you, but I didn't want you to feel like you were keeping me from work, or that I didn't want you with me. You have school to worry about, not traipsing across the country to watch me look at property. I need you next to me, so there was no way I would leave you here for two days. Who told you, anyways?"

I unlocked the door and opened it, looking at the floor. "Sara."

He put his hands on his hips. "Of course she did. What does she have planned?" His voice came out in a groan.

"You don't sound happy. Why, it's your birthday?"

"I don't celebrate my birthday."

I slipped my hands around his waist, lacing my hands together on his back. He was still a little damp from his shower. "What do you want for your birthday?"

I felt him tense up again. "As long as I have you, I don't need anything else."

My heart surged wanting to jump out of my chest. "So, you weren't going to tell me you canceled a trip?"

He took my shoulders, pushing me back a little, so I was looking in his eyes. "Bre, honey, I was going to do my best to cancel, but if I couldn't, I would be taking you. I just didn't want to drag you away from your rehearsals, or make you feel like you had to choose. I know your spring workshop is coming up."

"Oh, ya, that..."

He leaned down to lightly kiss my lips. "Yes, that." He pulled me into a hug. I reached down and squeezed his ass.

"Oh, no, no you don't. I have to go to work. If you start, I won't stop, and you have to go to school."

I moaned and tried again. He lightly pushed me away and spun me around to usher me to get ready. "Yes, Dad." I said mockingly, as I started to walk away, but he grabbed my arm and pulled me back into his embrace, planting a kiss on me that made me weak in the knees. Finally, breaking the kiss, he pushed me forward a bit and smacked my ass as I walked away from him.

"Don't test me, Sabrina."

I looked over my shoulder, as I dropped my robe and entered the shower.

His face was torn. I saw him check the time and I knew I had him. He quickly dropped his towel and in a few quick motions was behind me in the shower. Spinning me around, he swiftly lifted me up and pinned me to the wall. In one motion he was in me. The water was hitting my breasts and there was a body jet hitting my ass just perfectly. The whole sensation set me off quicker than ever before.

Caston followed behind me. Stilling once he was finished, he rested his head on my neck. "You'll be the death of me and my business."

I laughed at him. "What a way to go, though, huh?"

I felt him smile into my neck, and he laughed.

I didn't have a car, usually relying on public transportation to take me to school, so he preferred to have Terrance drive me. He was drinking his coffee when I walked downstairs to grab my bags and head off to class.

"You know I wouldn't have to have Terrance drive me around if you let me take the bus, like I used to," I said, as I grabbed a bagel.

"True, but then I can't make sure you are safe."

Shaking my head, I walked over and kissed his cheek. "Bye, Cass. Don't work too hard."

Sliding into the backseat of the Jeep, I opened my bag and smiled, as I touched Caston's SD card from his camera. Terrance slid into the driver seat. I knew he was my only chance to get Caston an unforgettable birthday gift.

"Terrance," I sing-songed his name, "will you help me?"

Shaking his head, he responded, "Why do I think I'm going to regret this?"

"Well, it's Caston's birthday this weekend. I want to give him something special. So...I need access to photo editing machines. Can you get someone at Black Hollywood's editing department today to help me do something?"

He caught my eye in the rearview mirror. Shaking his head, he pulled out his cell phone, "Rick, I'm bringing someone to BH... She needs to edit some pictures... I know... Mr. Black does not need to be notified... Rick...come on man... Fine... Thank you." He hung up.

"Well?'

"You're in."

"Eeek! Thank you, Terrance." I leaned forward and hugged him around the seat.

"You owe me one. I have to go on a date with his sister."

I pulled my lips in and covered my mouth, so he wouldn't see me giggle.

Black Hollywood's editing room was amazing. Rick showed me around. He was uneasy with leaving me in there by myself, but Terrance assured him I wasn't going to hack into, or steal, anything. I also assured him I've been taking photography and editing classes throughout my college career. He smiled, slightly, and nodded. I quickly got to work on the pictures Caston took of me only a few days ago.

It didn't take me long. Caston is a magnificent photographer. A tweak here and there. I sent the pictures to Black Hollywood's printing department. Walking out into the hall, I saw Rick sitting in the lunch room.

"Thank you, Rick. I really appreciate your help. I sent my project down to the photo lab, so they'll be ready..."

"In about an hour, or so. Maybe less," Rick said, moving to stand.

I did a small jump for joy. "Great. I think I'll hang out here and eat some lunch, while I wait. If that's okay with you?"

"Suit yourself." He turned to walk down the hall, now that the editing room was once again his.

I pulled my iPod out of my bag and put the earphones in. My attention was completely tuned into the music and my book. I didn't even hear anyone walk in...until it was too late.

I was knocked over the head with something hard. Face planting on to the table, I whipped out my ear buds and spun around. Beverly. Her eyes were black as coal. Fury burning behind them.

"Beverly. How?" I squeaked out.

"What the fuck are you doing here?" She spoke low, controlled, but wicked.

"I... I was just..." I was barely able to make a sound out of fear.

She shoved me off the chair and I scrambled into the corner of the room on my hands and knees.

"Spit it out, you stupid bitch."

Turning around, I hugged my knees to my chest and made myself as small as possible. I just shook my head. I wasn't going to answer her.

Her arm came out and pulled me up by my neck. I could barely breathe.

"I told you three times now, LEAVE CASTON, OR YOU WILL REGRET IT."

There was a commotion outside of the room. Terrance burst through the door and tackled Beverly to the ground. Her hand suddenly leaving my neck made me fall to the ground, hitting my head on the counter on the way down. I was coughing and hysterically sobbing. My head was killing me. It felt warm. Reaching up, I touched my head and my hand felt something warm and gooey. Pulling my hand back, it was covered in blood. Seeing that much blood made me feel very lightheaded, then everything went black.

I opened my eyes and Terrance was sitting next to me on the couch in the lunch room with an ice pack on my head.

"There you are?" His warm smile made me feel okay.

I moved to try to get up, but my head throbbed horribly and I collapsed back on the couch. "Oh my God, my head hurts."

"You're one tough girl. I think you'll be okay, though."

I bit my lip. "Does Caston have to know about this?"

"Unfortunately, he's already on his way here. I'm sorry, Sabrina. I'm already in trouble. Don't want to lose my job."

"It's okay, Terrance," I said with a smile.

That is when Caston walked into the room looking frantic. "Sabrina!"

I cringed. "Hey, Cass… Surprise?"

He rushed to my side, where Terrance had been not five seconds ago. "What the hell, Sabrina? What are you doing here?"

I thrust myself into his embrace. "Before I tell you, tell me Terrance isn't going to lose his job? It wasn't his fault. I made him bring me here."

He took a deep cleansing breath. "Fine."

"I wanted to give you something special for your birthday. It was supposed to be a surprise. I took the memory card from your camera and edited the pictures you took of me the other day. They really were beautiful. I guess the surprise was on me, though. I thought I was safe."

He lightly kissed the cut on my head. "Oh, Sabrina, what would I do without you keeping me on my toes? Beverly should still be in jail, but someone posted bail. Fucking idiots. I'll fire whoever let her in here. There is a restraining order against her for you, and me, including all of my businesses."

Moving to sit next to him on the couch, I hung my head, not looking at him. "I still don't understand why she acts like this. You haven't told me everything, have you?"

"No." He got up hastily and walked to the other side of the room.

I looked up at him. His hands on his hips, facing away from me, I could tell he was having an internal struggle with himself. I knew he needed me, needed my strength. I walked over to him and snaked my hands around his waist, resting my head on his broad back. Instantly I felt him relax. "Whatever it is, Caston, I won't leave you. I love you."

Pulling my hands away from him, he spun me around to face him. He looked me over to see if I was okay. Thankfully, I didn't think I had a concussion. I was between him and the counter. His beautiful eyes searched mine for answers. Not looking away, I wanted him to see that it was the truth. I wasn't going anywhere.

"Oh, Sabrina," he brought his lips down to mine. I opened to him as soon as he brushed his tongue on my lips. The lightness made me shiver, sending a warm fuzzy feeling between my legs. He deepened his kiss, sliding his hands over my cheeks, entwining his fingers in my hair. Finally, pulling back he whispered against my lips, "I promise, I'll tell you on the way to Vegas."

"Vegas? So no cancelling then?"

He lightly kissed me again. "No, unfortunately I can't. You'll be coming with me."

I pulled his head down to my lips, kissing him hard. "I can't wait!"

My head felt tingly. I wasn't sure if it was because of head injury, or because of the kiss.

Someone cleared their throat in the background. Caston swung his head around. It was Rick. He was holding the portfolio I sent down to be printed. Stepping around Caston, I walked over and grabbed the package from him.

"Good job on these," he whispered.

Turning back around, I handed Caston the book. "Well, since my birthday gift is ruined, I might as well give these to you now. I'll just have to come up with something else for your actual birthday."

I handed the package to him. My stomach was in knots. I wished I could have at least looked them over first.

Slowly taking the gift from me, Caston sat on the couch again and opened it up. I couldn't watch. My heart was beating so hard, I thought it was going to come out of my damn chest. Hearing an audible gasp, I turned around.

His eyes met mine. There was a heat in them that was indescribable. "Sabrina, my God, did you edit these yourself?"

I nodded, feeling timid.

"They are magnificent. Come sit." He patted the seat next to him.

He started the book over again. A huge smile crossed my face. They really were beautiful. "I had a good photographer."

"No, the photographer had a good subject."

I laughed and shook my head no.

"Seriously, Sabrina, you have a job here anytime if you can do this with pictures. I'd like to see you edit some other pictures that we have had problems with to see what you can do with them."

I shrugged. Never thought my photography classes would come in handy. "Sure."

He turned to look back over the pictures. Closing the book he turned to look at me, "Sabrina, these pictures are the best gift anyone has ever given me."

I laughed so loud and hard it made my head hurt. When I noticed he was serious I stopped. "You can't be serious."

"I'm serious. No one is more special to me than you. These pictures are so personal, and for you to take it upon yourself to edit and print them for me... I love you, Sabrina."

My heart fluttered, he was serious.

Chapter Thirty-Two

Caston

Even though her head injury was pretty bad, the doctor said Sabrina didn't have a concussion. Over the next few days we spent our time together, laying by the pool, talking about my work with the community and her childhood and her parents. My heart swelled when she would talk about them and the love they had for her, and she for them. Our nights were quiet, spent cuddled up on the couch in front of the fire. Sabrina would read, or watch television, and I would do what I do best, work. Just cuddling up to her made me feel whole. It was perfect.

Sabrina was able to return to school relatively quickly, but it was affecting her balance. She held it together, though. I was so proud of her. Professor Lee wasn't happy with the extra security, but I assured her I would make it worth her inconvenience. My angel had to be kept safe.

Quicker than I wanted it to be, we were leaving for Vegas. I'd promised her I would finish my story about Beverly during our trip. Fucking bitch, I hope she rots in hell.

Terrance was bringing Sabrina home from school soon. Our bags were already packed, ready to go, but I knew she would want to freshen up before we headed out.

I was sitting in the great room with my laptop. The machine was on, but I wasn't able to concentrate on it. The velvet box in my pocket was burning a hole in my leg.

The door slammed shut. I closed down the laptop and met her by the stairway. I swept her up into my arms, planting the biggest kiss on her velvet lips.

It's been too long since I've felt her and our kiss turned hotter. I slid her bag down her arm, as I was lifting her shirt from the other side. Our lips only parted long enough for me to slide the shirt over her head. Grabbing her backside, I lifted her up, so she could put her legs around me.

She wasn't wearing a bra, her nipples were hard as pebbles. They lightly grazed my chest as she pulled my shirt off. I bent over sucking the swells of her breasts. She tasted salty sweet from sweat. I moved my kisses up to her neck. Her breath quickened when I kissed her in the dip where her neck and collarbone met.

I needed inside her. Walking her over to the couch, I set her down, then kneeled in front of her. I kissed down her chest, over to her nipples, taking one then the other in my mouth and nibbling them in to harder peaks. When I reached the skin right above her shorts, I licked my way along the band. Her stomach sucked in, because she's ticklish there. The little chuckle that came from her lips made my dick twitch. She expected me to immediately remove her shorts, but I surprised her. I moved my way down and kissed her thighs along the opening of the shorts. She groaned wanting my touch. Her hips were grinding, trying to get any sort of relief between her legs. I could smell her arousal and I licked my lips. Looking up, I saw her playing with her breasts.

I could sit and watch her forever. Her small perky breasts, the smooth abs defining her stomach. Hidden in her shorts was the most beautiful pussy I've ever seen. Perfect. Light pink, bare. I couldn't wait any longer. I needed to taste her. I ripped her shorts off, taking her light blue thong with them. Her pussy was already covered in her moisture. I pushed her legs up and used my hands to spread her open to me. The glistening juice called to me. I sunk my tongue into her pussy. She let out a deep moan. I felt her muscles contract around me right before a flood of fluid coated my mouth.

Quickly undoing my shorts I let them fall to my knees. "This is going to be quick, Sabrina. We don't have much time."

I plunged into her. Her fingernails raked up my back, pulling a cavernous groan out of me. Her warm pussy inviting me in with each thrust. Her eyes were closed, but I could see them fluttering behind her eyelids.

"Open your eyes, Bre, I want to see you when I come inside you."

Her eyes opened. They were on fire. My heart clenched. "Oh, Caston," she screamed as she came hard. I sealed my lips upon her and danced my tongue with hers, as I spilled into her.

I heard footsteps coming through the kitchen, and I felt my stomach clench. Why do people always seem to walk in on us? Thankfully, Sabrina, hasn't heard them yet.

I righted myself, seeing Jon in the kitchen. Pulling up my pants, as I stood, I gave him the 'get the fuck out' look. Seeing that I was half-naked and putting my clothes on Jon stopped in his tracks, he held up his hand to me, and I nodded slowly indicating we would be out in five.

I looked back down to Sabrina, still seated on the couch.

"Sabrina, honey, we have to go."

I reached my hand out to her and she placed her hand in mine. Surprising her, I pulled her up and swung her over my shoulder. She let out a laugh, and I smacked her ass on the way to our bedroom.

I sat on the bed, waiting for her to finish getting ready. I didn't care that we were running behind. The plane was mine, so they had to wait for me. Sara and Jon kept texting me, though. They weren't happy we are taking forever.

"Oh, Caston, I'm afraid I'm forgetting something." She looked so cute, looking through her bags frantically.

"Sabrina, we aren't going out of the country. We can just go buy it, if you forgot something."

She stopped and looked up at me like she had never considered that scenario. "You're right. Why am I freaking out?"

I got up and walked over to her. I slid my arms around her waist, pulling her to me. Brushing her hair behind her ear, I noticed she didn't put any earrings on, as usual.

"You know," I said, leaning down to kiss her earlobe, "I think there is something missing."

She backed out of my embrace, looking around at the bags. "Really, what?"

I pulled the box out of my pocket and opened it. "These."

She turned around and gasped. "Oh my God! Caston! These are gorgeous."

Her hands lightly brushed the aqua blue box. Any girl would recognize it. Tiffany & Co®. She was a girl with simple taste, so I got her simple cushion cut diamond solitaire earrings. "Do you like them?" My voice trembled. What the hell?

"Like them," she looked up at me, "I love them! Oh my God. I can't accept these, Caston."

I had to laugh at her response. I removed them from the box and put them in her ears.

She pushed her hair back, so she could see them. They sparkled like her eyes. I looked over her shoulder at our reflections in the mirror.

"Not as beautiful as you, but they'll do."

She turned and planted a kiss on my lips. I started to deepen it, but there was pounding on the door and Jon barged in.

"What the fuck dude! Not again. I mean, if you guys are fucking at least let Sara and me join."

Sabrina hid her face in my chest.

"We're coming."

"Hi, Sabrina," Jon said, laughing.

Not showing her face, she picked up her hand and waved mumbling, "Hey, Jon."

"Hey, fucker, grab some bags. It'll get us down there faster."

When Jon left, I grabbed her hands and kissed them. "Ready?"

"Yes," she said, taking a deep breath, "Do you remember what you promised me?"

I nodded. "When we get on the plane, and are able to get alone time, my story is yours to hear."

A tentative smile inched across her face. "You know, I never... Never mind."

We walked down the stairs. "What? You can tell me anything."

She blushed. "I've never joined the mile high club."

"Well, my dear, we'll have to rectify that won't we?" My cock stirred, thinking about it.

Jon, Sara, Sabrina, and I all sat in the seats on my private jet. Sabrina grabbed my hand and squeezed it. Looking over to her she looked a little green. "Are you okay?" I asked concerned.

"Yup," she swallowed roughly, "I'll be fine as soon as we are leveled off. I hate takeoff and landing."

I leaned over and kissed her cheek.

I couldn't help staring at her. She had her head leaned back on the seat. Her eyes were closed and she was taking deep breaths. It was so cute how nervous she was. Finally, the announcement came that we were at flying altitude and we could move about the cabin. I unbuckled and crouched over her, kissing her eyelids. "Can I get you anything?"

She opened her eyes, holding me with her hazel gems. She shook her head no.

Jon got up and pulled Sara up against him. Her eyes were hooded and he leaned, kissing her deep. "I'm going to claim the bed, unless you want it first. It's going to be a long flight..."

"Or you could join us?" Sara said, looking right at Sabrina.

I had to cover my mouth at Sabrina's expression. "Maybe later, I need to talk to Sabrina," I said, seeing her relax in front of me.

"Suit yourself," Jon said, ushering Sara off to the back with a smack on her ass.

Turning back to Sabrina I said, "You'd never know those two have kids the way they act. I hope I can act like that when we have kids."

Sabrina's eyes went wide in shock before I realized what came out of my mouth. Shit, I just fucked up. *Too soon, Caston.*

Changing the subject quickly, I asked her if she was hungry, as I walked to get myself a snack.

I sat on the large couch on the other side of the plane. She was still buckled in the bucket seat. "Sabrina, you can unbuckle and come sit here. It's way more comfortable than that seat."

She nodded tentatively, unbuckling and standing up. She started walking just as we hit a pocket of turbulence. She froze, and I noticed her lips start to tremble. I rushed to her side. "Honey, it's okay. Just a little bump." I brought her over to the couch and held her on my lap.

Needing to take her mind off the fact that we were miles up in the air I began my story again.

"So where did I leave off with Beverly?"

I felt her relax in my lap. She closed her eyes and leaned over to rest her head in my lap. "You just told me your mom had died."

"Oh, yes. Okay, so, you know my parents have an open marriage, and Beverly is technically my aunt."

"Yes, that confused me." She sat up with her eyes glaring into mine.

"Beverly and my dad were always married. So when Beverly found out Rose was pregnant with her husband's child she freaked out. Beverly never told my dad about me. She shunned my mom, cut her off from everything, kept her from contacting my dad. How she got my mom's trust fund revoked I'll never know. I'm sure it was something to do with sex," I gritted my teeth. "Hence, how I grew up, poor. When my mom couldn't take care of me anymore, she somehow got a call to my dad, shocking the hell out of him with the news, begging him to take me. Beverly never wanted me. She would have preferred me put up for adoption. I'm thankful my dad stood up to Beverly and said no. Dad wanted to leave Beverly when he found out everything she did, but Beverly threatened him with blackmail if he left her. She has a way to brainwash people into thinking she's innocent all the time, which isn't the case. It sickens me, and being with you makes me realize that I was under her thumb for too long. She will not win this time."

"I still don't understand why your dad didn't leave Beverly. What was so bad that he couldn't recover from it?"

I take a deep breath and begin the story of my creation, "I asked him that once. We were in a huge fight. Something broke loose and I couldn't hold back anymore. I'd been holding a grudge for so long that I snapped asked him, 'What the hell could be so bad that he would abandon my mom?' He broke down sobbing. He told me how much he loved my mom, and that Rose was his soul mate, but he loved his son, too. He had an affair with her before the open marriage he and Beverly are in now. He was going to leave Beverly, but when Beverly found out she planted drugs, made it look like he used prostitutes, some under age, and God only knows what else to blackmail him. She would have made sure his life was in ruins, and he would have lost Jon.

"He said when he walked in that night Rose was sitting there with Beverly. Rose's face was streaked with tears. She held photos and papers of all the blackmail items that Beverly had fabricated against my Dad. The TV was on and my dad said he was flabbergasted to see a video of Beverly and him having sex the night before. Beverly convinced Rose that my dad was just using her. My dad said he turned to Rose to explain, but she was just sobbing and shaking her head. She got up and bolted out of the house. After that night he never heard from Rose again, and then she disappeared. He had no idea I existed. He told me he was devastated and didn't understand why she wouldn't even give her a chance to explain. That is why he was so cold to her when he picked me up that day. Dad decided that if Rose had really loved him, she would have known he hadn't done those things and if she had really wanted him she would have found a way to get back to him. He did hate her for keeping me from him. It wasn't until later that he was able to think about the situation and see what Rose had been facing. He regrets how he treated her. What he did was stupid, and I hated him for that for so long, but we've worked past it, and I do forgive him to a point now."

"So is this why you changed your name to Black?"

"Yes, pretty much, but also because it is Rose's last name. So, it really irks Beverly. In spite of everything my mom still loved my dad. She gave me his last name to give me a part of him. Later on she figured out what Beverly had done. At that point she was desperate she chanced getting in touch with my dad. The only way Beverly agreed to let my dad keep me was my mom could have no contact with me. When I decided to change my name I chose Black as my last name, not only to reflect my birth mother, but because there is a black hole in my soul, a dark void, that I can't fill because of Beverly." He paused, taking a deep breath, as if to gather his courage, before he continued, "There is more, though, can you handle more?"

She looked shell shocked. "Are you with me, Bre?"

Blinking, she brought herself back to me. She laid back down in my lap. I kept on with my story, as I stroked her hair.

"When Beverly found out I was attending her sex parties, she approached me. She asked me how long I had been spying on things. When I told her she flipped out on me. My dad usually wasn't home during the week because of his job, so I had to deal with her alone. That's about the time she noticed I was becoming a man and wanted to take advantage of it. Her slimy friends would come over and they would seduce me." I felt her gasp, but I kept going. I needed her to know.

"By this time I was sixteen-seventeen Jon was away at college. I thought the older women made me look cool. At parties I had women

227

all over me; men wanted me too, couples asking for me to join them. Well, any horny teen would jump at that. Beverly had me scheduled out. She always seemed to either be in the room, or part of the orgy that I was taking part in. I never thought anything of it…until one day I caught her after the fact counting out the money. I was disgusted with her for what she did to me. I confronted her. She told me she had videos of all of my encounters and records of how much money I was making. She blackmailed me into continuing, by threatening to destroy my life. I knew that would devastate my dad and Jon. I'm not proud of what I did, and I would take everything back if I could, but she left me alone any other time, which was fine with me, because I hated her for what she did to my mother. Once I was old enough to realize Beverly wouldn't do anything that would upset her own way of life, I stopped. I told her never again."

"Oh, Caston, I'm sorry," she whispered.

"Don't be sorry for me. I made it through." Brushing my thumb along her cheek I continued, "So it got worse when I was in college. I was going to school for business, and I met Sara," I felt her tense. "We hit it off. I brought her to a few of the parties, because Sara was very sexually open. The first time Beverly saw her, she left us alone. As things grew serious between us Beverly started to break in on our time. She would show up at my dorm, she would monopolize my time, she told me Sara couldn't come to the parties anymore. When she did that I told her if Sara couldn't come I wouldn't either. That is when she went crazy. Threatening Sara's life, saying she was going to expose me to my dad, and she pushed herself on me."

Sabrina sat up and held her stomach. I was repulsive. I knew it. Damn me, for having her trapped in this plane when I told her.

"Beverly caught me off guard one afternoon and started kissing me. My fucking body took over. I'd been pimped out so much, so to speak, that it was second nature for me. I never wanted to go there with her. Well, Sara walked in on us right before I went all the way with Beverly. Beverly's face was the devil. I scrambled to get off of her as Sara stood there in shock at what she was seeing. Beverly yelled out as if she was orgasming, and Sara ran out of my room. Before I could go after her, Beverly told me if I wanted her to live I'd let her go. Well, I cared very much for her. I sat on the floor of my room torn to pieces. I threw myself into school after that, eventually dropping out and starting a small company. Beverly stayed her distance from me when I would go to see my dad and Jon. However, every time a girl came into the picture she would flip her lid again. I decided it was better for all of us if I stayed single. I became my work. I became *the* Caston Black of Black Hollywood. She would let me be with other women, I just couldn't get serious."

I could see the tears in Sabrina's eyes. I needed her to know Beverly couldn't get to me, anymore. Facing her, I held her face in my hands. "No more, Sabrina, she can't get me to back away, anymore. I love you, Sabrina. You're my everything. You are the filler that I've been searching for. Beverly won't take you from me. Do you understand me?"

A tear fell down her cheek and I kissed it away. I touched the diamond earrings in her ears. She leaned into my hand. Her eyes softened. "I'm sorry, Caston."

"Don't be sorry for me. Yes, I didn't have the best life growing up, but it made me stronger, who I am today. I also met you, because the circumstances led me to you." I pressed my lips to hers. They were warm and soft, accepting of me. She parted her lips slightly. I took the invitation and dipped my tongue into her mouth. Slowly kissing her.

She slowly backed away, catching her breath. "What about Sara?" she asked, as she nodded her head toward the back of the plane.

"She's tough," I smiled. "After I explained what was really happening when she walked in, she wouldn't take Beverly's shit. She kept coming to the parties. We were together every so often, but once I introduced her to Jon, that part of our relationship ended. They hit it off. One thing led to another and they got married. Sara and Jon aren't just my family, they're my best friends and biggest supporters. Seven years later they have two kids. I still can't believe I'm an uncle."

"How did Jon never know what was going on?" She asking, looking very perplexed.

"He wasn't home. He was in college and then went right for his master's degree. The weekend he was home happened to be the one when Beverly tried to force herself on me and Sara left. I was so distraught, he had to physically peel me off of the floor. I didn't want to live for a while. I figured my life might as well be over. He transferred to my college and gave me the support I needed. He tried to confront Beverly about it, too, but she pulled some sort of blackmail on him as, well. To this day he still won't tell me."

I shifted slightly. My soul was now completely exposed.

"Caston," she straddled my lap, "thank you for telling me. I know that was hard for you." She kissed me, stroking the fires of my libido.

She lowered herself to the floor in front of me. Her fingers traced the hard bulge in my pants. It felt amazing.

Looking up at me, she unbuttoned my jeans and pulled them apart. She kissed the exposed skin in the opening. I lifted up, and helped her pull my pants down. My cock sprung free in front of her and she licked her lips, making a small purring sound. I felt myself tighten my thighs when she did that, and a small bead of liquid formed on my tip. Her hungry eyes saw it. She leaned over and devoured my whole length in one motion. My breath caught. I could feel the back of her throat, and she still wasn't gagging. I place my hand on the back of her head, caressing my fingers through her brunette hair. Resting my head on the back of the couch, I relished in the feeling of her warm mouth.

She cupped my shaft, moving her head lower. Sucking my balls into her mouth, she did something magical with her tongue. A growl came out of my mouth. My God, she was amazing. Her mouth moved lower, licking me under my balls. I shivered. I couldn't even describe what that felt like.

Working her mouth over my shaft her tongue and hands made me lose control. "Bre, I'm going to come. Oh God." She sucked me in to the back of her throat, and I spilled myself. She kept swallowing until nothing was left.

Looking up at me, she licked her lips. I reached down and drug her up my body. I took her mouth in mine and kissed her hastily, tasting myself on her tongue. My cock stirred again, as she straddled my hips. I wanted in her so bad.

"Bre, if we do this here, Jon and Sara might walk in on us." I said between kisses, while removing her clothes.

"Shut up, Caston," she responded.

Groaning, I knew that was her way of saying she could care less.

Just as I expected I wasn't even done removing her shirt when they walked out of the room in the back. Jon's face lit up, he reached down to adjust himself. Sara was the first over to us. She stepped up, helping me remove Sabrina's bra. Leaning over she pushed Sabrina's hair away from her shoulder and brushed a light kiss on it. She cupped Sabrina's breasts, manipulating her nipples. My cock twitched when Bre's head fell back and a soft whimper escaped her lips.

Jon was behind Sara, removing her shirt. He captured her lips in his.

Sabrina brought her attention back to me, looking me in the eyes. She looked as if she was in a trance, but I needed her to know I was here for her. I kissed her neck and licked up to her ear. Whispering to her, "If at any time you want to stop, say the word."

She turned her head and leaned back against Sara, closing her eyes. Sara leaned over and kissed Sabrina. Their tongues danced over one another. Sara snaked her hands around Sabrina, letting them dip to her clit, as Sabrina reached up and grabbed Sara's hair, pulling her in to deepen their kiss.

I thought my cock was going to explode right there. It was one of the sexiest things I'd ever seen. Jon groaned, I looked up at him, and he mouthed, *Fuck yes*. I smiled and my head fell back, taking in the feeling of Sabrina grinding on my cock, while she made out with Sara.

I moved to stand up, turning Sabrina around to face Sara. I quickly discarded my shirt. Somehow, Jon had already discarded his clothes as well. Sara and Sabrina kept kissing, exploring each other's bodies. I reached around Bre, pulling her back against my body, letting my hand trail down to her warm lips. Pushing my hand between them, I sunk two fingers into her wet pussy.

Jon mimicked everything I did to Sabrina on Sara. The moans that filled the cabin were orgasmic.

Pulling my fingers out of Sabrina, I held them up for Sara. She took them in her mouth, as Sabrina took Jon's fingers, sucking off Sara's juices. I felt pre-cum leak out of my cock at the site of the girls enjoying each other's taste. I bit down on Sabrina's shoulder, as I wrapped my other arm around her waist.

Jon and I slid into the girls from behind. My cock stretching Sabrina as I entered. Her head fell back on my shoulder. Sara leaned over and took Bre's nipples in her mouth. Sabrina turned her head to me, as I fucked her hard.

Moans and gasps filled the air. Balls slapping on wet pussies. Sara and Sabrina reached down to play with each other's clits. I could feel Sara's fingers so close to my cock, as I plunged into Sabrina's wetness. She let them slide a little further, and I felt her fingers join my cock inside Sabrina.

Not wanting to lose it too soon I pulled out. I guided Sabrina to the couch and laid her down. Sara walked by me never, losing eye contact with Sabrina, grabbed my cock and guided it into Sabrina's luscious mouth. I grabbed Sara's hair and shoved her down between Sabrina's legs. The noise that came out of Sabrina's mouth vibrated over my shaft, as Sara consumed her pussy.

Jon sat back a little, pumping his cock, watching the scene in front of him. Finally, not being able to take anymore, he quickly kneeled on the couch and entered Sara from behind. Her gasp made my balls tighten to me. I reached over and palmed Sabrina's breasts, rolling her hard peaks between my fingers.

I needed to feel her velvet pussy around my cock again. I withdrew and twisted to pull Sabrina from Sara. Turning her the other way Sabrina was now under Sara. Reaching up, she pulled Sara down to her mouth. I flung her legs over my shoulders and pounded into her. Watching her kiss Sara had me on fire. My fingers dug into her hips. I felt her walls squeezing me, as her orgasm took over.

"I'm going to explode," I grunted.

Jon nodded in understanding. We removed our cocks, placing the girls down in front of us. Mouths open, waiting for our warm, sticky come to bath their faces and breasts. We both came at the same time. The girls accepted our seed. Turning to Sabrina, Sara grabbed her, pulling her to her mouth. They kissed openly in front of us. Moving their hands down each other's body they rubbed their clits until they came apart, sinking to the ground out of exhaustion.

Collapsing back onto the couch, Jon and I stared at the girls covered in our release and cuddling after their orgasms. We both nodded and leaned our heads back to catch our breath.

Chapter Thirty-Three

Sabrina

Sara and I headed to the back of the plane hand in hand. We grabbed our clothes as we walked into the room, and she led me directly to the bathroom. We slowly cleaned each other off, occasionally placing kisses on the spaces we just cleaned. When we were finished, I collapsed on the bed, while Sara picked up our towels.

"I've never done anything like that before."

"How do you feel now?" Sara asked.

I sat up on the bed, facing her. "I don't know."

She walked over to me. "Do you regret it?"

"No."

"Would you do it again?"

I blushed and giggled. "Yes."

She bounced onto the bed next to me. "Oh, good."

We laughed and fell back on the bed, staring at the ceiling.

"Sara."

"Ya, honey."

"Caston told me everything about you and him. He also told me how Beverly interfered," I leaned up on my elbow and rolled to face her. "I can't say I'm sorry it didn't work out between you guys, but I hate that things happened that way."

She rolled to face me. "Don't be. He was looking out for me, and if we didn't break up I would never have met Jon. He gave me my precious children. Caston loves you. He won't let Beverly come between you guys. I've never seen him act like this before."

"Thanks, Sara."

I leaned over and placed a kiss on her breast. "Looks like you missed a spot."

Laughing, she took over wiping with the wash cloth she was holding. "Thanks."

I quickly got dressed and went out to the main room again. The boys were dressed and I felt myself blush as Jon caught my eye. I walked past him and placed my arms around Caston's waist. He was facing the bar area, pouring something to drink. Kissing him between his shoulder blades I whispered, "I love you."

He turned around, capturing my mouth with his. "I love you, too. More than you know."

He handed me a bottle of water and grabbed my hand. We walked back to the couch. When we sat, I snuggled into the crook of his arm.

I felt myself doze off. I felt so at peace in his arms.

Waking up to light kisses on my face made a smile inch across my face. "Mmm, Cass."

"Hey, Bre, wake up honey, we've landed," he whispered, so I wouldn't be startled.

My eyes fluttered open and there was his face, inches from mine. I leaned forward kissing him. "I'll never tire of waking up to your kisses."

"I hope not." He pulled me up and into his arms.

We embraced for a few minutes.

Someone came bounding up the stairs, interrupting us.

"Mr. Black, the limo is waiting," the short bouncy red head with triple Ds said to us.

Feeling slightly inadequate, I gave her a displeased look. I could tell she didn't expect to see someone with Caston when she walked in, because her mouth was agape when she noticed me. "Oh, sir, I'm so sorry to interrupt."

I could tell she was a spicy thing, a natural beauty. Her short grey skirt and white sleeveless shirt were flawless. Her hair was down in relaxed curls and she had just a hint of gloss on her lips. Caston smiled when he saw her, which made my blood boil. I really had to get my jealousy under control.

"Rae, no apologies, Sabrina and I were leaving." He led me closer to the door and her. "Rae, I'd like you to meet my Sabrina, Sabrina this is Rae, the head of my club and hotel here in Vegas."

Her shoulders squared off and she raised her hand to me. "Nice to meet you, Sabrina. Welcome to Las Vegas."

I could swear she wrinkled her nose at me, like I was beneath her, but I didn't want to jump to conclusions. "It is a pleasure, Rae."

She looked up at Caston. "I'll just leave you two. See you in the limo."

Turning on her heels, she headed back down the stairs to the tarmac.

"I don't think she likes me Caston."

He turned me to face him. "Sabrina, I love you, and that's all that matters."

Reaching into the seat, I grabbed my purse and let him lead me out into the hot Vegas sun.

The limo ride was fun. Jon, Sara, and I with our backs to the driver, and popped a champagne bottle. We had the music on and let it flow through us. I was a little sad Caston couldn't enjoy himself, like we were, but I knew the sooner he finished his work the sooner he would be back with me.

Getting a little silly, I spilled some champagne down the front of my cleavage. I scrunched my face, "It's pooling in my bra," I giggled.

Sara leaned forward and licked the trail from my cleavage up my chin to my lips. Jon sat back and watched us. He was pulling on his hard cock through his jeans. Desire heated my stomach, as she reached my lips and slowly licked them.

It suddenly went silent. Music was still blaring, but the talking from the other end of the limo seemed to come to a halt.

Rae looked like she was about to throw up, and Caston's face made me squeeze my thighs together. He looked like he wanted to devour me alive. I immediately noticed the bulge in his pants as well. The champagne was going to my head, so I started laughing uncontrollably. Sara joined in, together we were so out of breath we were gasping in a matter of seconds.

"Can you please pull it together, Sara," Rae spit out.

I sucked in my lips and my eyes widened. What? Who is this chick? Snapping my head over to Sara, I saw Jon put his hand on her arm. "Fuck off, Rae. Why did you even come to meet us at the airport anyways?"

"Honey, don't start," Jon whispered.

The triple Ds were moving up and down rapidly, as Rae took deep breaths. I could tell she wanted to say something back.

Wanting to change the subject, I noticed the Vegas Strip was now within sight. "Oh my God, it's magnificent."

Sara turned her attention to me and started pointing things out in the distance. I caught Caston's eye, and he mouthed, *Thank you.* I responded by winking and blowing a kiss to him.

We pulled up in front of a magnificent black glass building. I was relieved to see there were no photographers outside of the building. Sara, Jon, and I barreled out of the limo and stood, while the driver unloaded our suitcases.

The dry heat was slightly overwhelming, but it felt good on my skin. I placed my sunglasses on, so I could keep an eye on the limo without being noticed, since Caston and Rae still haven't emerged.

Sara was talking on her phone and Jon had suddenly disappeared. Feeling alone I just stood there, slightly antsy. I'm sure it was only a few minutes, but it felt like hours. Caston ducked out of the limo and rushed over to my side, swooping me up in a huge hug. He grabbed my hand and started walking into the building.

I'm not sure why, but I glanced over my shoulder to see Rae crawling out straightening her skirt and buttoning a few of her buttons on her shirt. She also wiped at her mouth, while she glanced nervously from side to side, before taking off to a side door entrance.

I saw red and the hand that was holding Caston's suddenly felt heavy and gross.

"Morning, Mr. Black. Good to see you, Mr. Black." Everyone we passed greeted Caston. I played the happy girlfriend and did the nod with a smile to each and every one.

Reaching the elevator Caston pressed his thumb to the reader above the button. The doors sprung open and we stepped inside. As soon as they shut, I yanked my hand out of his and crossed them over my chest. Moving to separate myself from him.

"Sabrina, what's wrong?" I could see the confusion in his eyes.

Thankfully, I hadn't taken my sunglasses off, because my eyes began to tear, and I didn't want him to see me cry again.

I turned my head to face the wall, instead of him.

Caston reached out and smacked the red stop button, sounding an alarm for a few second. I jumped at the sound and at the anger that flashed across Caston's face.

"What the fuck, Sabrina? You're fine on the plane, I spill my guts to you, we have amazing sex, you make out with Sara in the limo and have a laughing fit, now you're cold and distant?"

Still keeping my arms crossed, I spit out, "You should know."

He spins me to look at him. The turn was rough and he pushed me up against the wall and ripped my sunglasses off, so I would look him in the eyes. "Obviously, I don't."

I grabbed onto to the cold metal railing behind my back, as he pressed his body into mine. His hard cock pressing into me made me moan slightly.

Rage washed over me, and I found the strength to push him off of me. "NO! Damn it, Caston, I can handle you looking at other women for work, I can even handle you meeting with and working with them. I CANNOT handle standing by a few feet away while you make out and do God only knows with them, basically right under my nose. No. Fucking. Way." I had my finger dug into his chest, and his back against the wall this time. What pissed me off worse is that he acted as if he still didn't understand what I was saying.

"What?" he yelled back.

"Rae! What the fuck were you doing with her in the limo when we got out? I saw her leave the limo, Caston. Is it a little Vegas welcome to get felt up and who knows what else, like a lei, when you get to Hawaii?"

I watched his jaw tense up and release. "Damn it, Sabrina, women throw themselves at me all the time. I didn't do shit with her. I told her if she tries it again she is fucking done. Fired."

I stayed, pressing him up against the wall in his face for a little while longer.

His eyes darkened and he looked hungry. My breath caught and my heart sped up, he lifted me up and slammed me on the opposite wall, as he reached between my legs and ripped the crotch out of my thong. Fumbling with the zipper of his pants, he finally released his hard shaft and plunged into me hard, taking my breath away. I was caught off guard, but it was exactly what I needed. His cock was steel and his thrusts were deep and fast. I felt myself heading toward my climax, as Caston growled my name and pumped his hot fluid inside me. I was so close, but thought I wasn't going to get relief, until he bit my neck, hard, as he thrust one last hard time into my wet folds. I felt the hot liquid of my own release coat his cock, shudders coursed through my entire body.

Still buried deep in me, he reached to the side and hit the red button, restarting the elevator car.

He kept his head in the crook of my neck, as he let himself slip from me, still holding me against the wall, he tucked his cock back into his jeans. "Thank God, you had a skirt on."

I started to laugh, as I held onto his hard arms. "I'm still not happy with that Rae chick."

"Want me to fire her?" Caston was serious when he raised his head back to look me in the eye.

"No," I whispered. "Cass…"

"Ya?"

"Can you put me down? Shouldn't we get to our floor soon?"

He laughed and put me down, handing me a few tissues from his pocket to wipe up.

"Thanks, always prepared, huh?"

He winked at me. "You know it. And that, my dear, is the official Vegas welcome…no one, but I can give it to you, okay?"

"Deal," I said just as the doors slid open.

I blinked a few times to make sure I wasn't dreaming. The door opened to a two story sky villa. The place was huge with jaw dropping floor to ceiling windows, showcasing the Vegas strip skyline and private terraces off the main rooms. I walked ahead of him to take in the whole space.

"There's a pool, Caston!" I yelled.

He just laughed at me, as I kicked off my flip flops and stepped into the warm water. The pool was enclosed in glass and looked as if it ran over the side of the wall to flow down the hotel below. It seemed as if you would fall over the edge if you got too close. Skinny dipping is definitely on my to-do list.

Actually, I think I'll do it now. I set my purse on the edge and grab my tank top and pull it over my head, exposing my white lace bra. I pulled the rubber band out of my hair and ran my fingers through the waves. Caston caught on to what I was doing. Looking at him, I unbuttoned my skirt and carefully stepped out of it, so I wouldn't get it wet. I never lost eye contact with him. He bit his lip and slowly started to walk toward me. I turned toward the windows and reached behind me, unsnapping my bra and threw it over my shoulder to land on a chair that was close to the poolside.

Caston is getting close to me. I can feel his presence. I ease what is left of my pink thong down my legs and turn around. He's about three feet away. Making the thong into a sling shot, I shoot it right in Caston's face. I busted out laughing, as I turned and dove into the pool, swimming to the other end.

Emerging, I pull myself up onto, the ledge and look over the city below us. Caston stands with his arms crossed waiting.

"I can't wait here all day," he huffed.

"Join me."

"Nope, that scares the shit outta me."

"What? You're kidding me. Why did you have it put in?"

"Because it's a big hit at the parties, and it looks cool." A big smile spreads across his face.

"So, no skinny dipping with me…" I make a pouty face, as I put my leg up on the ledge to expose myself to him.

He runs his hands through his hair in frustration. "This is totally not fair."

"Nothing can get you out here…" I pinch one nipple and let my other hand slowly run down my stomach until it reaches the tip of my pussy.

He growled, but I saw him start to remove his shoes.

I let my finger slid through my folds, "Oh God, Caston, I'm so wet." I bite my lip and let my head fall back as I play with myself.

Caston had his shirt and shoes off now and was pacing the side of the pool. "Sabrina, please come back here."

I almost felt bad for him, but I continued on, "This feels so good."

He slowly unbuttoned his pants and slid them down his muscular legs. I locked eyes with him, as he pumped his cock a few times, watching me from across the pool.

I could see the struggle going on inside of him. Do I make it easier on him and come to him, or do I push him out of his comfort zone?

Just as I was about to give in and put him out of his misery, Caston dove in. Watching his body slice through the water gave me the chills.

He was perfectly centered between my legs when he popped up for air, and instead of gasping for air, he dove right into my pussy. I fisted my hands into his wet hair and pushed him in deeper. His tongue twirled around and plunged into my depth making me cry out.

Before I could grasp what he was doing, he hooked his arms around my legs and threw me into the middle of the pool.

Coming back up, I was met by his fierce kiss, knocking me off my feet. He grabbed me, so I didn't fall under the water, again. Never breaking his kiss with me he walked me back, so we were at the stairs on the safe side of the pool.

I pulled back from him, as my body rested on the steps. "Nice move there Cass, but I got you to come out there."

"I almost passed out when I got to you."

I laughed. He bent down to kiss my neck, where my special heart pendant hung, and plunged into me. My laughing quickly ended and turned to lust for this incredible man. Coming together we held onto each other until our breathing returned to normal.

Hearing the elevator doors open, Caston jumped out of the pool and grabbed a few towels for us. He wrapped me up, so I was decent before attending to himself. "Bre, honey, why don't you head to the bedroom and take a relaxing bubble bath. I think that is our security for the weekend. I need to meet with. Then I promise you, I'm yours for the rest of the evening."

"Okay." I stretched up onto my tip toes and kissed him lightly. "Do we have any plans?"

"Dinner, and then whatever you want."

I saw two burly men appear in my line of sight, and I backed away slowly. I bent down to grab my purse, making sure I didn't show off my goodies to anyone and walked down the hall, not knowing exactly where I was going.

Chapter Thirty-Four

Caston

I watched her walk away, holding the towel tightly around her body. Her ass swayed back and forth. I wished I was chasing her down the hall, instead of meeting with security. Taking a deep breath, I grabbed another towel and ran it through my hair, then draped it around my shoulders.

"Welcome, gentlemen," I said, acknowledging the men that had come in.

"Sir," they said in unison.

"Please, show yourself to the office. I'll be right behind you."

They turned and stalked off in the opposite direction of Sabrina. I quickly grabbed my clothes and followed them. Reaching into my jean pocket, I pulled out my cell phone and noticed there were a few missed calls from Terrance. I sighed. If he called more than once it was important.

I quickly dialed, as I walked toward the office.

Terrance answered immediately. "Sir, I'm sorry to call so many times."

"It's okay, Terrance. What is wrong?"

"Beverly."

I sighed, leaning with my back against the wall. "What now?"

"She is causing a ruckus at Black Hollywood. She keeps getting in somehow. I need to find out what employee is under her spell."

"Have her arrested."

"Very well, sir. Have the security detail arrived yet?"

"Yes. I was just about to go into a meeting with them now, actually. "

"I'll let you know if anything changes. I'll also be in direct contact with Jake and Phillip at all times."

"Thank you, Terrance. Oh and Terrance, please get Will go destroy the video surveillance of the elevator to the suite from about an hour ago." Hanging up the phone I let my head fall back to the wall, as I took a couple deep breaths. What the fuck is her deal?

I pulled my jeans on and walked into the office, drying my hair a little more. The boys stood up, giving me their attention.

I stood behind my desk and addressed them. "Jake, Phillip, very nice to meet you. Both of you come highly recommended by my head of security, Terrance."

"Thank you, sir," Jake said, shifting on his feet. "Terrance has filled us in on the situation at hand. I've already met with hotel security and distributed Beverly's picture. A copy of the restraining orders have been filed with the local authorities. I believe we have everything underway, so the next few days here will be uneventful."

"Very good," I said, sitting. "However, I was just informed that Beverly is being arrested, probably as we speak, for trespassing at BH headquarters. She won't be a problem for us, thankfully. It's my birthday party I want to discuss. I want everyone to be as discreet as possible, so we do not pull attention. My birthdays can get crazy."

Phillip looked as though he wanted to interject, but I stopped him with my hand in the air. "I know there is a party. There always is. Sara, I'm sure thinks it's a surprise." I shook my head.

Phillip chuckled. "Okay, we'll make sure everyone is secure before they enter. You'll be back at what time with Ms. Bennett?"

"Eleven."

"Very good, sir." Phillip made a note in his phone.

"Anything else?" I asked, getting up to shake the men's hands.

"Nothing right now, Mr. Black," Jake said, "but I'll be sure to call you if anything comes up."

I nodded. "If you'll excuse me, I would like to get back to my girl."

Walking past them, I headed down the hall, past the pool. I was enjoying the quiet. One day, I'll have a quiet birthday. I sighed.

Stopping at the bar by the pool area, I poured myself a whisky, before continuing on to master bedroom to find Sabrina.

I pushed the bedroom door open and my heart clenched. Sabrina was sprawled out on the bed fast asleep. Her hair was draped across the pillow. I walked over to the side table and set my drink down. Slowly getting in bed, I drew her to me.

My phone ringing bought me out of my sleep. It was Terrance's ring. My stomach dropped. Hoping to not wake my love, I slid out of bed and quickly made my way into the hall.

"Hello?"

"I'm sorry, sir, did I wake you?"

"Don't worry about it, Terrance, what is the matter?"

"Beverly, she's MIA."

"Fuck!" I slid my hands through my hair. "Okay, keep an eye on it. I'm sure you have already contacted Jake and Phillip. Damn it!"

"I'm sorry, sir, I feel like I have failed you."

"Terrance, don't feel that way. Just find her."

I hung up the phone and walked back into the room. Sabrina was sitting up on the bed with the sheet pooled around her lower half.

She didn't look happy, "What's wrong, Caston?"

"Beverly is causing problems, and I'm worried."

She held her arms out to me. Walking over to her, I took comfort in her embrace. "Caston, I love you. Don't think you need to hold things back from me. I'm a big girl. I can handle it, we can handle it." She stroked my head and then kissed my forehead.

Sitting up out of her arms, I looked at her draped in the white sheet. She looked like an angel. I took my finger and traced her necklace, picking up the charm between my fingers. Her breath caught, as my light touch grazed her skin.

"I wish it was just us tonight," I murmured. She looked at me confused. "Sabrina, I know Sara has a party planned for me. She thinks she surprises me every year, and she never does. I have to know everything, for security reasons."

"But she..."

"I'm a good actor," I said, flashing my sly smile.

"Well, you still have a few more hours to yourself, what would you like to do?"

"If I do what I'd like, we would never leave this room, but I have a few things planned, so we need to get up and get moving."

Still holding on to her charm, I snaked my other hand around her neck and brought her to me. Her lips parted slightly and her eyes shut. I paused millimeters away from her. Her hot breath bathed my lips. Our hungry lips and tongues mingled wildly. Pushing her back onto the bed, my hands cupped her breasts, and I brushed her nipples with my fingers. Her moan into my mouth fuelled my fire. Never parting our lips, I kicked off my jeans and entered her. She was so ready for me. Her slick liquid slid over my cock, making my motions effortless. Each quiver in her muscles I felt brought me higher. Her hands slide down my back and grabbed at my ass, pushing me harder into her. I felt like I couldn't get deep enough.

"Oh, Bre, I love you."

She dug her nails into my back, and I felt her tighten around me. I knew she was flying over the edge, and I followed her into sated bliss.

Feeling her giggle, I caught her eye questioning her with just my look.

"We aren't off to a good start on leaving this room, are we?"

"I guess not," I responded, laughing.

We laid in each other's arms for a while longer. I wanted to give her the next gift, but I was very nervous. I wasn't sure how she would react to it.

"Sabrina," I mumbled into her shoulder.

"Mmm, hum"

"I want to give you your next present."

I feel her smile. "Okay," she whispered.

I got up and walked to where the suite butler placed our bags. Reaching in, I felt the hard book wrapped up in beautiful paper. I felt as though I was going to puke.

Padding back to the bed, I handed her the package. Her smile was contagious. I was praying it would stay there.

She took the green sparkly box from me. Her hands touched it so tenderly. She slowly turned it over and found the seam in the paper. Sliding her finger under it, she loosened it making one side fall open. My heart sped up. Here it comes. Flipping it back over, she removed the paper. Her eyes went wide and her hand flew up to her open mouth.

She wasn't saying anything. I bit my lip, trying to judge her reaction. Was she upset? "Sabrina?"

Tears fell from her eyes. "Sabrina, honey, I can call and change it. This doesn't have to go to publication."

She held her finger up to me to silence me. Shit! I knew I shouldn't have done this.

She picked up the mockup of Black Hollywood. She opened the book to the pages with her pictures from the meadow. Her hazel eyes glistened, her hair spread out above her. The smile on her face was so sexy, I had to share her with the world. "It's the September issue, so it won't interfere with school, but if you still want me to cancel it, I will," I whispered.

Most of the pictures Sabrina edited for me were there, all tasteful and not showing too much. I didn't want too much shown to the world, because she was mine after all, to cherish.

"I love it," she whispered so low I almost did not hear her.

"What?"

She looked up at me with tears fall down her face. "Don't cancel it. It's beautiful."

"Really? You're okay with this?"

She nodded and swung her arms around my neck. "Thank you."

"Well, I told you those pictures were some of the best I've ever seen. How could I not show them to the world?"

She sobbed into my arms. "Bre, what's the matter?"

"I just thank God I met you. When I think about where I was when you came into my life and what my life was like, I feel like I'm in a fairytale waiting to wake up. I love you, Cass. Are you sure you're real, Caston?"

"I can remind you again, if you want?"

She giggled and leaned back to look me in the eyes. "What am I going to do with you?"

Wrapping her in my arms, again, I pulled her down to the bed to remind her how real I am.

Once ready, we sat in the kitchenette and ate some lunch. "I have something I'd like to discuss with you, Sabrina."

She looked nervous. I smiled, but felt my heart clench that she was still so insecure.

"Honey, would you consider coming to work at Black Hollywood? You would work under Rick, for now, so you wouldn't be reporting directly to me. He and I were so impressed by the editing you did on your pictures. We think you have potential, with the right training. I meant it when I said, you would be an asset to the company. Rick told me he would only like to work for a few more years before he retires, and I thought he could train you to take over for him, when the time comes."

Her mouth was open, and she was staring at me like I had two heads. "But dance. I want to do it professionally, Caston. It's all I've ever wanted to do."

"I know you want to dance professionally, but we can work around your school schedule and whatever may come afterward. I really think you'll enjoy the work and the people in the company."

She blinked a few times, but still hadn't answered me.

"What do you think?"

Silence.

"Sabrina, I'm not accustomed to waiting when I offer someone a job."

Finally, a smile spread on her face. She reached over and felt my forehead. "Are you serious? I think you might be coming down with something."

I laughed hard. "Sabrina, I've never been more serious."

She launched herself into my arms. I caught her before we tumbled onto the floor. "Oh my god, Caston! Yes! I'll definitely take the job!"

Her smile and happiness were contagious. I held her in a hug for a long time. I didn't think it can get any better than this.

Finally pulling away from her, I asked, "What would you like to do now?"

She tapped her chin as if in deep thought. "I want to sightsee. I want to walk the strip from one end to the other."

"Done." I took her hand and headed toward the elevator where Phillip and Jake were waiting.

Chapter Thirty-Five

Sabrina

I was in complete shock when I opened the package Caston had for me. My pictures, the ones I edited, in Black Hollywood. They looked magnificent. Beautiful even. My heart swelled with pride. He was unreal. Then he offers me a job. This really isn't happening. My life doesn't fall into place like this. I really was going to wake up and have this be all a dream.

Heading down in the elevator with security, I realized that this was real. I squeezed Caston's hand as we moved to walk out of the elevator. Phillip and Jake walked out first, letting us pass them, then fell in step with us, about four feet back. Caston wrapped his arm around my waist, as we moved through the crowded lobby and out the door, virtually unnoticed.

I saw a few groups of girls start whispering, and I was praying they would not go all fan girl on him. He had sunglasses on and a cap turned backwards, so he was a little harder to recognize. He looked absolutely yummy and made my insides clench. I leaned my head on his chest, as we walked and he looked over to me, planting a kiss on the top of my head.

"Have I told you that I love you, recently?"

I looked up at him, as we waited for the crosswalk to change. "I love you, too."

The hustle and bustle of the strip moved about us while we were in our own slow-motion world. Coming to a high end boutique, I pulled Caston to the window to do a little window shopping. I pointed out a few things that were stunning.

"You'd look beautiful in those items."

I blushed. "I couldn't pull those off."

"Let's go see," he said, pulling me into the store.

"Good afternoon, sir, ma'am, anything I can help you with today?" the snooty store clerk sneered in way of greeting us.

I cowered behind Caston, because I felt completely out of place. "Afternoon, my girl saw some items in your window, and she would like to try them on."

Caston removed his hat and glasses and the mood of the clerk immediately changed. Like a light switch. "Oh, Mr. Black, I didn't recognize you. Anything for you, sir."

I rolled my eyes and shook my head when she turned to lead us to the dressing areas.

"What's wrong?" Caston whispered.

"She thought we were trash until you took your glasses off. That's bullshit."

I saw him thinking about what I said. "You're right, Sabrina."

He showed me to a chair and turned around to the clerk. "I'd like to see your manager, while you get Sabrina the items she wants to try on."

"Of course, sir." She scurried off to get the items that I requested.

Once she set up the dressing room with the dresses, shirts, skirts, and shoes I'd picked out, I was ushered behind the curtain. I was overwhelmed. These garments were so expensive. One shirt in the stack had a price tag that was more than all the clothes in my closet combined, well, except for the ones Caston gave me. The clerk left me alone to start trying on the items.

"Sabrina, I want to see all those items. No hiding in there, or I'll come in after you."

"Maybe that's what I want," I whispered back, so only he could hear me.

He groaned deeply. "Don't tempt me."

Before I had a chance to try anything on a new clerk stepped in to the room. "I'm Ashlee, I'll be taking care of Mr. Black and you while you're here. Where do you want to start?"

Her enthusiastic voice and smile were infectious, I was suddenly excited to do a fashion show for Caston.

Ashlee got me dressed and corseted in a beautiful long midnight black dress. It was strapless with a slight sweetheart neckline. The top pushed up my cleavage just enough. It was fitted through the bodice with a flair toward the bottom and a train off the back. The back was very low cut, showing off the muscles in my back. There was black and diamond crystal details that lined the back of the dress and moved around to the front of my waist. It accented the choker Caston gave me. I looked at myself in the mirror and I didn't recognize myself. Ashlee pulled up my hair and twisted it to get it pinned up, so my neck and back were one long line.

"I've got just the shoes, hold on a second." She quickly exited. I just kept staring at myself. This was not me. How did I win the lottery like this?

Ashlee walked back in the room holding a pair of heels. They were black satin. A simple piece went over the toes but the ankle strap is what set the shoes into a category of their own. There were two rows of large diamond like crystals fastened to them. "They are perfect," I whispered.

She bent down to help me into the shoes. I touched my necklace, as I turned around to stare back at the girl looking back at me in the mirror.

"May I draw the curtain, so you can show Mr. Black?"

I nodded slowly. I stayed facing the mirror, as the curtain was pushed to the side.

Caston was sitting in a chair with his phone in his hand when the red velvet fabric was pulled to the side. I studied his face. When he looked up his mouth fell open. Immediately setting the phone down, he uncrossed his legs and leaned forward.

"Sabrina…"

I rendered him speechless. Slowly turning around, I dropped my hand to my side, so he could see the front. I've never felt this beautiful in my life.

"Well?" I questioned with a slight shoulder shrug once I faced him.

"I'm speechless, Bre, you're gorgeous. I think this dress was made for you." He got up and walked over to me. He ran his hand down the curve of my waist along the heavy satin fabric, "Simple, but stunning." His finger grazed my bare back and I shivered.

I closed my eyes and a slight moan slipped from my lips, as his hand continued up my other arm, stepping in front of me his finger moved across the swells of my breasts. He stopped in front of me and I opened my eyes, looking up at him. The desire was overwhelming. He was hungry for me. "We'll take it all," he said, never breaking his eye contact with me.

I swallowed hard and bit my lip; my mouth had suddenly gone dry. Slowly he leaned in, taking my chin in his thumb and finger, tipping my head up to meet his. The light kiss brushed my lips. Just a peck, but it communicated so much. The electricity from it was crackling around us. I even heard Ashlee in the corner of the room sigh when we parted.

"I want you to wear this tonight to dinner."

When we returned to our suite in the hotel, we were met by Sara and Jon. Caston was pulled one direction by Jon. I was pulled in the other by Sara to prepare for tonight. Our hands were holding each other until the last second. Even then we keep eye contact with each other over our shoulders, as we walked away.

Finally, turning my attention back to Sara I stopped her mid-sentence. "You know Caston really wanted a quiet birthday, don't you?"

She shooed me over to the waiting hair dresser. "He says that every year. He never means it."

She sat down next to me and continued talking about the plans and what's going to happen tonight.

I stared off into the mirror in front of me, tuning her out. Caston told me he wanted a quiet birthday and that's exactly what I planned on giving him. The party was in our room, so I would have to come up with another plan. The wheels started turning.

Hours later my hair was done. That was an experience I didn't want to endure again, if I didn't have too. I could have done the same thing to my hair in half an hour. Sara tried ushering me to the make-up person next, but I excused myself, saying I needed to use the restroom. No way was I going to look like a clown all done up in layers of makeup.

I stepped into the hall and shut the door behind me. Jake was sitting in a chair down the way. Hoping he could help me, I approached him quickly.

"Jake, I need your help?"

"Yes, Ms. Bennett?" he said, standing.

"Let's go in here, so no one hears us," I said, walking into the nearby unoccupied room.

Shutting the door behind me, I turned to face him. He looked a little confused and nervous.

"Plans for tonight need to change." He looked as if he wanted to interject, but I kept going, "Caston doesn't want a surprise party. He wanted a nice quiet evening. I want to give that to him, and this is where I need your help. Obviously, Sara's party is here, so we can't come back here after dinner tonight. Please, acquire another suite in the hotel, so we have someplace to go."

"But, ma'am…"

"No buts, make it happen, radio Phillip and get him down here if needed. I need this to happen. Mr. Black does so much for everyone, I want him to get something he really wants."

I was so nervous I was wringing my hands in front of me. It wasn't like me to give orders like this.

"Okay, Ms. Bennett. I'll make sure it happens. I'll give you the new key when you arrive to dinner and fill you in on the room number."

"Thank you, Jake," I squealed and hugged him, "I'm so excited!"

"Anytime, Ms. Bennett," he patted my back awkwardly.

Laughing, I backed up and headed out the door back to the room, so I could finish getting ready. I skipped, thinking of how happy I was and how happy Caston will be to finally get a quiet evening on his birthday.

Stepping out of the room I felt like I was floating on air. Walking into the main room it suddenly went silent. I looked up slowly to see everyone had turned toward me. My vision tunneled right to Caston. He took my breath away in his crisp black tux with a black vest and tie and a white shirt. His hair was perfectly messed up in a way only Caston could pull off.

He walked over to me. "You look breathtaking, Sabrina."

Cocking my head to the side, I responded, "I could say the same to you, birthday boy."

He held out a box for me to take. "I don't think I could make you any more beautiful than you are, but I already had this for you."

I smiled and took the box from him opening it. "Oh, Caston, wow."

It was a black diamond tennis bracelet. It matched my necklace and earrings. "This is gorgeous."

Taking it from my hands, he latched it around my small wrist. "Not as gorgeous as you."

His hand cupped my cheek, and I leaned into it. The warmth spread through my whole body. Leaning over he kissed me.

The room was still silent, making me a little uncomfortable, knowing everyone was sharing in our intimate exchange.

"Caston," I whispered. "Everyone is staring at us."

I felt him smile on my cheek. "Let them."

Even though the dinner was supposed to be celebrating Caston's birthday, it turned into a business dinner. It was raining outside, but the view from the private room in the restaurant was spectacular. Some of the other men at the table got a little heated, and I tensed up feeling uncomfortable.

"Don't worry, Sabrina, they're all talk," he whispered in my ear.

I gave him a weak smile and a light kiss on the lips. He stroked my cheek, ignoring everyone at the table.

"I have an announcement," he said, clutching my hand on the table, waiting for everyone to quiet, "Sabrina has agreed to come to work for Black Hollywood as an apprentice photo editor."

The heat in my cheeks made my face feel on fire. Everyone just gawked at me.

There were many congratulatory messages being passed my way, but one of the men directly across from me scowled. "What the fuck, Caston, making your fuck buddy an editor? That's a new low, even for you."

His wife leaned over to try to quiet him. Caston's face was furious. The two men became very heated, and I didn't want to hear anymore. I feared tears were going to escape my eyes.

"If you'll excuse me, please," I said, as I stood up, grabbing my purse and headed toward the bathroom. Thankfully, the exit was also in the same direction.

I hurried myself before the drips started falling. I put my head down, and ended up colliding with Jake, who caught me by my arms.

"Oh my gosh, I'm so sorry." I wiped the tears from my eyes.

"Ms. Bennett, is everything okay?"

"Yes, Jake, just a drunk asshole at the table. Caston might need you to remove him, though."

"Yes, ma'am. Oh, and here is the other key for you. It is room 3132."

"Thank you, Jake." I pushed away from him and continued my way down the hall, stepping out into the outdoor tent to get fresh air.

Chapter Thirty-Six

Caston

Damn assholes! Drunk bastard making Sabrina feel like I only want her working for me because we're involved. She's a talented woman. Where is she?

I excused myself, after telling Dan his things from BH will be packed up and returned to him by Monday. I do not want him back at BH ever again. I don't tolerate shit like that, drunk or not.

Seeing Jake come toward me I felt a slight panic, thinking something had happened to her.

"Jake, what is the matter? Where is Sabrina?"

"She just stepped outside. She told me there might be a problem with someone at dinner?"

"Just Dan being the fuck up he usually is. Please, remove him without making too much of a scene."

"Very well, sir."

I headed toward the doors. I saw her under the tent on the terrace. Her hair was piled high on her head and her figure was to die for in that dress. The light from the tent filtered around her and she looked like an angel standing before me.

I opened the door and walked up behind her. The electricity from the storm combined with connection between my love and me charging the air. I slid my arms around her waist, cuddling her to my chest.

She quickly swiped at her eyes, trying to hide that she was crying.

"Sabrina, please don't take what he said to heart. He's an asshole, who no longer works for me."

"But, Caston, I'm sure he spoke what everyone at that table thought. No one has seen my work, yet."

"And they don't need to see your work. I'm the only one that does. It's my business."

"Are you sure this is what you want?"

The question was baited and heavy. I felt as though we weren't talking about the job anymore. My heart broke and my stomach turned over.

"What?" I whispered.

She turned in my arms. Her face so solemn. "I don't think this will work. I'm so out of place with your group. No one takes me serious. They all think I'm only with you for your money."

More tears began filling her eyes. No, this is not happening.

"You can't leave me." The words struggled to come out.

"Why, Caston? You'd be better off not having to deal with me; Beverly would get off your case, your employees wouldn't think you were going over the deep end, and well ..."

I stepped back, holding her at arm's length. Was I wrong about where we were heading? I saw the look in her eye, and I knew she was just trying to be brave. She was torn up inside. I couldn't take it.

I dropped to one knee, reached into my coat pocket, and retrieved a black velvet box that I had placed there earlier. Her eyes went wide in realization of what I was doing.

"Sabrina Marie Bennett, I know we haven't known each other long, but life is too short to spend a single minute unhappy without you. You've overcome a difficult past, and so have I. It's not the things that have happened to us in life that define us, it's how we handle them. And I don't want us to handle them alone. I had a dark void in my life that you filled, you lit my life up, giving me hope for the future. I'm here for you. I will stand by you on your good days and bad. I'll spend every minute trying to make your bad days good. I want you to be with me until the end. You are my everything; please accept my proposal, be my partner in life…my…other half?"

Tears were falling from her eyes, but her smile engulfed her face. I held the ring box open for her, displaying the three caret round brilliant diamond with a black diamond bridge that graces the center. Diamonds curve up to cradle the center diamond.

Her breath caught when I displayed the ring to her. She started nodding her head. "You're crazy, do you know that?"

"Only about you. What's your answer?"

"Yes, oh my God, yes!" She held her hand out to me, and I slid it onto her thin finger.

Standing up, I picked her up in a hug and spun her around. Her laugh was magical. Setting her down, I took her face in my hands and placed a kiss on her lips. As if on cue fireworks started in the background.

She started laughing and crying against my lips. "You really think of everything."

"Well, I wish I could take credit for the fireworks, but that wasn't me," I laughed.

She laughed too, wiping her eyes. Her lips were wet and swollen from our kisses. I held her in my embrace as we watched the show.

"I wish we didn't have to go back to my party. I'd much rather devour you instead of cake."

"Good thing I watch out for my fiancée's best interests," she said, as she held up a key she produced from her purse.

"But… How… What?" I was having trouble speaking coherently.

She shrugged. "You told me you always wanted a quiet birthday."

I spun her around and captured her mouth in mine again. "No one has ever been able to surprise me. You, my dear, have surprised me numerous times. I love you, so much."

I offered her my arm and we walked back into the building to the elevator, bypassing the rest of the dinner party. I wanted to worship her body for the rest of the night.

Stepping into the elevator, our bodies slammed together. Her hands were in my hair, I pressed her up against the bulge in my pants. I had to have her. We never parted on our way to our new room. Thankfully, no one else joined us in the elevator. When the doors slid open, I grabbed her hand and pulled her along the hall, quickly trying to get to the room.

Entering the room I held her against the wall. Her hands undid my tie, as I kissed along her neck and jaw. The sweet taste of her skin made me hungry. Her skin broke out in goose bumps. I loved the way she reacted to me. She slid the tie from my neck, and I stuffed it in the pocket of my pants. Her arms pushed my jacket off, letting it fall to the floor. Reaching around to her ass, I grabbed at it through the satin material of her dress. This was killing me. Still kissing, not wanting to part too long, we made our way to the bed. I turned her around and pulled her into me, kissing along the back of her neck, as I started to undo the back of her dress. The small moans coming from her lips were like music.

Finally freeing her of the material, I pushed it down her body. She was naked from the waist up. I snaked my arms around her, pulling her back into me. One hand found and stroked her breast, as the other moved up around her neck, pulling her head to the side to give me better access to the spot that made her come apart in my hands.

"Oh, Caston," she moaned.

I nibbled and sucked her neck, sending a tremble through her body. She slowly moved out of my arms and turned to face me. Her body was perfect. She removed the dress, and was now standing before me in her black G-string and gorgeous shoes.

She bent down to remove the shoes, but I couldn't have that. "Leave the shoes on," I growled.

She strutted toward me, pulling at her hair, releasing it into a waterfall of brunette curls over her shoulders and back.

Taking my shirt buttons in her hands she slowly started to undo the buttons. I slid my hands in her hair, kissing her luscious lips. I couldn't get enough of her. When she got my shirt off, I knew I wouldn't last much longer. I flipped her onto the bed, quickly removing my pants.

My cock sprung free and I crawled up her body. "I can't take it much longer. I need you, now. Then I can spend the rest of the night worshiping you."

I removed the scrap of material claiming to be her panties with my teeth, pausing to take a taste of her, as I passed by her mound. She was soaked.

I crawled up her body, kissing her soft flesh as I moved along. Once at her neck, I snaked my arms around her waist and rolled to place her on top of me. I wanted to see her take control. She straddled my cock and took it in with one push. Her clit hit my skin, it felt on fire. Her muscles clenched around me. I could tell she was just as close as I was. I wanted all of her. She was mine. I couldn't wait to make her my wife.

Her hips rolled and she moved up and down my cock, coating me with her juices. I sat up and tangled her hair in my hand, pulling back on it. She gasped, and I felt a flow over my cock. I loved how responsive she was.

"Caston." My name sounded breathless.

"Oh Sabrina, I love you." I grunted, as I pushed into her a few more times before spilling myself in her. Her own release followed mine as she clenched me hard.

She sank down to pull me into a hug. I continued holding her until I felt the spasms around my cock subside.

"I'm glad we made it to the room. I wanted to rip that dress off of you in the elevator."

She giggled, then yawned. I laid her on the bed and I got up. Walking over to the bathroom, I cleaned up. When I was finished I brought a washcloth back and wiped her, gently. I removed her shoes, making a note that she will definitely have to wear these again, and I crawled in bed next to her, pulling her onto my chest.

I stroked her back lightly with my fingertips, as I watched her admiring her ring.

"Do you like it?"

She placed her hand on my chest and looked up at me. "Love it. It's beautiful Caston. I love you more than anything. Thank you."

I kissed the top of her head, "Go to sleep, now. We have to fly back home tomorrow, and I intend to make you very tired over the next few hours."

She giggled, but yawned, again. Laying her head back down it was only a few seconds before she fell fast asleep on me. This is how it should be, how it will be from now on.

Chapter Thirty-Seven

Sabrina

We have been home a few weeks and the engagement news hit the tabloids before we even left Vegas. I was now known to everyone. Even though it was scary, it was a thrill, too. Caston kept me level headed. I continued dancing to prepare for my spring workshop, and I was also working at Black Hollywood, so we hardly saw each other during the day, lately. We both lived for night, it was when we were alone together and could show each other how much we loved one another.

Last night was particularly spicy, which has kept me very distracted today. My midnight wake-up call from Caston is keeping me blushing in all the right places. My iPhone pings and I'm quickly brought back to earth.

From: Caston Black
Subject: I see you blushing.
Date: June 5, 2012
To: Sabrina Bennett

My dear fiancée,
I know you're still blushing from last night's wake-up call. I know you all too well. Just wait until you come home tonight. Have I told you lately how lucky I am to have found you?
XOXO
Cass

I'm smiling even bigger than I was, and at that moment I decide I cannot stay here one minute longer. Quickly packing up my bags, I grab my jacket, and head for the door. "Good night, Hannah. I'm heading out early. As soon as you're finished with what you're doing you may leave as well." I race to the elevator, but it was too slow for me right now, so I turn to head down the stairs. Just as I entered the stairway my phone rings. It's a number I'm not familiar with.

"Sabrina Bennett," I said, answering it anyways. There is no one there. "Hello? Hello?" I look at the phone and I have good reception. "Hello?" Shrugging I hang up.

Oh, well, I'll have Terrance look into it when I get home. As I make my way to the parking garage I see my new Bentley Caston bought me as an engagement present and think just how great my life is. I hit the unlock button and get in. Turning to put my bags in the passenger seat and I almost crush the two dozen long steam red roses sitting on the seat. I have a goofy school girl smile gracing my face. Is everyone really this in love with their fiancée, or are we special? I carefully put my bags on the floor and reach for the card, but before

I'm able to open it my iPhone rings again, and I answer it without looking. "Oh, honey, you shouldn't have. These flowers are beautiful." I say before I even looked at the number.

"I know. I wanted to see your face when you saw them," the voice said. My blood ran cold. This wasn't Caston. Who was this? I almost dropped the phone, but managed to hold on to it while I opened the card.

I'm back, did you miss me?

"Who is this?" I yelled.

"You know all too well. Don't try to call your lover. He can't help you, now."

The phone hung up. I quickly tried to dial Caston. I had no service. What the hell?!? I was just talking to someone on the phone! My hands start shaking and my stomach is turning. Whoever that said they wanted to see me when I saw the flowers. They are here somewhere. I frantically start looking at all the cars around me, but there is no one in here. Frozen, I didn't know what to do. Do I get out and run back to the office, or try to leave and get to someplace that is safe? Leave, is what I decided.

I quickly try to start the car, but it doesn't turn over. "Oh, come on" I'm screaming and hitting the steering wheel. Then panic flooded through my veins. I scramble out of the car and fall scrapping my knees. I get up, and just as I'm almost to the doors of the office...

BOOM

The power of the blast throws me into the glass doors of the lobby entrance of the garage. The noise, the sound, the glass exploding, I go black. I feel hands pulling me through the doorway. The cold marble floor on my back and the tugging brings me back to a foggy reality. I start struggling to get away from whoever is pulling me. Who was pulling me, and was I going to safety?

"No, no, get away" I scream. "Please. Leave me alone!"

"Sabrina, Ms. Bennett, are you okay? Oh my God! Sabrina!" It's Hannah. I go back into the darkness, since I know I'm with someone safe.

My head hurts…where am I? The sirens. Oh God, make it stop. Where's Caston? I want Caston. There is so much commotion around me, I open my eyes in the back of an ambulance. Paramedics are all around taking my vital signs.

"Who did this", I hear off in the distance. "I want some fucking answers, like ten minutes ago. Terrance, this is NOT OKAY."

My Caston is here. He's mad. "Sir, she's waking up," one of the paramedics says. Caston is instantly by my side, scooping me up in his arms. His strong, protective arms.

"Sir, sir, you can't move her… Sir." I hear.

"She's my fiancée. I'll damn well do as I please." Caston huffs back at the guy, fumbling to follow him, so he doesn't rip the IV out of my arm.

I try to giggle, "Ugh, that hurts. Cass, what's going on?" I whispered, since that is as loud as my voice will go.

"Shh, Sabrina, it's okay. Don't talk now. I'm here. I'll never leave you. Ever."

I snuggle into his arms, as he brushes the blood matted hair from my face. "Oh, Sabrina, I'm so sorry. I promised I'd protect you and it always seems you're the one to get hurt. I'm a failure."

"No, no, baby. You're not..." I try to protest, but he puts a finger over my lips to quiet me.

"Rest now. No talking"

I close my eyes, but that voice is ringing through my head. That cold voice. I snuggle closer to my safety. His hands trace my face so tenderly. His fingers go over every little scrape and cut on my face, arms, and legs taking them all into his memory. He's so gentle. I hear him sniffle. Opening my eyes, I peak up at him. He has tears coursing down his cheeks. I lift my hand up to wipe them away. His eyes lock with mine, and I give him a weak smile. His eyes are so big and unprotected. He looks lost and scared.

He leans his head into my hand. "Sabrina, what would I ever do without you?"

This time I'm the one to quiet him with my finger. "I'm never going to leave you, Caston. Just remember that."

"Sir?" I hear Terrance behind me, but he doesn't want to look away.

I pull my hand back from his face, and he finally breaks my eye contact. "Yes, Terrance." He sighs, not because he's annoyed, he's exhausted.

"Sir, whoever did this knew the garage. He knew where the security cameras were, knew how to get in and out without being detected."

I hear Caston grumble. "I want him fucking caught, Terrance, you hear me!"

"Not him" I mumble. Caston and Terrance both look at me. "Not him, her"

"Her?" Caston says "Bre, how do you know it was a her?"

"I talked to her, Cass. She called me when I got in the car, when I found the flowers. She was watching me…"

"Who was, babe, who was watching you?"

"She said she wanted to see my face when I found the flowers. Oh God, Caston. She was here, somewhere. She did something to my phone, so I couldn't call you when she hung up. I tried to get away. I tried, but the car wouldn't start. Oh God, if I hadn't gotten out…" I start sobbing. He pulls me closer to him rocking me, like a little child.

Terrance turns and I hear him yelling into his phone. "Will, I need to track all the incoming calls to Sabrina's cell phone in the last hour. Yes, she is doing okay, just really scraped up. Okay. Thank you. Send Mr. Black and me the report."

Caston pulls me closer, and I wince. "I'm sorry, Sabrina, did I hurt you?"

"No, just a little sore" I say.

"Don't worry we'll find whoever did this." His iPhone pings.

I look up at him as he opens the email. His face goes pale. I instantly sit up in his lap. The pain becomes a distant memory. "What is it, Caston? What's in that email?" I turn to look at Terrance, who has the same face as Caston. I snap back to look at Caston. He is frozen. I've never seen him like this. Time pauses. Terrance goes running, yelling something I cannot make out, because everything is mumbled. I grab Caston's cell phone and look at what made time stand still. It's Sara and Jon. They were blindfolded and tied up in a room that was dirty and dingy. They look as if they have been beaten and are bleeding.

I feel myself go limp. Caston catches me before I hit the ground. The world seems to stop moving. *Please, let them be okay. Oh God, please!*

275

More sirens. More hustle. Who could have done this? Then silence. It is deafening. This hurts my head more than the commotion. Caston whisked me into the small tent outside of Black Hollywood, while the evacuation of the building was taking place. The paramedics were still fawning over me making me annoyed. This is too close to home. I start shaking uncontrollably.

"Sabrina, honey, look at me. Look at me, Bre," Caston is yelling. Slowly I meet his eyes. "We will find them. We will." He takes my head between his hands and slowly massages my temples. My breathing finally slows and I am not shaking as hard.

"Sara and Jon," I cry.

"Shhh, try to relax"

"Here you go, Sabrina" Terrance hands me a bottle of water. I take it, but I am too stunned and numb inside to drink it.

"Who did this, Terrance?"

I look up at him. He looks down avoiding my glare. "I'm not sure. There hasn't been a single threat, or murmur of a threat, against you, Mr. Black, or family in months."

"Sabrina, can you remember anything about the voice that called on the phone? Was there any background noises? Anything distinctive?" Caston asks much too calmly.

I think he's putting up a brave front for me. Shutting my eyes, I bring myself back to the car. That voice. High pitched cold voice... Then it hits me... I know who it is. "Beverly!"

Caston gets up and walks to the other side of the tent. Terrance follows him. I cannot hear what they're saying. I can only see the heated discussion going on between them. Terrance looks defeated. Caston runs his hands through his hair. I cup the water in my hands trying to occupy them.

Not wanting to be alone anymore, I get up and walk over to Caston. I need him and his strength. "Has Will found anything, yet?" I ask.

"No, damn it." Caston yells. I'm startled. Turning to me he says, "I'm sorry, Sabrina, I didn't mean to scare you. I'm just so fucking mad and scared." He wraps his arms around me, and I snuggle into his chest, as he rests his chin on my head. We stand there for what seems like hours. Not moving, holding each other and keeping each other as calm as we can.

Terrance says, "No luck on the cell phone calls. They were made from a prepaid phone, like I suspected, but the tower location tells us she was within a mile of BH. I'm not sure how she got out of jail and got past security."

Just as he opens his mouth to say something there is a commotion outside of the tent. I look up at Caston, as he looks down at me. Caston flies past Terrance, who already has his gun drawn. I was forced to stay behind because my IVs were limiting me.

Oh My God. Why didn't it dawn on me that she could still be in the building? "Sara and Jon were put in the elevator by someone." I said to whoever was listening.

I get up to go searching. Someone grabs my arm, "Where are you going?"

"I'm going to find her. She is here. Where the fuck is she? Where's Caston? Why does she think she can get away with this?" I run out pulling free of my IVs. "What the fuck do you want with me? I'm here. Show yourself." I irrationally scream.

I sink to the ground, sobbing. Suddenly there is disorder behind me. I see Terrance in the distance grabbing for his gun. Oh God No. Everything seemed to be in slow motion now. Turning I look straight into her cold, empty eyes. Everyone is rushing around me, running away. Why? Then I see it, a gun. She was pointing a gun at me. My mouth opens to say something, but nothing comes out.

What just happened? Why does my leg hurt so badly? Oh my God, stop the pain. Beverly was being tackled to the ground by Terrance. Oh God, why the pain?

"Sabrina, are you okay? Sabrina talk to me." Caston is pleading, pulling me into his lap, rocking me. Paramedics are once again swarming me. Caston's covered in blood. My blood. I can't say anything to him, but I want to calm him down.

Caston rides with me to the emergency room. Nothing is said between us, we just hold hands.

Arriving in the ER we're immediately swarmed by nurses. Caston is frantically trying to get answers. I'm losing so much blood that I keep getting dizzy.

"Why the fuck is she still bleeding? Where is the fucking doctor?" Caston screams pacing the hall.

"Please, move out of the way, Mr. Black. We must get her up to surgery. She is losing too much blood," a doctor in blue scrubs and a plastic mask says.

I hold onto Caston's hand as long as I can.

"Don't give up on me, baby." Caston whispers in my ear just as our hands are being pried apart by the nurses.

Through my fog I see Caston sink to his knees. *Baby, I'm okay. I'm going to be okay. I won't give up.* I thought I said before falling into darkness.

Caston & Sabrina's story continues …

I Won't Give Up
On you

Coming 2014

Acknowledgements

To my editor, Liz, with Book Peddler's Editing. You were always there no matter what time of the day to ask and bounce questions off of. I can't thank you enough for all your hard work. Your suggestions helped make the book flow much better.

https://www.facebook.com/BookPeddlersEditing?ref=br_tf

To Michael, Dawn, with Digital Mitchall Event Photography and Rob, with Rob Miller Photography. Your work on the cover photo was amazing. You were so much fun to work with and I cannot wait to do it again. Thank you for also designing the fabulous cover. It turned out exactly like I dreamed!

https://www.facebook.com/digitalmitchell

https://www.facebook.com/pages/Rob-Miller-Photography/296918773705422

To Kristine, good luck on your competition! Without you my cover would not look the way it does. You were the perfect model for the job.

https://www.facebook.com/pages/Kristine-Kowalski-NPC-Bikini-Competitor/203007306535089

To Angela, with Fictional Formats. You took a huge weight off my shoulders. I was able to rest easy knowing that once I hit that publish button my baby would look nice and pretty.

https://www.facebook.com/FictionalFormats

To Jen, you helped me so much all throughout the book. Thank you for letting me bounce ideas off of you, helping me work through tough spots, being my first editor, and overall your encouragement throughout this entire process.

To Renee, Jenn, and all my other crazy book addicts. Without you ladies I probably wouldn't have this book out today. You started this crazy process in my head with the group stories and it all snowballed from there. So thank you for making me remember how much I loved writing!

To all the blogs and Facebook pages who have helped promote me along the way. Thank you for all your hard work and dedication.

To all my beta readers, thank you for all of the constructive feedback you gave me to make my book better.

To anyone I may have forgotten, THANK YOU! I love you!

www.ingramcontent.com/pod-product-compliance
Lightning Source LLC
Chambersburg PA
CBHW062136170626
46813CB00002B/716